Garden Spells

Sarah
Addison
Allen

RANDOM HOUSE
LARGE PRINT

Copyright © 2007 by Sarah Addison Allen

All rights reserved.
Published in the United States of America by
Random House Large Print in association with
Bantam Dell, New York.
Distributed by Random House, Inc., New York.

Library of Congress Cataloging-in-Publication Data
Allen, Sarah Addison.
Garden spells / by Sarah Addison Allen.
p. cm.
ISBN: 978-0-7393-2743-2
1. Sisters—Fiction. 2. North Carolina—Fiction.
3. Large type books. 4. Domestic fiction. gsafd I. Title.
PS3601.L4356G37 2007b
813'.6—dc22
2007027866

www.randomhouse.com/largeprint

FIRST LARGE PRINT EDITION

10 9 8 7 6 5 4 3 2 1

This Large Print edition published in accord with
the standards of the N.A.V.H.

Jacket art © Melody Cassen
Hand-lettering by Carol Russo
Jacket design by Jamie S. Warren Youll

For my mom. I love you.

ACKNOWLEDGMENTS

Thanks to my dad for these stubborn writing genes, and for the stories of his grandfather that brought Lester to life. Endless gratitude to the wonderful, magical Andrea Cirillo and Kelly Harms. Big butter biscuit thanks to Shauna Summers, Nita Taublib, Carolyn Mays, and Peggy Gordijn. Much love to the loopy Duetters, and to Daphne Atkeson for encouraging me to write this, then make it better.

Thanks to Michelle Pittman (two times!) and Heidi Hensley, who deserve tiaras for their patient friendship. A special shout out to the eponymous Miss Snark. And I bow to Dawn Hughes, hairdresser extraordinaire, for helping me get my salon facts straight.

GARDEN SPELLS

PART ONE

Hindsight

CHAPTER
1

Every smiley moon, without fail, Claire dreamed of her childhood. She always tried to stay awake those nights when the stars winked and the moon was just a cresting sliver smiling provocatively down at the world, the way pretty women on vintage billboards used to smile as they sold cigarettes and limeade. On those nights in the summer, Claire would garden by the light of the solar-powered footpath lamps, weeding and trimming the night bloomers—the moon vine and the angel's trumpet, the night jasmine and the flowering tobacco. These weren't a part of the Waverley legacy of edible flowers, but sleepless as she often was, Claire had added flowers to the garden to give her something to do at night when she was so wound up that frustration singed the edge of her nightgown and she set tiny fires with her fingertips.

What she dreamed of was always the same. Long roads like snakes with no tails. Sleeping in the car at night while her mother met men in bars and honky-tonks. Being a lookout while her mother stole shampoo and deodorant and lipstick and sometimes a candy bar for Claire at Shop-and-Gos around the Midwest. Then, just before she woke up, her sister, Sydney, always appeared in a halo of light. Lorelei held Sydney and ran to the Waverley home in Bascom, and the only reason Claire was able to go with them was because she was holding tight to her mother's leg and wouldn't let go.

That morning, when Claire woke up in the backyard garden, she tasted regret in her mouth. With a frown, she spit it out. She was sorry for the way she'd treated her sister as a child. But the six years of Claire's life before Sydney's arrival had been fraught with the constant fear of being caught, of being hurt, of not having enough food or gas or warm clothes for the winter. Her mother always came through but always at the last minute. Ultimately, they were never caught and Claire was never hurt and, when the first cold snap signaled the changing colors of the leaves, her mother magically produced blue mittens with white snowflakes on them and pink thermal underwear to wear under jeans and a cap with a droopy ball on top. That life on the run had been good enough for Claire, but Lorelei obviously thought Sydney deserved better, that Sydney deserved to be born with roots.

And the small scared child in Claire hadn't been able to forgive her.

Picking up the clippers and the trowel from the ground beside her, she stood stiffly and walked in the dawning fog toward the shed. She suddenly stopped. She turned and looked around. The garden was quiet and damp, the temperamental apple tree at the back of the lot shivering slightly as if dreaming. Generations of Waverleys had tended this garden. Their history was in the soil, but so was their future. Something was about to happen, something the garden wasn't ready to tell her yet. She would have to keep a sharp eye out.

She went to the shed and carefully wiped the dew off the old tools and hung them on their places on the wall. She closed and locked the heavy gate door to the garden, then crossed the driveway at the back of the ostentatious Queen Anne-style home she'd inherited from her grand-mother.

Claire entered the house through the back, stopping in the sunroom that had been turned into a drying and cleaning room for herbs and flowers. It smelled strongly of lavender and peppermint, like walking into a Christmas memory that didn't belong to her. She drew her dirty white nightgown over her head, balled it up, and walked naked into the house. It was going to be a busy day. She had a dinner party to cater that night, and it was the last Tuesday in May, so she had to deliver her end-of-the-month shipment of lilac and mint and rose-petal jellies and nasturtium and chive-blossom vinegars to the farmers' market and to the gourmet grocery store on the square, where the college kids from Orion College would hang out after classes.

There was a knock at the door as Claire was pulling her hair back with combs. She went downstairs in a white eyelet sundress, still barefooted. When she opened the door, she smiled at the fireplug of an old lady standing on the porch.

Evanelle Franklin was seventy-nine years old, looked like she was one hundred and twenty, yet still managed to walk a mile around the track at Orion five days a week. Evanelle was a distant relation, a second or third or fourteenth cousin, and she was the only other Waverley still living in Bascom. Claire stuck to her like static, needing to feel a connection to family after Sydney took off when she was eighteen and their grandmother died the same year.

When Claire was young, Evanelle would stop by to give her a Band-Aid hours before she scraped her knee, quarters for her and Sydney long before the ice cream truck arrived, and a flashlight to put under her pillow a full two weeks before lightning struck a tree down the street and the entire neighborhood was without power all night. When Evanelle brought you something, you were usually going to need it sooner or later, though that cat bed she gave Claire five years ago had yet to find its use. Most people in town treated Evanelle kindly but with amusement, and even Evanelle didn't take herself too seriously. But Claire knew there was always something behind the strange gifts Evanelle brought.

"Well, don't you look eye-talian with your dark hair and Sophia Loren dress. Your picture should be on a bottle of olive oil," Evanelle said. She was in her green velour running suit, and slung over her shoulder was a rather large tote bag full of quarters and stamps and egg timers and soap, all things she might feel the need to give someone at some point.

"I was just about to make some coffee," Claire said, stepping back. "Come in."

"Don't mind if I do." Evanelle entered and followed Claire to the kitchen, where she sat at the kitchen table while Claire made the coffee. "You know what I hate?"

Claire looked over her shoulder as steam carrying the smell of coffee curled around the kitchen. "What do you hate?"

"I hate summer."

Claire laughed. She loved having Evanelle around. Claire had tried for years to get the old lady to move into the Waverley house so she could take care of her, so the house wouldn't feel as if the walls were moving out of her way as she walked, making the hallways longer and rooms bigger. "Why on earth would you hate summer? Summer is wonderful. Fresh air, open windows, picking tomatoes and eating them while they're still warm from the sun."

"I hate summer because most of them college kids leave town, so there aren't as many runners and I don't have any nice male backsides to look at when I walk the track."

"You're a dirty old lady, Evanelle."

"I'm just sayin'."

"Here you go," Claire said, setting a coffee cup on the table in front of Evanelle.

Evanelle peered into the cup. "You didn't put anything in it, did you?"

"You know I didn't."

"Because your side of the Waverleys always wants to put something in everything. Bay leaves in bread, cinnamon in coffee. I like things plain and simple.

Which reminds me, I brought you something." Evanelle grabbed her tote bag and brought out a yellow Bic lighter.

"Thank you, Evanelle," Claire said as she took the lighter and put it in her pocket. "I'm sure this will come in handy."

"Or maybe it won't. I just knew I had to give it to you." Evanelle, who had twenty-eight sweet teeth, all of them false, picked up her coffee and looked over at the covered cake plate on the stainless-steel island. "What have you made over there?"

"White cake. I stirred violet petals into the batter. And I crystallized some violets to put on top. It's for a dinner party I'm catering tonight." Claire picked up a Tupperware container beside it. "This white cake, I made for you. Nothing weird in it, I promise." She set it on the table next to Evanelle.

"You are the sweetest girl. When are you going to get married? When I'm gone, who will take care of you?"

"You're not going anywhere. And this is a perfect house for a spinster to live in. I'll grow old in this house, and neighborhood children will vex me by trying to get to the apple tree in the backyard and I'll chase them away with a broom. And I'll have lots of cats. That's probably why you gave me that cat bed."

Evanelle shook her head. "Your problem is routine. You like your routine too much. You get that from your grandmother. You're too attached to this place, just like her."

Claire smiled because she liked being compared to her grandmother. She had no idea about the security of having a name until her mother brought her here, to this house where her grandmother lived. They'd been in Bascom maybe three weeks, Sydney had just been born, and Claire had been sitting outside under the tullip tree in the front yard while people in town came to see Lorelei and her new baby. Claire wasn't new, so she didn't think anyone would want to see her. A couple came out of the house after visiting, and they watched Claire quietly build tiny log cabins with twigs. "She's a Waverley, all right," the woman said. "In her own world."

Claire didn't look up, didn't say a word, but she grabbed the grass before her body floated up. **She was a Waverley.** She didn't tell anyone, not a soul, for fear of someone taking her happiness away, but from that day on she would follow her grandmother out into the garden every morning, studying her, wanting to be like her, wanting to do all the things a true Waverley did to prove that, even though she wasn't born here, **she was a Waverley too.**

"I have to pack some boxes of jelly and vinegar to deliver," she said to Evanelle. "If you'll wait here for a minute, I'll drive you home."

"Are you making a delivery to Fred's?" Evanelle asked.

"Yes."

"Then I'll just go with you. I need Cokecola. And some Goo Goo Clusters. And maybe I'll pick up some tomatoes. You made me crave tomatoes."

While Evanelle debated the merits of yellow tomatoes versus red, Claire took four corrugated boxes out of the storeroom and packed up the jelly and the vinegar. When she was done, Evanelle followed her outside to her white minivan with **Waverley's Catering** written on the side.

Evanelle got in the passenger seat while Claire put her boxes in the back, then Claire handed Evanelle the container with her plain white cake in it and a brown paper bag to hold.

"What's this?" Evanelle said, looking in the brown bag as Claire got behind the wheel.

"A special order."

"It's for Fred," Evanelle said knowingly.

"Do you think he'd ever do business with me again if I told you that?"

"It's for Fred."

"I didn't say that."

"It's for Fred."

"I don't think I heard you. Who is it for?"

Evanelle sniffed. "Now you're being Miss Smarty Pants."

Claire laughed and pulled out of the drive.

Business was doing well, because all the locals knew that dishes made from the flowers that grew around the apple tree in the Waverley garden could affect the eater in curious ways. The biscuits with lilac jelly, the lavender tea cookies, and the tea cakes made with nasturtium mayonnaise the Ladies Aid ordered for their meetings once a month gave them the ability to keep secrets. The fried dandelion buds over marigold-petal rice, stuffed pumpkin blossoms, and rose-hip soup ensured that your company would notice only the beauty of your home and never the flaws. Anise hyssop honey butter on toast, angelica candy, and cupcakes with crystallized pansies made children thoughtful. Honeysuckle wine served on the Fourth of July gave you the ability to see in the dark. The nutty flavor of the dip made from hyacinth bulbs made you feel moody and think of the past, and the salads made with chicory and mint had you believing that something good was about to happen, whether it was true or not.

The dinner Claire was catering that night was being hosted by Anna Chapel, the head of the art department at Orion College, who gave a dinner party at the end of every spring semester for her department. Claire had catered these parties for her for the past five years. It was good exposure to get her name out among the university crowd, because they only expected good food with a splash of originality, whereas the people in town who had lived there all their lives came to her to cater affairs with a specific agenda—to get something off your chest and be assured the other person wouldn't speak of it again, to secure a promotion, or to mend a friendship.

First Claire took the jelly and vinegar to the farmers' market on the highway, where she'd rented shelf space at a booth, then she went into town and parked in front of Fred's Gourmet Grocery, formerly Fred's Foods, as it had been called for two generations, before a posher college and touristy crowd started shopping there.

She and Evanelle walked into the market with its creaking hardwood floors. Evanelle headed for the tomatoes, while Claire went to the back to Fred's office.

She knocked once, then opened the door. "Hello, Fred."

Sitting at his father's old desk, he had invoices in front of him, but judging by the way he jumped when Claire opened the door, his mind had been on other things. He immediately stood. "Claire. Good to see you."

"I have those two boxes you ordered."

"Good, good." He grabbed the white blazer hanging on the back of his chair and put it on over his short-sleeved black shirt. He walked out to her van with her and helped her bring the boxes in. "Did, um, did you bring that other thing we talked about?" he asked as they walked to the stockroom.

She smiled slightly and went back outside. A minute later she came back in and handed him the paper bag with a bottle of rose geranium wine in it.

Fred took it, looking embarrassed, then he handed her an envelope with a check in it. The act was completely innocuous, because he always gave her a check when she delivered her jelly and vinegar, but this check was a full ten times what his normal check to her was. And the envelope was brighter, as if filled with lightning bugs, lit by his hope.

"Thank you, Fred. I'll see you next month."

"Right. Bye, Claire."

Fred Walker watched Claire wait by the door for Evanelle to pay the cashier. Claire was a pretty woman, all dark hair and eyes and olive complexion. She didn't look anything like her mother, whom Fred had known in school, but then, neither did Sydney. They obviously took after their fathers, whoever their fathers were. People treated Claire politely, but they thought of her as standoffish and they never stopped her to talk about the weather or the new interstate connector or how sweet this year's crop of strawberries was. She was a Waverley, and Waverleys were an odd bunch, each in his or her own way. Claire's mother had been a troublemaker who left her children to be raised by their grandmother and then died in a car pileup in Chattanooga a few years later, her grandmother rarely left the house, her distant cousin Evanelle was forever giving people strange gifts. But that was just how the Waverleys were. Just like Runions were talkers, and Plemmons were shifty, and Hopkins men always married older women. But Claire kept the Waverley house in good shape, and it was one of the oldest homes around and tourists liked to drive by it, which was good for the town. And most importantly, Claire was there when someone in town needed a solution to a problem that could be solved only by the flowers grown around that apple tree in the Waverleys' backyard. She was the first in three generations to openly share that particular gift. That made her okay.

Evanelle walked over to Claire, and they left together.

Fred clutched the bag containing the bottle and walked back into his office.

He took off his blazer and sat back at the desk, staring again at the small framed photo of a handsome man wearing a tux. The photo had been taken at Fred's fiftieth birthday party a couple of years ago.

Fred and his partner, James, had been together for over thirty years, and if people knew the true nature of their relationship, it had gone on so long now that no one cared. But he and James had grown apart lately, and little seeds of anxiousness were starting to take root. Over the past few months, James had been staying overnight in Hickory, where he worked, a few nights a week, saying he was working so late that commuting back to Bascom didn't make sense. This left Fred at home alone far too often, and he didn't know what to do with himself. James was the one who always said, "You make wonderful pot stickers, let's have that for dinner tonight." Or, "There's a movie I want us to see on television." James was always right, and Fred questioned every little thing when he wasn't there. What should he have for dinner? Should he set the things he needed to take to the dry cleaner out at night or wait for the morning?

All his life Fred had heard things about the Waverleys' rose geranium wine. It signaled in the drinker a return to happiness, remembering the good, and Fred wanted back the good thing he and James had. Claire made only one bottle a year, and it was damn expensive, but it was a sure thing, because Waverleys, for all their blindness to their own way of living, were extremely accurate in helping other people see.

He reached for the phone and dialed James's work number. He needed to ask him what he should make for dinner.

And what meat did you serve with magic wine?

Claire arrived at Anna Chapel's home late that afternoon. Anna lived in a cul-de-sac neighborhood just outside Orion College, and the only way to get to it was through the campus. The neighborhood had been for the instructors at the college, the houses built at the same time the campus was constructed a hundred years ago. The intention was to keep the academic community as insular as possible. A wise move, considering the opposition to a college for women at the time. Today, the chancellor still made his home there, and a few professors, including Anna, lived in the original houses. But the neighborhood was dominated now by young families who had no association with the college. They simply liked the privacy and security of the place.

"Claire, welcome," Anna said when she opened the front door to find Claire on her porch, carrying a cooler of things that needed to be refrigerated immediately. She stepped aside and let Claire enter. "You know the way. Do you need help?"

"No, thank you. I'm fine," Claire said, though late spring and summer were her busiest seasons and the time when she had the least help. She usually hired first-year culinary students at Orion to help her during the school year. They, after all, were not from Bascom and the only questions they asked were culinary ones. She'd learned the hard way to avoid hiring anyone local if she could help it. Most of them expected to learn something magic or, at the very least, get to the apple tree in the backyard, hoping to find out if the local legend was true, that its apples would tell them what the biggest event in their lives would be.

Claire went to the kitchen, put away the things in the cooler, then opened the kitchen door and brought in the rest of the things through the back entrance. Soon the farmhouse-style kitchen was alive with the steamy warmth and crafty scent that eventually flowed through the house. It welcomed Anna's guests like a kiss on the cheek from their mothers, like coming home.

Anna always wanted to use her own dishes—heavy pottery ones that she'd made herself—so Claire arranged the salad on the salad plates first and was ready to serve when Anna told her everyone was seated.

The menu tonight was salad, yucca soup, pork tenderloins stuffed with nas-turtiums and chives and goat cheese, lemon-verbena sorbet between dishes, and the violet white cake for dessert. Claire was kept busy, monitoring the food at the stove, arranging the food on the plates, serving and then deftly and quietly taking plates away when the guests had finished a course. This was as formal as any affair she catered, but these were art professors and their spouses, casual and intelligent people who poured their own wine and water and appreciated the creativity of the meal. When she had to work alone, she didn't focus on the people, just what she had to do, which was painfully exhausting that evening considering she had slept the night before on the hard ground of her garden. But it had its positive side. She was never very good with people.

She was aware of **him,** though. He was seated two places down from Anna, who was at the head of the table. Everyone else watched the food as it entered the room, as it was placed in front of them. But **he** watched her. His dark hair almost touched his shoulders, his arms and fingers were long, and his lips were fuller than she'd ever seen on a man. He was . . . trouble.

As she was serving dessert, she felt something almost like anticipation the closer she got to sliding his plate in front of him. She wasn't quite sure if it was his anticipation or hers.

"Have we met?" he asked when she finally made it to his place. He was smiling such a nice, open smile that she almost smiled back.

She put his plate in front of him, the piece of cake so perfect and moist, the crystallized violets spilling over it like frosted jewels. It screamed, **Look at me!** But his eyes were on her. "I don't think so," she replied.

"This is Claire Waverley, the caterer," Anna said, happy with wine, her cheeks pink. "I hire her for every department gathering. Claire, this is Tyler Hughes. This is his first year with us."

Claire nodded, extremely uncomfortable that all eyes were on her now.

"Waverley," Tyler said thoughtfully. She started to move away, but his long fingers wrapped gently around her arm, not letting her move. "Of course!" he said, laughing. "You're my neighbor! I live beside you. Pendland Street, right? You live in that large Queen Anne?"

She was so surprised he'd actually touched her that all she could do was give a jerky nod.

As if aware that she'd gone stiff or of the slight shiver along her skin, he immediately let go of her. "I just bought that blue house next to you," he said. "I moved in a few weeks ago."

Claire just looked at him.

"Well, it's nice to finally meet you," he said.

She nodded again and left the room. She washed up and packed away her things, leaving the last of the salad and cake in the refrigerator for Anna. She was moody and distracted now and she didn't know why. But as she worked, she kept running her fingers unconsciously along her arm where Tyler had touched her, as if trying to brush something off her skin.

Before Claire took her last box out to her van, Anna came to the kitchen to rave about the food and to tell Claire what a good job she'd done, either too drunk or too polite to mention Claire's odd behavior with one of her guests.

Claire smiled and took the check from Anna. She said good-bye, picked up the box, and left by the back entrance. She slowly walked down the short driveway to her van. Fatigue was settling low in her body like sand, and her steps were slow. It was a nice night, though. The air was warm and dry, and she decided she was going to sleep with her bedroom windows open.

When she reached the curb, she felt a strange gust of wind. She turned to see a figure standing under the oak tree in Anna's front yard. She couldn't make him out clearly, but there were tiny pinpricks of purple light hovering around him, like electrical snaps.

He pushed himself away from the tree, and she could feel him stare at her. She turned and took a step to her van.

"Wait," Tyler called.

She should have kept walking; instead, she turned to him again.

"Do you have a light?" he asked.

Claire closed her eyes. It would be much easier to blame Evanelle if the old woman actually knew what she was doing.

She set the box down and reached into

her dress pocket and brought out the yellow Bic lighter Evanelle had given her earlier that day. **This** was what she was meant to do with it?

She felt like she had water against her back, pushing her toward the deep end, as she walked toward him and extended the lighter. She stopped a few feet away, trying to keep as much distance as possible, digging her heels in as whatever force it was tried to take her closer.

He was smiling, easygoing, and interested. He had an unlit cigarette between his lips, and he took it from his mouth. "Do you smoke?"

"No." She still had the lighter in her outstretched hand. He didn't take it.

"I shouldn't. I know. I'm down to two a day. It's not a very social habit anymore." When she didn't respond, he shifted from one foot to the other. "I've seen you around. You have a wonderful yard. I mowed my yard for the first time a couple of days ago. You don't talk much, do you? Or have I done something to offend the neighborhood already? Was I out in my yard in my underwear at any point?"

Claire gave a start. She felt so protected in her home that she frequently forgot that she had neighbors, neighbors who could, from their second stories, see down into her sunroom, where she'd taken off her nightgown that morning.

"It was a wonderful meal," Tyler said, still trying.

"Thank you."

"Maybe I'll see you again?"

Her heart started to race. She didn't need anything more than she already had. The moment she let something else into her life, she would get hurt. Sure as sugar. Sure as rain. She had Evanelle, her house, and her business. That was all she needed. "Keep the lighter," Claire said, handing it to him and walking away.

When Claire pulled into her driveway, she stopped by the front yard instead of pulling around back. There was someone sitting on the top step of the porch.

Claire got out, leaving her headlights on and the car door open. She jogged across the yard, all her earlier fatigue gone in a panic. "Evanelle, what's wrong?"

Evanelle stood stiffly, the glow from the streetlights causing her to look frail and ghostly. She was holding two packages of new bed linens and a box of strawberry Pop-Tarts. "I couldn't sleep until I brought you this. Here, take them and let me sleep."

Claire hurried up the steps and took the things, then she wrapped an arm around Evanelle. "How long have you been waiting?"

"About an hour. I was in bed when it hit me. You needed fresh sheets and Pop-Tarts."

"Why didn't you call me on my cell phone? I could have picked these things up."

"It doesn't work like that. I don't know why."

"Stay the night. Let me make you some warm sugar milk."

"No," Evanelle said curtly. "I want to go home."

After those feelings Tyler had stirred in her, Claire wanted to fight even more for the things she had, the only things she wanted in her heart. "Maybe these sheets mean I'm supposed to make up a bed for you," she said hopefully as she tried to turn Evanelle toward the door. "Stay with me. Please."

"No! They're not for me! I don't know what they're for! I never know what they're for!" Evanelle said, her voice rising. She took a deep breath, then said in a whisper, "I just want to go home."

Despising herself for feeling so needy, Claire patted Evanelle gently, reassuringly. "It's okay. I'll take you home." She set the sheets and the Pop-Tarts on the wicker rocker by the front door. "Come on, honey," she said, leading the sleepy old lady down the stairs and to the van.

When Tyler Hughes got home, Claire's house was dark. He parked his Jeep on the street and got out, but then he stopped on the walkway to his house. He didn't want to go in yet.

He turned when he heard the clicking of small dog feet on the sidewalk. Soon, a tiny black terrier skittered past, hot on the trail of a moth that was popping from one streetlight to the next.

Tyler waited for what was coming next.

Sure enough, Mrs. Kranowski, a spindly old woman with a hairdo that looked like vanilla soft-serve ice cream, appeared. She was chasing after the dog, calling, "Edward! Edward! Come back to Mama. Edward! Come back here now!"

"Need help, Mrs. Kranowski?" Tyler asked as she passed.

"No, thank you, Tyler," she said as she disappeared down the street.

This neighborhood spectacle, he'd quickly discovered, happened at least four times a day.

Hey, it was good to have a routine.

Tyler appreciated that better than most. He would be teaching classes that summer, but there were a couple of weeks between the spring and summer semesters, and he always got restless when he didn't have a routine. Structure had never been his strong suit, though he took a lot of comfort in it. Sometimes he wondered if he was made that way or simply taught. His parents were potters and potheads, and they had encouraged his artistic streak. It wasn't until he started elementary school that he realized it was wrong to draw on walls. It had been such a **relief.** School gave him structure, rules, direction. Summer vacations had him forgetting to eat because he spent hours and hours drawing and dreaming, never moderated by his parents. They had loved that about him. His had been a good childhood but one where ambition ranked right up there with Ronald Reagan as taboo subjects. He'd always assumed that, like his parents, he could make a meager living from his artwork and be happy with that. But school was nice, college even better, and he didn't like the thought of leaving it.

So he decided to teach.

His parents never understood. Making good money was almost as bad as becoming a Republican.

He was still standing there on his walkway when Mrs. Kranowski came back down the sidewalk with Edward now wiggling in her arms. "That's a good Edward," she was saying to him. "That's Mama's good boy."

"Good night, Mrs. Kranowski," he said when she passed him again.

"Good night, Tyler."

He liked this crazy place.

His first position after getting his master's was at a high school in Florida, where they were so desperate for teachers that they were paying premium salaries, living expenses, plus moving expenses from his home in Connecticut. After a year or so, he also started teaching night art classes at the local university.

It was serendipity that eventually led him to Bascom. He met a woman at a conference in Orlando, an art professor at

Orion College in Bascom. There was wine, there was flirtation, there was a wild night of sex in her hotel room. A few years later, during a restless summer break, he found out about an opening in the art department at Orion College, and that night came back to him in beautiful and vivid images. He interviewed for and got the position. He didn't even remember the woman's name, it was simply the romance of the thing. By the time he arrived, she had moved on, and he never found her.

The older he got, the more he thought about how he hadn't married, about how what brought him to this town in the first place was another restless summer and a dream of a life with a woman with whom he'd had a one-night stand.

Okay, was that really romantic or just pitiful?

He heard a thud come from around the side of his house, so he took his hands out of his pockets and headed to the backyard. When he'd mowed a couple of days ago, the grass had been high, so there were big wet clumps of grass clippings all over the yard.

He should probably rake it all up. But then what would he do with all that grass? He couldn't just leave it in a big clump in the middle of his yard. What if all the cut grass dried and killed the live grass under it?

One day out of school and he was already obsessively preoccupied with his lawn. And it would probably get worse.

What was he going to do with himself until the summer session started?

He had to remember to make notes to himself to eat. He'd do it tonight, so he wouldn't forget. He'd stick them to the refrigerator, the couch, the bed, the commode.

The light from the back porch illuminated the backyard—a small yard, not nearly as large as the one next door. The Waverleys' metal fence, covered with honeysuckle, separated the two yards. Twice since he'd moved in, Tyler had pulled kids off the fence. They were trying to get to the apple tree, they said, which he thought was stupid because there were at least six mature apple trees on Orion's campus. Why try to go over a nine-foot fence with pointy finials when they could walk to Orion? He told the kids this, but they just looked at him like he didn't know what he was talking about. That apple tree, they said, was special.

He walked along the fence, taking deep breaths of sweet honeysuckle. His foot hit something and he looked down to see he had kicked an apple. His eyes then followed a trail of apples to a small pile of them close to the fence. Another one hit the ground with a thud. This was the first time he'd ever had apples fall on his side of the fence. Hell, he couldn't even see the tree from his yard.

He picked up a small pink apple, rubbed it to a shine on his shirt, then took a bite.

He slowly walked back to his house, deciding that he would put the apples in a box tomorrow and take them to Claire, tell her what happened. It would be a good excuse to see her again.

It was probably just another instance of following a woman to a dead end.

But what the hell.

Do the things you do best.

The last thing he remembered was putting his foot on the bottom step of the back porch.

Then he had the most amazing dream.

CHAPTER
2

Ten days earlier
Seattle, Washington

Sydney walked over to her daughter's bed. "Wake up, honey."

When Bay opened her eyes, Sydney put her finger to the little girl's lips.

"We're going to leave, and we don't want Susan to hear, so let's be quiet. Remember? Like we planned."

Bay got up without a word and went to the bathroom and remembered not to flush the commode, because the two town houses shared a wall and Susan would be able to hear. Bay then put on her shoes with the soft, quiet soles and dressed in the layers Sydney had set out for her because it was colder that morning than it would be later, but there wouldn't be time to stop and change.

Sydney paced while Bay dressed. David had gone to L.A. on business, and he always had the older lady in the town house next door keep an eye on Sydney and Bay. For the past week, Sydney had been taking clothes and food and other items out of the house in her tote bag, not deviating from the routine David held her to, the one Susan kept watch over. She was allowed to take Bay to the park on Mondays, Tuesdays, and Thursdays and to go to the grocery store on Fridays. Two months ago she met a mother at the park who'd had the nerve to ask what the other mothers couldn't. Why so many bruises? Why so jumpy? She helped Sydney buy an old Subaru for three hundred dollars, a good chunk of the money Sydney had managed to save in the past two years by taking one-dollar bills out of David's wallet every so often, collecting the change in the couch cushions, and taking back items for cash that she'd bought with a check, the account for which David kept a sharp eye on. She'd been taking the food and clothes to the lady in the park, to be put in the car. Sydney hoped to God that the lady, Greta, hadn't forgotten to park the car where they'd agreed. The last she'd talked to her was Thursday, and it was Sunday. David would be back that night.

Every two or three months, David would fly to L.A. to check in person how the restaurant he'd bought into was running. He always stayed to party with his partners, old college buddies from his UCLA days. He'd come home happy, still a little buzzed, and that would last until he wanted sex and she wouldn't compare with the girls he'd been with in L.A. She used to be like those girls, long ago. And dangerous men had been her specialty, just as she always imagined it had been for her mother—one of the many reasons she left Bascom with nothing but a backpack and a few photos of her mother as a traveling companion.

"I'm ready," Bay whispered as she walked into the hallway where Sydney was pacing.

Sydney went to her knees and hugged her daughter. She was five already, old enough to realize what was going on in her house. Sydney tried to keep David from having any sort of influence on Bay, and by unspoken agreement he didn't hurt Bay as long as Sydney did what he said. But it was a terrible example Sydney was setting. Bascom, for all its faults, was safe, and going back to a place she despised was worth Bay finally knowing what security felt like.

Sydney pulled back before she started crying again. "Come on, honey."

She used to be good at leaving. She used to do it all the time before she met David. Now the fear of it was making it hard to breathe.

When she first left North Carolina, Sydney had gone straight to New York, where she could blend and no one thought she was strange, where the name Waverley meant nothing. She moved in with some actors, who used her to perfect their Southern accents while she worked on getting rid of hers. After a year she went to Chicago with a man who stole cars for a living, a good living. When he was caught, she took his money and moved to San Francisco and lived on it for another year. She changed her name then, so he wouldn't find her, and she became Cindy Watkins, the name of one of her old friends from New York. After the money was gone, she went to Vegas and served drinks. The girl she'd traveled from Vegas to Seattle with had a friend who worked at a restaurant called David's on the Bay, and she got jobs for them both.

Sydney had been wildly attracted to David, the owner. He wasn't handsome, but he was powerful and she liked that.

Powerful men were thrilling, until the point that they turned frightening, and that was when she always left. She became so good at touching fire and not getting burned. Things with David started to get scary about six months after she started seeing him. He would bruise her sometimes, tie her up in bed and tell her how much he loved her. Then he started following her to the grocery store and to friends' houses. She made plans to leave him, to steal some money from his restaurant and go to Mexico with a girl she'd met at the Laundromat, but then she found out she was pregnant.

Bay arrived seven months later, named by David after his restaurant. The first year of Bay's life, Sydney resented the quiet baby for everything that had gone wrong. David disgusted her now, frightened her well beyond the limit she thought there was to being scared. And he sensed it and hit her more. This hadn't been part of her plan. She didn't want a family. She'd never counted on staying with any of the men she met. Now she had to stay because of Bay.

One day everything changed. They were still living in the apartment she and David had shared before moving to the town house. Bay was barely a year old, and she was playing quietly with the clean laundry in the basket on the floor, draping washcloths on her head and towels over her legs. Suddenly Sydney saw herself, playing alone while her mother wrung her hands and paced the floor at the Waverley house in Bascom, before her mother left again without a word. A powerful feeling surged through her, and her skin prickled and she let out a deep breath that came out like frost. That was the moment she let go of trying to be her mother. Her mother had tried to be a decent person, but she had never been a good mother. She had left her daughters with no explanation, and she never came back. Sydney was going to be a good mother, and good mothers protected their children. It had taken her a year, but she finally realized that she didn't have to stay because she had Bay. **She could take Bay with her.**

She'd been so good at running in the past that she'd been lulled into a false sense of security, because no one had ever come after her. She actually made it through beauty school before walking out of the salon in Boise where she'd gotten her first job and finding David in the parking lot. Before she noticed him standing there by his car, she remembered turning her face into the wind and smelling lavender and thinking she hadn't smelled that since Bascom. The scent seemed to be coming from the salon itself, as if trying to get her to follow it back in.

But then she saw David and he dragged her to his car. She was surprised but didn't struggle, because she didn't want to be embarrassed in front of her new friends in the salon. David drove off and parked behind a fast-food restaurant, where he hit her with his fists so many times she lost consciousness, and she woke up while he was fucking her in the backseat. He rented a motel room afterward and let her clean up, telling her how it was all her fault as she spit a tooth into the bathroom sink. They later went to pick up Bay at daycare, where David had discovered Bay was enrolled and was how he found them. He was charming and the teachers believed him when he said Sydney had been in a car accident.

Back in Seattle, his anger would come on so suddenly. Bay would be in the next room and Sydney would be making her a peanut butter sandwich, or she'd be in the shower, and suddenly David would appear and hit her in the stomach or pin her against the counter and rip down her shorts, then he'd pound into her, telling her she would never leave him again.

For the past two years, ever since he'd dragged her back from Boise, Sydney would walk into a room and smell roses, or she would wake up and taste honeysuckle in the air. The scents always seemed to be coming from a window or a doorway, a way out.

It was only one night while watching Bay sleep, crying quietly and wondering how she was going to keep her child safe when they were in danger if they stayed and in danger if they left, that it suddenly made sense.

She'd been smelling home.

They had to go home.

She and Bay walked silently downstairs in the predawn dark. Susan next door could see both the front and back doors, so they went to the window in the living room that over-looked the small strip of side yard that Susan couldn't see. Sydney had earlier popped out the screen, so all she had to do was quietly open the window and lower Bay out first. Next she tossed down her tote bag, another suitcase she'd packed, and Bay's small back-pack, which she'd let Bay pack on her own, full of secret things that brought her com-fort. Sydney crawled out and led Bay through the hydrangea bushes and into the parking lot by their house. Greta from the park said she was going to leave the Subaru in front of the 100 block of town houses one street over. She was going to put the keys above the visor. No insurance and a dead tag, but that didn't matter. All that mattered was that it would get them away.

It was drizzling as she and Bay jogged along the sidewalk, skirting the shine of the streetlights.

Sydney's bangs were dripping into her eyes when they finally stopped at the 100 block of town houses. Her eyes darted around. Where was it? She left Bay and ran up and down the parking lot. There was only one Subaru, but it was too nice to be worth only three hundred dollars. It was locked too, and there were papers and an Eddie Bauer coffee mug inside. It belonged to someone else.

She ran around the parking lot again. She checked one street over, just to be sure.

It wasn't there.

She ran back to Bay, out of breath, appalled that her panic made her leave her daughter even for a minute. She was getting sloppy, and she couldn't do that. Not now.

She sat on the curb between a Honda and a Ford truck and buried her face in her hands. All that courage wasted. How could she take Bay back, back to the way things were? Sydney couldn't, wouldn't, be Cindy Watkins anymore.

Bay came to sit close beside her, and Sydney wrapped an arm around her.

"It will be okay, Mommy."

"I know it will. Let's just sit here for a minute, okay? Let Mommy figure out what to do."

At four in the morning, the parking lot was quiet, which was why Sydney jerked her head up when she heard a car approaching. She scooted Bay over as close to the pickup as possible to avoid detection. What if it was Susan? What if she'd told David?

The lights from the car slowly approached, as if searching for something. Sydney shielded Bay and closed her eyes, as if that would help.

The car stopped.

A car door slammed.

"Cindy?"

She looked up to see Greta, a short blond woman who always wore cowboy boots and two large turquoise rings.

"Oh, God," Sydney whispered.

"I'm sorry," Greta said, kneeling in front of her. "I'm so sorry. I tried parking here, but the guy living over there caught me and told me he was calling a tow truck. I've been driving by every half hour, waiting for you."

"Oh, God."

"It's okay." Greta pulled Sydney to her feet and led her and Bay to a Subaru wagon with plastic over a broken window on the passenger side and rust spots from fender to fender. "Be safe. Go as far as you can."

"Thank you."

Greta nodded and got into the passenger seat of the Jeep that had followed her into the parking lot.

"See, Mommy?" Bay said. "I knew it was going to be okay."

"Me too," Sydney lied.

The morning after Anna Chapel's party, Claire went to the garden for a basket of mint. She was going to start on the food for the Amateur Botanists Association's annual luncheon in Hickory on Friday. Being botanists, they liked the idea of edible flowers. Being a bunch of rich eccentric old ladies, they paid well and could give a lot of referrals. It was a coup to get the job, but it was a big job, and she was going to have to buck it up and hire someone local to help her serve.

The garden was gated by heavy metal fencing, like a gothic cemetery, and the honeysuckle clinging to it was almost two feet thick in some places, completely closing in the place. Even the gate door was covered with honeysuckle vines, and the keyhole was a secret pocket only a few could find.

When she entered, she noticed it right away.

There, in the cluster of Queen Anne's lace, tiny leaves of ivy were sprouting.

Ivy in the garden.

Overnight.

The garden was saying that something was trying to get in, something that was pretty and looked harmless but would take over everything if given the chance.

She quickly pulled the ivy out and dug deep for the roots. But then she spied a hairy vine of it sneaking up a lilac bush, and she crawled over to it.

In her haste, she hadn't closed the garden gate behind her, and a half hour later she jerked her head around in surprise when she heard the crunch of footsteps on the gravel pathway that snaked around the flowers.

It was Tyler, carrying a cardboard milk box and looking around as if he'd entered someplace enchanted. Everything bloomed here at once, even at a time of year when it wasn't supposed to. He stopped suddenly when his eyes found Claire on her knees, digging up the roots of the ivy under the lilac bush. He gave her a look like he was trying to make her out in the dark.

"It's Tyler Hughes," he said, as if she wouldn't recognize him, "from next door."

She nodded. "I remember."

He walked over to her. "Apples," he said, crouching beside her and putting the box on the ground. "They fell over the fence. There are at least a dozen here. I didn't know if you used them for your catering, so I thought I'd bring them over. I tried your door, but no one answered."

Claire scooted the box away from him as subtly as possible. "I don't use them. But thank you. You don't like apples?"

He shook his head. "Just occasionally. I can't figure out for the life of me how they got in my yard. The tree is too far away."

He didn't mention a vision, which relieved her. He must not have eaten one. "Must have been the wind," she said.

"You know, the trees on campus don't have mature apples on them at this time of year."

"This tree blooms in the winter and produces apples all spring and summer."

Tyler stood and stared at the tree. "Impressive."

Claire looked over her shoulder at it. The tree was situated toward the back of the lot. It wasn't very tall, but it grew long and sideways. Its limbs stretched out like a dancer's arms and the apples grew at the very ends, as if holding the fruit in its palms. It was a beautiful old tree, the gray bark wrinkled and molting in places. The only grass in the garden was around the tree, stretching about ten feet beyond the reach of its branches, giving the old tree its room.

Claire didn't know why, but every once in a while the tree would actually throw apples, as if bored. When she was young, her bedroom window looked out over the garden. She would sleep with her window open in the summers, and sometimes she would wake in the morning to find one or two apples on the floor.

Claire gave the tree a stern look.

Occasionally that worked, making it behave. "It's just a tree," she said, and turned back to the lilac bush. She resumed pulling at the roots of the ivy.

Tyler put his hands in his pockets and watched her work. She'd been working alone in the garden for so many years that she realized she missed having someone there. It reminded her of gardening with her grandmother. It was never meant to be a solitary job. "So, have you lived in Bascom long?" Tyler finally asked.

"Almost all my life."

"Almost?"

"My family is from here. My mother was born here. She left but moved back when I was six. I've been here ever since."

"So you are from here."

Claire froze. How could he do that? How could he do that with just five little words? He just said to her the very thing she'd always wanted to hear. He was getting in without even knowing how he did it. He was the ivy, wasn't he? She very slowly turned her head and looked up at him, his lanky body, his awkward features, his beautiful brown eyes. "Yes," she said breathlessly.

"So, who are your guests?" he asked.

It took a moment for the words to penetrate. "I don't have any guests."

"As I was coming around the front of the house, someone pulled up to the curb with a car full of boxes and bags. I thought they were moving in."

"That's strange." Claire stood and took off her gloves. She turned and walked out of the garden, making sure Tyler was following her. She didn't trust the tree alone with him, even if he didn't eat apples.

She walked along the driveway curving beside the house, but then she came to a sudden stop beside the tulip tree in the front yard. Tyler came up behind her, close, and put his hands on her arms, as if aware that her legs had turned boneless.

More ivy.

There was a little girl, about five years old, running around the yard with her arms stretched wide like an airplane. A woman was leaning against an old Subaru wagon parked on the street, her arms crossed tightly over her chest, watching the little girl. She looked small, frail, with unwashed light-brown hair and deep circles under her eyes. She seemed to be holding herself to keep from trembling.

Claire wondered absently if this was how her grandmother felt when her daughter came home after years away, when pregnant Lorelei showed up on her doorstep with a six-year-old clinging to her leg. This relief, this anger, this sadness, this panic.

Finally making her legs move, she crossed the yard, leaving Tyler behind.

"Sydney?"

Sydney pushed herself away from the car quickly, startled. Her eyes went all over Claire before she smiled. That insecure woman with her arms wrapped around her was gone, replaced by the old Sydney, the one who always looked down her nose at her family name, never realizing what a gift it was to have been born here. "Hi, Claire."

Claire stopped on the sidewalk, a few feet

away from her. She could be a ghost, or maybe someone who looked incredibly like Sydney. The Sydney Claire knew would never let her hair look like that. She wouldn't be caught dead wearing a T-shirt with food stains on it. She used to be so meticulous, so put together. She always tried so hard not to look like a Waverley. "Where have you been?"

"Everywhere." Sydney smiled that spectacular smile of hers, and suddenly it didn't matter what her hair or clothes looked like. Yes, this was Sydney.

The little girl from the yard ran up to Sydney and stood close to her. Sydney put her arm around her. "This is my daughter, Bay."

Claire looked at the child and managed to smile. She had dark hair, as dark as Claire's, but Sydney's blue eyes. "Hello, Bay."

"And this is . . . ?" Sydney asked suggestively.

"Tyler Hughes," he said, extending a hand past Claire. She hadn't realized he'd come up behind her again, and she gave a start. "I live over there, next door."

Sydney shook Tyler's hand and nodded. "The old Sanderson place. It looks good. It wasn't blue the last time I saw it. Just a hideous moldy white."

"I can't take credit for it. I bought it like that."

"I'm Sydney Waverley, Claire's sister."

"Nice to meet you. I'll just be going. Claire, if you need me for anything . . ." He squeezed Claire's shoulder, then left. She was confused. She didn't want him to go. Yet of course he couldn't stay. But now she was alone with Sydney and her quiet daughter, and she had no idea what to do.

Sydney wagged her eyebrows. "He's hot."

"Waverley," Claire said.

"What?"

"You said your last name was Waverley."

"Last time I checked."

"I thought you hated the name."

Sydney shrugged noncommitally.

"What about Bay?"

"Her name is Waverley too. Go play some more, honey," Sydney said, and Bay ran back to the yard. "I can't believe how great the house looks. New paint, new windows, new roof. I never imagined it could look so good."

"I used Grandma Waverley's life-insurance money to remodel."

Sydney turned away a moment, ostensibly to watch Tyler climb the stairs to his front porch and then walk into his house. She had stiffened, and it occurred to Claire that this was shocking news to Sydney. Had she really expected to find their grandmother here, alive and well? What **was** she expecting? "When?" Sydney asked.

"When what?"

"When did she die?"

"Ten years ago. Christmas Eve, the year you left. I had no way to contact you. We didn't know where you went."

"Grandma knew. I told her. Say, do you mind if I pull this clunker behind the house?" Sydney knocked on the hood with her fist. "It's sort of an embarrassment."

"What happened to Grandma's old car, the one she gave you?"

"I sold it in New York. Grandma said I could sell it if I wanted to."

"So that's where you've been, New York?"

"No, I only stayed there for a year. I've been around. Just like Mom."

They locked eyes, and suddenly everything was quiet. "What are you doing here, Sydney?"

"I need a place to stay."

"For how long?"

Sydney took a deep breath. "I don't know."

"You can't leave Bay here."

"What?"

"Like Mom left us here. You can't leave her here."

"I would never leave my daughter!" Sydney exclaimed, a touch of hysteria tinging her words, and Claire was suddenly aware of all that wasn't being said, of the story Sydney wasn't telling. Something big had to have happened to bring Sydney back here. "What do you want me to do, Claire, beg?"

"No, I don't want you to beg."

"I don't have anywhere else to go," Sydney said, forcing the words out, like spitting sunflower-seed shells to the sidewalk, where they stuck and baked in the sun, getting harder and harder.

What was Claire supposed to do? Sydney was family. Claire had learned the hard way that you weren't supposed to take them for granted. She'd also learned they could hurt you more than anyone else in the world. "Have you had breakfast yet?"

"No."

"I'll meet you in the kitchen."

"Come on, Bay, I'm pulling the car around back," Sydney called, and Bay ran to her mother.

"Bay, do you like strawberry Pop-Tarts?" Claire asked.

Bay smiled, and it was Sydney's smile made over. It almost hurt Claire to look at, remembering all the things she wished she could take back from when Sydney was a child, like chasing Sydney out of the garden when she wanted to see what Claire and their grandmother were doing and hiding recipes on high shelves so Sydney would never know their secrets. Claire had always wondered if she was the one who made Sydney hate being a Waverley. Was this child going to hate everything Waverley too? Bay didn't know it, but she had a gift. Maybe Claire could teach her to use it. Claire didn't know if she and Sydney would ever reconcile, or even how long she was going to stay, but maybe she could try to make up for what she'd done with Bay.

In mere minutes, Claire's life had changed. Her grandmother had taken in Claire and Sydney. Claire would do the same for Sydney and Bay. No questions asked. It's what a true Waverley did.

"Pop-Tarts are my favorite!" Bay said.

Sydney looked startled. "How did you know?"

"I didn't," Claire said, turning toward the house. "Evanelle did."

Sydney parked the Subaru beside a white minivan at the back of the house, in front of the detached garage. Bay hopped out, but Sydney got out a little slower. She took her tote bag and Bay's backpack, then she went around to the back of the car and un-screwed the Washington State license plate. She stuffed it into her bag. There. No clues as to where they'd been.

Bay was standing in the driveway that separated the house from the garden. "This is really where we're going to live?" she asked, for about the sixteenth time since they'd pulled in front of the house that morning.

Sydney took a deep breath. God, she couldn't believe it. "Yes."

"It's a princess house." She turned and pointed to the open gate. "Can I go see the flowers?"

"No. Those are Claire's flowers." She heard a thud and watched an apple roll out of the garden and stop at her feet. She stared at it for a moment. No one in her family ever found anything odd about having a tree that told the future and threw apples at people. Still, it was a better welcome than Claire had given her. She kicked the apple back into the garden. "And stay away from the apple tree."

"I don't like apples."

Sydney went to her knees in front of Bay. She pushed the little girl's hair behind her ears and straightened her shirt. "Okay, what's your name?"

"Bay Waverley."

"And where were you born?"

"On a Greyhound bus."

"Who is your father?"

"I don't know who he is."

"Where are you from?"

"Everywhere."

She took her daughter's hands. "You understand why you have to say these things, don't you?"

"Because we're different here. We're not who we were."

"You amaze me."

"Thank you. Do you think Claire will like me?"

Sydney stood, then took a moment to steady herself when dark spots appeared in front of her eyes and the world tilted off its axis for a moment. Her skin felt prickled, as if with goose bumps, and it hurt to blink. She was so tired she could hardly walk, but she couldn't let Bay see her like that, and she certainly couldn't let Claire see her like that. She managed to smile. "She'd be crazy not to."

"I like her. She's like Snow White."

They walked into the kitchen through the sunroom and Sydney looked around in awe. The kitchen had been remodeled, taking over most of what had been the dining room beside it. It was all stainless steel and efficiency, and there were two commercial refrigerators and two ovens.

They wordlessly went to the kitchen table and sat, watching Claire put on coffee and then slide two Pop-Tarts into the toaster. Claire had changed—not in big ways but small ones, like the way light changed throughout the day. A different slant, a different hue. She carried herself differently; she no longer had that greedy, selfish way about her. She seemed comfortable, the way their grandmother used to seem comfortable. Don't-move-me-and-I'll-be-fine comfortable.

Watching her, it suddenly occurred to Sydney that Claire was beautiful. Sydney had never realized her sister was so beautiful. The man she was with earlier, the man from next door, thought so too. He was clearly attracted to Claire. And Bay was captivated by her, not taking her eyes off her even when Claire put warm Pop-Tarts and a glass of milk on the table in front of her.

"So, you run a catering company?" Sydney finally asked when Claire handed her a cup of coffee. "I saw the van."

"Yes," Claire said, turning away in a swish of mint and lilac. Her hair was longer than it used to be, and it veiled her shoulders like a shawl. She used it for protection.

If there was one thing Sydney knew, it was hair. She loved beauty school and loved working in the salon in Boise. Hair said more about people than they knew, and Sydney understood the language naturally. It had surprised her that some other girls at beauty school thought it was hard. To Sydney it was second nature. It always had been.

She didn't have the energy to keep talking to Claire when Claire was making it so difficult, so she took a sip of the coffee and found it had cinnamon in it, just like Grandma Waverley used to make it. She wanted to drink more, but her hand started shaking and she had to set the cup down.

When was the last time she'd slept? She'd made sure Bay slept, but she was too scared to sleep more than small pockets at a time at rest stops and Wal-Mart parking lots along the way. Miles of highway ran on a permanent loop in her mind, and she still felt the hum of the road in her bones. It had taken them ten days, surviving on the food she'd packed, white bread and gingersnaps and cheap packages of peanut butter and crackers, the ones where the peanut butter tasted oily and the crackers crumbled at the touch. She wasn't sure she could last much longer before she broke down in tears.

"Come on, Bay," Sydney said the moment Bay finished her breakfast. "Let's go upstairs."

"I left new sheets from Evanelle on the beds," Claire said.

"Which room?"

"Your room is still your room. Bay can sleep in my old room. I sleep in Grandma's now," she said, her back to them as she began to bring down large canisters of flour and sugar from the cabinets.

Sydney led Bay straight to the staircase, not looking around, because she was disoriented enough and didn't want to discover what else had changed. Bay ran up the stairs ahead of her and waited, smiling.

It was worth it. All this was worth it, just to see her child like this.

Sydney led her to Claire's old room first. The furniture was different, mismatched. The sewing table used to be in the sitting room downstairs, and the bed used to be in their grandmother's room. Bay ran to the window. "I like this room."

"Your aunt Claire used to spend hours at that window, staring out at the garden. You can sleep with me, if you want to. My room has a view of the blue house next door."

"Maybe."

"I'm going to start bringing in our things. Come with me."

Bay looked at her hopefully. "Can I stay up here?"

She was too tired to argue. "Don't leave this room. If you want to go exploring, we'll do it together."

Sydney left Bay, but instead of going downstairs to get the boxes and bags left in the car, she walked to her old room. When she was young she spent a lot of time by herself in her room, sometimes imagining that she was trapped there by her evil sister, like in a fairy tale. For two years after her mother left, Sydney even slept with sheets tied into a rope under her bed so she could crawl out the window when her mother came back to save her. But then she grew older and wiser and realized her mother wasn't coming back. She also realized that her mother had the right idea by leaving in the first place. Sydney couldn't wait to leave, to follow her boyfriend Hunter John Matteson to college, because they were going to be in love forever, and even if they came back to Bascom it would be okay, because he had never treated her like a Waverley. Not until the very end, at least.

She took a deep breath and entered the room reverently, a church of old memories. Her bed and dresser were still there. The full-length mirror still had some of her old stickers on it. She opened the closet and found a stack of boxes full of old linen that mice had gotten into. But the room didn't have an air of neglect. There wasn't any dust, and it smelled old and familiar, like cloves and cedar. Claire had taken care of it, hadn't turned it into a sitting room or filled it full of things she didn't need or use anymore or taken Sydney's old furniture out.

That did it.

Sydney went to the edge of the bed and sat. She put a hand over her mouth as she cried so Bay, singing quietly in the next room, wouldn't hear.

Ten days on the road.

She needed a bath.

Claire looked prettier, and cleaner, than she did.

Grandma Waverley was gone.

Bay liked it here, but she didn't yet realize what being a Waverley meant.

What was David doing?

Did she leave behind any clues?

So much had changed, but her room was exactly like she'd left it.

She crawled to the pillow at the top of the bed and curled into a small ball. She was asleep seconds later.

CHAPTER
3

There was an art to the male posterior. That's all there was to it.

Well, that was most of it.

The young runners on the university track had such verve and tone and, probably best of all, if Evanelle ever felt the need to give them something, she could never catch them. Obviously her gift knew that and never decided to kick in at the track during the school year. But in the summer there were slower, older people on the track, and sometimes Evanelle had to give them little packets of ketchup and tweezers. She even had to give one old woman a jar of sourwood honey one day. They gave her strange looks on the track in the summer.

That morning, instead of going to the track, Evanelle decided to walk downtown before the shops opened. There were always runners around the square. She followed a few of them until she came to Fred's Gourmet Grocery and happened to look in the window. It was well before he normally showed up for work, but there was Fred, in his stocking feet, getting a container of yogurt out of the dairy section. His rumpled clothing was an obvious indication that he'd spent the night there. Evanelle supposed the rose geranium wine didn't work on James, or maybe Fred decided not to use it after all. Sometimes people who had been together for a long time got to imagining that things used to be better, even when they weren't. Memories, even hard memories, grew soft like peaches as they got older.

Fred and James were a steadfast couple, everyone knew that. The fact that they were gay had been overlooked a long time ago, when it was obvious they were one of the always-togethers, a distinction usually reserved for very old couples. She knew Fred. She knew that what people thought was important to him. He was a lot like his father that way, though he'd never admit it. Once someone told him something critical, he would hold on to it for a long time, change everything he did just so he wouldn't face the same criticism again. He would hate for anyone to know that he and James were having problems. He was an always-together. He had so many expectations to live up to.

She knew she should leave, but she decided to wait for a moment to see if her gift would kick in. She stared at him, but nothing occurred to her. She had nothing to give him but advice, and most people weren't inclined to take that too seriously. Evanelle was neither as mysterious nor as clever as her Waverley relatives who had always lived in the Queen Anne home on Pendland Street. But she did have the gift of anticipation. From the time she was a little girl, she brought her mother dishcloths before the milk was spilled, she closed the windows before there was even a hint of a storm, and she gave the preacher a cough drop before he had a coughing spell during the sermon.

Evanelle had been married once, a long time ago. The first time she met her husband they were six years old, and she gave him a small black stone she'd found on the road that day. That night he used it to tap on her window to get her attention, and they became the best of friends. After thirty-eight years of marriage and not once feeling the need to give him something again, she was seized with the need to buy her husband a new suit. It turned out to be because he didn't have a decent one to be buried in when he died the following week. She tried not to think too hard about her gift, because then she would think about how frustrating it was not to know why people needed the things. Sometimes at night when her house felt particularly empty, she still wondered what would have happened if she hadn't bought her husband that suit.

She watched Fred go to the picnic-supply aisle and open a box of plastic utensils. He took out a plastic spoon and opened his cup of yogurt. She really should be moving on, but then she got to thinking about how nice it would be to live in a grocery store, or better yet a Wal-Mart, or better still a mall, because they had beds in the linen departments of the stores and a big food court. She suddenly realized that Fred had stopped short, the plastic spoon in his mouth, and he was looking back at her through the window.

She smiled and gave him a little wave.

He walked to the door and unlocked it.

"Can I help you with something, Evanelle?" he said, stepping outside.

"Nope. I was just passing by when I saw you."

"Is there something you want to give me?" he asked.

"Nope."

"Oh," he said, as if he really wanted something, something that would make everything all better. But relationships were hard. There was no cure for them. He looked around to see if anyone on the street had seen them, then he leaned forward and whispered, "I've asked him to be home early for the past two nights, and the past two nights he hasn't come home at all. I don't know what to do with my time at home when he's not there, Evanelle. He's always so good at making the decisions. Last night I couldn't even figure out what time I should eat. If I ate too early and he came home, then I couldn't eat with him. But if I waited too long, it would be too late to eat. At around two o'clock this morning I figured I should get things ready to fix breakfast in case he came in. That would be a nice gesture, right? I came here to pick some things up, but James usually leaves me a grocery list, so when I got here I wasn't sure what to get. I kept thinking, what if he doesn't want grapefruit? And what if I brought home coffee beans he doesn't like? I ended up falling asleep on the couch in my office. I don't know what I'm doing."

Evanelle shook her head. "You're putting it off is what you're doing. When you have to do something, you have to do it. Putting it off only makes it worse. Believe me, I know."

"I'm trying," Fred said. "I bought rose geranium wine from Claire."

"What I'm saying is you have to talk to him. Don't wait for him to come home. Call him and ask the serious questions. Stop putting it off." Fred got a stubborn look to him, and Evanelle laughed. "Okay. You're not ready for that. Maybe the wine will work, if you can get him to drink it. But no matter what you decide to do, you should probably do it with shoes on."

Fred looked down at his stocking feet, horrified, and hurried back into the store.

With a sigh, Evanelle walked up the sidewalk, looking in windows. Most of the morning joggers were gone, so maybe she would just go home and clean up before she went to visit Sydney. Claire was a little panicked, though she tried to hide it when she called Evanelle last night to tell her about Sydney's arrival. Evanelle calmed her down and told her everything was going to be all right. She reminded Claire that coming home was a good thing. Home was home.

Evanelle passed the White Door Salon, where women with too much time on their hands and too much money in their purses paid way too much for haircuts and hot-stone massages. Then she stopped in front of Maxine's next door, the posh clothing shop that the women from the White Door liked to shop in after their hair was done. There in the window was a button-down silk shirt.

She walked in, even though they hadn't put out the open sign yet. Her gift was like an itch, like a mosquito bite in the center of her body, and it wouldn't go away until she did what it demanded.

And it suddenly, insistently, demanded that she buy Sydney that shirt.

Sydney woke up with a start and checked her watch. She hadn't meant to fall asleep. She stumbled to the bathroom and drank water from the sink, then she splashed her face.

She left the bathroom and stopped to check in on Bay, but Bay wasn't in her room. Her bed was made, though, and some of her favorite stuffed animals were sitting on the pillows. She checked all the rooms upstairs, then jogged downstairs, trying to stave off panic. Where did she go?

Sydney walked into the kitchen and froze.

She'd just walked into heaven. And her grandmother was right there, in every scent.

Sugary and sweet.

Herby and sharp.

Yeasty and fresh.

Grandma Waverley used to cook like this. When Sydney was young, Claire always found a way to run Sydney out of the kitchen, so Sydney would sit in the hallway outside the kitchen and listen to the bubble of sauce boiling, the sizzle of things in skillets, the rattle of pans, the mumble of Claire and Grandma Waverley's voices.

There were two big bowls, one full of lavender and one full of dandelion greens, on the stainless-steel island. Loaves of bread sat steaming on the counters. Bay stood on a chair by Claire at the far counter, and she was using a wood-handled artist's brush to carefully paint pansy flowers with egg whites. One by one, Claire then took the flower heads and delicately dipped them in extrafine sugar before setting them on a cookie sheet.

"How did you manage this in just a couple of hours?" Sydney said incredulously, and Claire and Bay both turned.

"Hi," Claire said, looking at her warily. "How do you feel?"

"I'm fine. I just needed a little nap."

Bay jumped down from her chair and ran to Sydney and hugged her. She was wearing a blue apron that dragged on the ground and had **Waverley's Catering** written on it in white. "I'm helping Claire crystallize pansies to put on top of custard cups. Come look." She ran back to her chair by the counter.

"Maybe later, honey. Let's go get our things from the car and let Claire do her work."

"Bay and I brought everything in yesterday," Claire said.

Sydney looked at her watch again. "What're you talking about? I was only asleep two hours."

"You arrived yesterday morning. You've been asleep for the past twenty-six hours."

Sydney's heart lodged in her throat, and she stumbled to the kitchen table and sat.

She'd left her daughter alone for twenty-six hours? Did Bay say anything to Claire about David? Did Claire care for Bay? Did she tuck her in, or had Bay been huddled, afraid and lonely, in her room all night in a strange house? "Bay . . ."

"Has been helping me," Claire said. "She doesn't say much, but she's a fast learner. We cooked all day yesterday, she had a bubble bath last night, then I put her to bed. We started cooking again this morning."

Did Claire think she was a bad mother? The one thing Sydney could be proud of, and she was already messing it up. This place messed her up. She was never sure of who she was here.

"Have some coffee," Claire said. "Evanelle said she was stopping by today to see you."

"Stay, Mommy. Watch what I can do."

Get yourself together, she told herself. "Okay, honey. I'm not going anywhere." She went to the coffeepot and poured a cup. "How is Evanelle?"

"She's fine. She's anxious to see you. Have some lavender bread. Bay and I have been eating on that last loaf there. There's some herb butter too."

Was Claire concerned about her? She'd thought a lot about Claire over the years. Mostly they were thoughts of how adventurous Sydney was being and how poor, pitiful Claire could do nothing but stay at home in stupid Bascom. It was cruel, but it made her feel better because she'd always been jealous of Claire's comfort with who she was. Claire had been so happy to see her leave. Now she was worried about her. Telling her to eat. Sydney tried to slice the bread slowly, but she was so hungry she ended up tearing most of it off. She spread some herb butter on the bread and closed her eyes. After her third slice, she started walking around the big kitchen. "This is impressive. I didn't know you could do this. Are these Grandma's recipes?"

"Some of them. The dandelion quiche and the lavender bread were hers."

"You never let me see them when I was little."

Claire turned from the counter and wiped her hands on her apron. "Listen, this is for a job in Hickory tomorrow. I've called two teenage girls who sometimes help me in the summer, but if you need some money, you can help me with it instead."

Sydney looked at her strangely. "You want me to help you."

"Normally, I can do this alone. But for bigger jobs I have to call people. Are you still going to be here tomorrow?"

"Of course I am," Sydney said. "What? You don't believe me?"

"While you're here, I could use your help."

"I guess it's pretty obvious I need the money."

Claire smiled slightly and Sydney liked that, the small connection it formed.

Encouraged, she said congenially, "So, tell me about that Tyler guy."

Claire lowered her eyes and turned around. "What about him?"

"Has he come by today?"

"He doesn't come by every day. Yesterday was the first time. He was bringing some apples that fell on his side of the fence."

"Did you bury them?"

"We always bury the apples that fall off the tree," Claire said, and Bay looked at Claire curiously. Sydney felt a sense of dread, wanting to hold off Bay knowing things for as long as possible. Sydney had traded any chance of Bay being considered normal for her safety. How exactly did you tell a child, even a child like Bay, that?

"So, Tyler," Sydney said before Bay could start asking questions. "Is he single?"

"I don't know." Claire took the cookie sheet with the pansies on it and put it in a barely warm oven.

"Are you interested in him?"

"**No,**" Claire answered vehemently, like a middle-school girl.

"He belongs here," Bay said.

Claire turned to her.

"It's this thing she does," Sydney said. "She has very firm opinions on where things belong."

"So that explains it. I asked her to get me a fork and she went right to the drawer. When I asked her how she knew it was there, she said because that's where it belonged." Claire looked at Bay thoughtfully.

"No," Sydney said. "It's not that. Don't force that on her."

"I wasn't," Claire said, and she seemed hurt. "And no one forced it on you. In fact, you ran as far away as you could from it and no one stopped you."

"The whole town forced it on me! I tried to be normal and no one would let me." The pots hanging on the rack above the kitchen island began to sway anxiously, like an old woman wringing her hands. Sydney watched them swing for a moment, then she took a deep breath. She forgot how sensitive the house could be, how floorboards vibrated when people got mad, how windows opened when everyone laughed at once. "I'm sorry. I don't want to argue. What can I do to help?"

"Nothing right now. Bay, you can go too." Claire untied Bay's apron and took it off her. "Do you have a black skirt and white blouse to wear to help me serve tomorrow?" she asked Sydney.

"I have a white blouse," Sydney said.

"You can borrow one of my skirts. Have you ever served before?"

"Yes."

"Is that what you did after you left? Waitressed?"

Sydney ushered Bay out of the kitchen. Running, stealing, **men.** Those had never been Claire's areas of expertise. Sydney wasn't going to tell Claire about her past. Not yet, anyway. It wasn't something you shared with just anyone, not even your own sister, if you didn't think she'd understand. "It was one of the things I did."

Later that afternoon, Sydney sat on the front porch while Bay did cartwheels in the yard. She saw Evanelle come down the sidewalk and smiled. Evanelle was in a blue running suit, that familiar large tote bag over her shoulder. Sydney used to love to guess what was in it. She hoped Bay would love that too. There weren't many high points to being a Waverley, but Evanelle was definitely one of them.

Evanelle stopped to talk with Tyler next door, who was in his front yard, contemplating a big clump of grass clippings. He was bored; Sydney recognized the signs. His hair was longish, obviously to hold down the natural curl. That meant he had a creative nature he tried to control, and he was trying to control it by spending most of his day raking a big pile of cut grass from one side of his yard to the other.

She couldn't imagine ever wanting another relationship with a man after David, but looking at Tyler, her heart felt sort of strange. She didn't want him, and he was clearly attracted to her sister, but the simple idea of a good man made her feel hopeful somehow. Maybe not for herself, but for other people, other women. Luckier women.

As soon as Evanelle left Tyler, Sydney hurried down the steps to meet her. "Evanelle!" she said as she embraced the old lady. "Claire told me you were stopping by. Oh, it's good to see you. You look exactly the same."

"Still old."

"Still beautiful. What were you doing over there with Tyler?"

"Is that his name? He looked like he needed some lawn bags. Lucky I had some on me. He was real nice-like about it. Here's his phone number." She handed Sydney a small piece of notebook paper.

Sydney looked at the paper uncomfortably. "Evanelle, I'm not . . . I don't want . . ."

Evanelle patted Sydney's hand. "Oh, honey, I don't know what you're supposed to do with it. I just knew I had to give it to you. I'm not trying to set you up."

Sydney laughed. What a relief.

"I have something else for you." Evanelle rooted around in her tote bag for a moment, then handed Sydney a shopping bag with the name of an upscale shop on the square. Sydney remembered it well. Girls at school whose parents had money bought things at Maxine's. Sydney used to work all summer in order to shop there too, to look like she belonged. She opened the bag and brought out a beautiful blue silk shirt. It was about three sizes too big, but she hadn't had something so decadent in a long time, not since she took all that money from her boyfriend the car thief and lived on it for a year. David had money, but he'd never been a gift giver, never big on rewards, remorse, or apologies.

Sydney sat on the steps and put the shirt to her nose and smelled that wonderful wealthy scent of the shop. It smelled like fine paper and English perfume. "It's so beautiful."

Evanelle lowered herself to the step beside Sydney and rummaged through her tote bag again. "I know it's too big. Here's the receipt. I was walking downtown this morning trying to find some nice male backsides. There was Maxine's, and I thought of you, and I knew I had to get you this. This shirt. This size."

Bay had approached and was shyly fingering the soft shirt in Sydney's hands. "Evanelle, this is my daughter, Bay."

Evanelle chucked her chin and Bay giggled. "She looks just like your grandmother when she was young. Dark hair, blue eyes. She's got Waverley in her, that's for sure."

Sydney put an arm around Bay protectively. **No, she doesn't.** "Strawberry Pop-Tarts are her favorite. Thank you for them."

"Nice to know when things find a good purpose." She patted Sydney's knee. "Where is Claire?"

"Busy in the kitchen, preparing for a luncheon."

"Are you going to help her?"

"Yes."

Evanelle's sharp eyes were on her. Sydney had always loved Evanelle. What child doesn't love an old lady who gives presents? But Claire always seemed to understand Evanelle better. "Keep this in mind about Claire. She hates to ask for anything." Bay ran back to the yard and did cartwheels for them, and they complimented her. Some time passed before Evanelle said, "It's not an easy thing to do, ask for help. You were brave to come here. I'm proud of you."

Sydney met the old woman's eyes, and knew that she knew.

It was nearly five o'clock in the afternoon on Friday when Claire, Sydney, and Bay arrived home from catering the luncheon in Hickory. Bay had fallen asleep in the van. Sydney thought Claire might be peeved at having to take Bay along, but she didn't argue at all when Sydney said she didn't want to leave Bay with Evanelle just yet. They'd only been in town three days. She wasn't leaving her daughter alone in a strange place. Claire had said, "Of course not. She'll come with us." Just like that.

Bay had enjoyed herself. The old ladies in the Amateur Botanists Association loved having her there, and every time Claire and Sydney came back from collecting plates or refreshing drinks, Bay had cleaned up the area or organized the coolers in that way she did, instinctively knowing where things were supposed to be.

Sydney carried Bay upstairs and put her on her bed, then turned on one of the floor fans Claire had brought down from the attic because summer was filling the house, tightening it with heat. She changed into shorts and a T-shirt, thinking Claire was going to do the same before unloading the things from the van.

But when Sydney went back downstairs, Claire had, in that short time, brought everything into the kitchen and was loading the dishwasher and filling the carafes with baking soda and hot water to soak. She was still in her blouse and skirt, the blue apron still over her clothes.

"I was going to help you," Sydney said.

Claire looked surprised to find her there. "I can do this. When I hire people, it's only to help serve. You can relax. I didn't know if you'd prefer a check or cash, so I went with cash. The envelope is there." She pointed to the kitchen table.

Sydney paused a moment. She didn't understand. Wasn't it a good day? Didn't they work well together? The ladies at the luncheon loved Claire's food, and they complimented Sydney on what a nice job she did serving. Sydney had been nervous at first. Back when she waitressed, she used to steal from customers, not giving them back money from their checks. She would smile and flirt and try to smooth things over if they called her on it. And it never hurt that she was usually sleeping with the manager of the establishment, so he would always side with her if the complaint got that far. She could con with the best of them. She'd been worried that serving again might bring that time in her life back to her, might make her want it again. But it didn't. It felt good to work honestly and hard. It reminded her instead of what was probably the best time in her life, in Boise, when she worked at the salon. She remembered her aching feet and the cramps in her hands and the shorn hair that would get under her clothes and itch and poke her skin. She loved it all.

But now Claire was saying she didn't need her help anymore. Sydney stood there while Claire continued to work. What was she supposed to do? She would go crazy if she couldn't do more than just help Claire out every once in a while. Claire didn't even let her do housework. "Can't I help you with anything?"

"I've got this covered. This is my routine."

Without another word, Sydney picked up the envelope and walked outside through the back to her Subaru. She leaned against it as she counted the money in the envelope. Claire had been generous. Sydney could go out and do something with this. That's probably what Claire expected her to do. Put some gas in the car. Go see someone.

But she didn't have a tag and she might get pulled over.

And there was definitely no one she wanted to see again.

Folding the envelope, she put it in the back pocket of her cutoffs. She didn't want to go back into the house and watch Claire work, so she walked around the driveway, kicking gravel, which Claire would probably smooth over later with a rake, putting everything back in order.

She walked to the front yard and looked over to Tyler's house. His Jeep was parked on the curb. Impulsively, she crossed the yard and walked up his steps. She knocked on his door and waited, stuffing her hands deeper into her pockets the longer he took. Maybe he was asleep. That meant she had to go back home.

But then she heard footsteps and

smiled, taking her hands out of her pockets as he opened his door. He was wearing paint-splattered jeans and a T-shirt, looking sort of rumpled and forgetful, as if perpetually wondering where time went.

"Hi," she said after he stared at her a few moments, confused. "I'm Sydney Waverley, from next door."

He finally smiled. "Oh, right. I remember."

"I thought I'd come by and say hello." His eyes drifted behind her, then to her side. He finally stuck his head out the door and looked over to the Waverley house. Sydney knew what he was doing, and she wondered how Claire had managed to make this guy so smitten. Maybe he had a thing for control freaks. "Claire's not with me."

He looked chagrined. "I'm sorry," he said, stepping back. "Please, come in."

She'd been in the house a few times when she was young, when old lady Sanderson lived there. A lot had been done to the place. It was brighter, and it smelled a lot better. Old lady Sanderson had been feline friendly. There was a nice red couch and some comfortable chairs in the living room, but they were placed oddly, like that was where the movers had set them. There were rows and rows of unframed paintings propped against the walls, and cardboard boxes were everywhere. "I didn't realize you'd just moved in."

He ran a hand through his hair. "About a month ago. I've been meaning to unpack. I was just painting in the kitchen. What time is it?"

"A little after five. What color are you painting the kitchen?"

He shook his head and laughed. "No, no. I paint in the kitchen. That's where my easel is set up."

"Oh, you're a **painter** painter."

"I teach art at Orion." He moved some newspapers from a chair and set them on the floor. "Sit, please."

"How long have you been in Bascom?" she asked as she went to the chair.

"About a year." He looked around for

another place to sit, running his hand through his hair again, pushing it off his forehead.

"You know, I could trim your hair, if you want me to."

He turned to her with that chagrined look again. "I keep forgetting to get it cut. You could do it?"

"You're looking at a bona fide beauty-school graduate."

"Okay. Sure. Thank you." He moved a box off the couch and sat. "I'm glad you came by. I don't really know any of my neighbors yet. Well, except maybe Mrs. Kranowski, who seems to spend half her day chasing her dog, Edward, around the neighborhood."

"I remember Mrs. Kranowski. What is she, one hundred years old now?"

"And surprisingly fast on her feet."

Sydney laughed and congratulated herself. This was a good idea. "I'll bring my case over tomorrow to give you that trim. Do you mind if my daughter comes along?"

"Not at all."

Sydney studied him a moment. "So, you like my sister."

She'd caught him off guard, but it didn't seem to occur to him not to answer. "You cut to the chase, don't you? I don't know your sister very well. But I . . . yes, I like her. She **fascinates** me." He smiled and leaned forward, putting his elbows on his knees, open and enthusiastic. It was contagious, like a yawn. He made Sydney smile back. "I had this dream about her. It was like nothing I've ever dreamed before. Her hair was short, and she was wearing this headband—" He stopped and leaned back. "I'm going to stop now before I sound any more ridiculous."

He didn't sound ridiculous. He sounded nice, so nice it made her a little envious of Claire. "My daughter likes her too."

"You don't sound happy about that."

"No, I didn't mean it to sound that way." Sydney sighed. "It's just not what I expected. Claire and I fought a lot as kids. I think we were both thrilled when I left town. She didn't like me very much. I didn't think she'd like Bay."

"How long were you gone?"

"Ten years. I never thought I'd be back." She shook her head, as if to shake away the thoughts. "Do you mind my coming over? You like my sister, not me, so no pressure. I just need to get out of that house sometimes. Want to order pizza? My treat."

"Sounds good. I don't think I've eaten today." Tyler looked at her thoughtfully. "You can come by any time you want, but ten years is a long time to be away. There aren't any old friends you want to see?"

Old friends. She almost laughed. Two-faced, weak-willed backstabbers, yes. Old friends, no. "No. It's a part of that never-thinking-I-was-ever-coming-back thing."

"Burned bridges?" Tyler asked astutely. He wasn't nearly as oblivious as his lifestyle made him seem.

"Something like that."

CHAPTER
4

That night, across town, Emma Clark had no idea her world was about to turn upside down as she got ready for the fund-raiser ball. She was, in fact, looking forward to the evening because of the attention she always received.

Clark women craved the spotlight. They loved attention

from men, particularly. And it wasn't hard to get, considering their legendary sexual prowess. They **always** married well.

Emma Clark's husband, Hunter John Matteson, was the biggest catch in town and everyone knew it. He was outgoing, handsome, athletic, and heir to his family's manufactured-housing empire. Emma's mother, shrewd woman that she was, had positioned Emma to be his wife since Emma and Hunter John were toddlers. Their families mingled and traveled in the same circles, so it wasn't hard to plant suggestions and nudge them together. Their families had even spent a month together on Cape May one summer when Emma and Hunter John were ten years old. "Look how cute they are together," her mother said every chance she got.

The only problem was, despite her mother's maneuvering, despite Emma's beauty and social position, despite the fact that she had been amazing boys behind the bleachers since she was fifteen and that any sane man would want her, all throughout high school Hunter John had been hopelessly in love with Sydney Waverley.

Oh, he knew he shouldn't have anything to do with her. People of their caliber didn't socialize with Waverleys. But it was no secret to his friends how he felt about her. They knew by the way he looked at her and the tragic teenage way he would act sometimes, like life without love was not worth living.

When he turned sixteen, in his one and only act of rebellion, he finally asked Sydney out. To everyone's surprise, his parents let him go. "Let the boy have some fun," his father had said. "She's the pretty Waverley, and she doesn't seem to have their touch, so she's harmless. My boy knows what's expected of him when he leaves school. I diddled around too, before I knew I had to settle down."

It was the second worst day of Emma's life.

For the next two years, Hunter John's clique in school had no choice but to accept Sydney into their fold, because she and

Hunter John were inseparable. Emma's mother said to keep her mouth shut and her enemies close, so even though it killed her, Emma made friends with Sydney. She frequently invited her to spend the night. They had plenty of rooms, but Emma always told Sydney that she had to sleep on the floor. Sydney didn't mind, because she hated it at the Waverley house and anything was better than that. But more often than not, Emma ended up on her bedroom floor with Sydney, talking and doing homework. Sydney was just a Waverley, but she was smart and fun and had the best taste in hairstyles. Emma would never forget when she let Sydney style her hair once, and then everything went right that day, like magic. Hunter John had even commented on how pretty she looked. Emma could never replicate it herself. There was a time when Emma actually liked Sydney.

But then, on their sleeping bags on the floor one night, Sydney said that she and Hunter John were going to do it for the first time. Emma had almost been in tears.

It was more than she could bear. She'd spent years watching the boy she knew she was supposed to be with in love with someone else. Then she'd been forced to befriend the girl who had distracted him from her. Now Sydney was going to sleep with him? It was the one thing Emma knew she was better at than anyone else, and **Sydney** was going to get to him first. It had taken every bit of strength she had to wait until Sydney fell asleep before running to tell her mother.

She remembered how her mother held her and stroked her hair. Ariel was in bed, on her white silk sheets. Her room always smelled of candles, and the crystals on the chandelier sent sparkles of light around the room. Her mother was everything Emma wanted to be: a living, breathing fantasy.

"Now, Emma," Ariel said easily, "you have been doing it and doing it well for over a year. All Clark women are good in bed. Why do you think we marry so well? Stop worrying. So she has him right now.

You'll have him for the rest of your life. It's just a matter of time. You'll always be better, and it's good when men have a basis for comparison. That's not to say you can't spread a little false information. As hard as it is to believe, a lot of women are afraid of that first time."

That made Emma laugh. Clark women were never afraid of sex.

Her mother kissed her forehead, her lips cool and soft. Then she stretched back in her bed and said, "Now, go on. Your father will be home soon."

The next day Emma told Sydney all sorts of false and scary things about how it hurt, and she told her all the wrong ways to do it. She never pressed Sydney into giving her details after it happened, but the satisfied look on Hunter John's face the first time he and Emma had sex had been all she needed to know.

Sydney left town after Hunter John broke up with her at graduation. She'd been devastated to know that school was just a bubble, that she and Hunter John couldn't be together in real life, that the friends she'd made couldn't be her friends after they all graduated. They had to step out into Bascom society and do what their parents expected of them, become their family names. And Sydney was, in the end, just a Waverley. She'd been so hurt and angry. No one realized that she hadn't known the rules. She'd been in love with Hunter John. She thought it would be forever.

Emma would have felt sorry for her if it hadn't been obvious that Hunter John was hurting just as much. It took so much effort that summer to get him to come around. Even after they had sex and he'd been blown away, he still talked of leaving for college, sometimes even saying that Sydney had the right idea by leaving. He didn't need this town.

So Emma did the only thing she thought she could.

She stopped taking the pill without telling Hunter John, and she got pregnant.

Hunter John stayed home and married her, and he never complained. They even decided, together this time, that they should have a second child a few years later. He worked for his father, then took over the family manufactured-home construction plants when his father retired. When his parents moved to Florida, Emma and Hunter John moved into his family's mansion. Everything seemed perfect, but she was never really sure where Hunter John's heart was, and that always bothered her.

Which brings us to the worst day in Emma Clark's life.

That Friday night, Emma still didn't realize something big was about to happen, even though all the clues were there. Her hair wouldn't curl. Then a pimple popped up on her chin. Then the white dress she'd planned to wear to the black-and-white hospital-fund-raiser ball mysteriously developed a stain on it that the housekeeper couldn't get out, so Emma had to settle for a black dress. It was a stunning dress—all her dresses were—but it wasn't what she wanted, what she had planned on, and she felt uncomfortable in it.

When she and Hunter John arrived at the ball, everything seemed fine. Perfect, in fact. The hospital ball was always held at Harold Manor, a Civil War-era home on the national historic registry and **the** place for social gatherings. She'd been there countless times. It was a wonderful, fantasylike setting, like something out of time. Men wore suits so starched they couldn't bend at the waist, and women had handshakes as soft as tea cakes. Clark women were at home in such a setting, and Emma was immediately the center of attention, as she always was. But it felt different, like people were talking about her, wanting to be near her, for all the wrong reasons.

Hunter John didn't notice, but then he never did, so she looked immediately for her mother. Her mother would tell her she was beautiful and that everything was all right. Hunter John kissed her cheek, then made a beeline to the bar, where his buddies were gathered. Young men at gatherings like this were like dust skittering to corners, trying to get away from the movement of skirts and the breath of ladies' laughter.

She ran into Eliza Beaufort while searching for her mother. Eliza had been one of her best friends in high school. "Keep the Beauforts as friends," Emma's mother always said, "and you'll know what people are saying about you."

"Oh, my Lord, I couldn't wait for you to get here," Eliza said. Her lipstick was smudged and lopsided from talking out of the side of her mouth. "I want to know all about how you heard."

Emma smiled slightly, distracted. "How I heard what?" she asked, looking over Eliza's shoulder.

"You don't know?"

"Know what?"

"Sydney Waverley is back in town." She almost hissed the words, like a curse.

Emma's eyes darted to meet Eliza's, but she didn't move a muscle. Was that why everyone was acting strangely tonight? Because Sydney was back and everyone here couldn't wait for Emma to arrive in order to get her reaction? That disturbed her for many reasons, the most important of which was that people thought she would even **have** a reaction, that this warranted some kind of concern on her part.

"She came back Wednesday and she's staying with her sister," Eliza continued. "She even helped Claire on a job in Hickory this afternoon. You really didn't know?"

"No. So she's back. So what?"

Eliza raised her brows. "I didn't think you'd take it this well."

"She was never anything to us, anyway. And Hunter John is very happy. I have no worries. I need to find my mother. We'll do lunch next week, yes? Kiss, kiss."

She finally found her mother seated at one of the tables, sipping champagne and entertaining people who stopped by to see her. Ariel looked queenly and elegant and ten years younger than her real age. Like Emma, her hair was blond and her boobs were big. She drove a convertible, wore diamonds with denim, and she never missed a homecoming game. She was so Southern that she cried tears that came straight from the Mississippi, and she always smelled faintly of cottonwood and peaches.

Her mother looked up as Emma approached, and Emma knew right away that she knew. Not only did she know, she wasn't happy about it. **No, no, no,** Emma thought. **There's nothing wrong. Don't make this wrong, Mama.** Ariel stood and left Emma's father with a provocative smile that would have him waiting eagerly for her return.

"Let's take a stroll out to the veranda," Ariel said, hooking her arm in Emma's and firmly leading her outside. They smiled as they passed some small groups of people who had come out to smoke, because smiling meant everything was okay. Once in a far corner, Ariel said, "No doubt you've heard about Sydney Waverley. Don't worry. Everything will be all right."

"I'm not worried, Mama."

Ariel ignored her. "Here's what I want

you to do. First, treat Hunter John extra special. Call more attention to yourself. I'm going to throw you a party at your house next weekend. Invite all your closest friends. Everyone will see how wonderful you are, how special. Hunter John will see how envied you are. We'll go shopping on Monday and buy you a dress. Red is your best color, and Hunter John loves you in red. Speaking of dresses, why did you wear black? You look better in white."

"Mama, I'm not worried about Sydney being back."

Ariel cupped Emma's face with both her hands. "Oh, sugar, you **should** be worried. First loves are powerful loves. But if you keep reminding your husband why he chose you, you won't have a problem."

Late that night, Emma couldn't wait to get Hunter John in bed, with a fervency she assured herself had **nothing** to do with Sydney being back. Once they arrived home, she checked on their boys, asleep in their rooms, and said a distracted good night to the nanny. She started undressing the moment she entered the master suite, then stood naked except for her heels and the pearl necklace Hunter John had given her for her twenty-seventh birthday last year.

Hunter John entered a few minutes later with a sandwich and a beer. "Ball food," as he called it, always left him hungry. He did this every time they came home from a function, and while Emma didn't particularly care for the habit, it wasn't worth arguing over. He did, after all, come up to bed to be with her and eat instead of doing it alone in the kitchen.

He didn't seem surprised to find her naked. Emma wondered when that had happened, when he'd begun to expect it instead of desire it. But he smiled as she sauntered up to him and took the beer bottle and the sandwich plate out of his hands. She put them on the table by the door and pulled him toward the bed, tugging at his dinner jacket and shirt as they went.

He laughed and let her push him onto the mattress.

"So what brought this on?" he asked as she pulled down his zipper.

She straddled him, looking down at his face. She paused for a moment, not meaning to incite his anticipation. But he expected such skill from her that he naturally assumed it was for his pleasure, and that excited him. His hands tried to coax her hips down and he began to move under her, but she remained motionless.

She enjoyed sex, and she knew she had a gift, a skill in bed. But was her mother right? Was this all she had? If she didn't have this, would he still be here? **Should** she be worried that Sydney was back? "Hunter John," she whispered, leaning down to kiss him, "do you love me?"

His laugh ended in a groan as he got himself worked up by what he thought was foreplay. "Okay, what did you do?"

"What?"

"Did you buy something?" he asked indulgently. "Something expensive? Is that what this is all about?"

He assumed this was because she wanted something from him. And to be fair, it was. It always was. She always got what she wanted from him through this. All except one thing. It didn't escape her that Hunter John hadn't answered her question. He didn't tell her he loved her.

But he had loved Sydney, which meant she had to do what her mother said. Work harder to keep what she had.

"I want to buy a red dress," she said, feeling like a bird caught in a briar bush— prickly, scared, **mad.** "A beautiful red dress."

"I can't wait to see you in it."

"You will. And then you'll see me out of it."

"That's what I like to hear."

Monday afternoon, Claire hung up the phone at her work desk in the storeroom, but she kept her hand resting on the receiver.

When you know something's wrong, but you don't know exactly what it is, the air around you changes. Claire felt it. The plastic of the phone was too warm. The walls were sweating slightly. If she went out to the garden, she knew she'd find the morning glory blooming in the middle of the day.

"Claire?"

Claire turned to find Sydney in the doorway to the storeroom. "Oh, hi," Claire said. "When did you get back?" Sydney and Bay had been to visit Tyler again, the fourth day in a row.

"A few minutes ago. What's wrong?"

"I don't know." Claire took her hand off the warm phone. "I just got a call to cater a party at Mr. and Mrs. Matteson's house this weekend."

Sydney crossed her arms over her chest. Then she dropped her arms to her sides. She hesitated before asking, "The Mattesons who live in that large Tudor home on Willow Springs Road?"

"Yes."

"Short notice," Sydney said cautiously, curiously.

"Yes. And she said she'd double my normal fee because of it, but only if I had enough help for the night."

"I always liked Mrs. Matteson," Sydney said, a spark of something popping in her words, like static. Something, something like hope, was trying to make itself clear. "Are you taking the job? I'll help you."

"Are you sure?" Claire asked, because things still seemed wrong. Sydney used to have a relationship with Hunter John, and she used to be friends with Emma. If she'd wanted to see them again, she would have gone before now instead of spending all her time cloistered in the house or hiding over at Tyler's.

"Of course I'm sure."

Claire shrugged. She must be reading too much into things. "Okay, then. Thank you."

Sydney smiled and turned on her heel. "No problem."

Claire followed her into the kitchen.

There were some things that hadn't
changed about Sydney, like her light-
brown hair that had just enough natural
curl to make it look like waves of caramel
icing on a cake. And her beautiful lightly
tanned skin. And the freckles across her
nose. She'd lost weight but still had a stunning figure, petite in a way that always
made Claire, who was four inches taller,
feel heavy and clumsy.

Those were the familiar things.

The rest of Sydney was a mystery. She'd
been here almost a week now and Claire
was still trying to figure her out. She was a
terrific mother, that much was clear.
Lorelei hadn't been a great example, and
their grandmother had tried, but they
were nothing like Sydney. She was loving
and attentive, knew where Bay was at all
times but still let her have her space, let her
dream and play. It was an emotional thing
to watch her little sister be such a great
parent. Where did she learn it?

And where had she been? Sydney was
jumpy, and she never used to be jumpy.

Just last night, when Claire couldn't sleep and went out to the garden, she found herself locked out, because Sydney would get up several times every night to make sure everything downstairs was locked up tight. What was she running from? It did no good to ask her questions; Sydney only changed the subject when asked about the last ten years. She left and went to New York. That was all Claire knew. What happened after that was anyone's guess. And Bay wasn't giving up any secrets. According to her, she was born on a Greyhound bus and she and her mother never lived anywhere. No, they lived **everywhere.**

Claire watched Sydney walk to the pot of soup steaming on the stove. "Oh, I forgot what I came in here to tell you. I invited Tyler over for dinner," Sydney said, taking a whiff of the chamomile chicken soup.

Claire gaped at her. "You did what?"

"I invited Tyler over for dinner. That's okay, isn't it?"

Claire didn't answer and made a beeline

to the bread keeper, not meeting Sydney's eyes. She took out a loaf of wheat bread and started slicing it for sandwiches.

"Claire, come on," Sydney said, laughing. "Give the man a break. He's thin. He has these notes all over his house, reminding him to eat. He told me he forgets. He showed me some of his artwork yesterday, and it's phenomenal. But, I swear to God, if he asks me one more question about you I'm going to suggest therapy. Tyler's nice. If you don't want him, tell him so he'll stop mooning over you and I'll have a chance."

Claire looked up immediately. "Is that why you're spending so much time over there? You want Tyler?"

"No. But why don't you?" Claire was saved from answering by a knock at the front door. "It's for you," Sydney said.

"He's **your** guest."

Sydney smiled and went to the door.

Claire set the bread knife down and strained to hear Tyler's voice. "Thanks for the invitation," she heard him say. "Great house."

"Want a tour?" Sydney asked, which made Claire anxious. She didn't want Sydney showing Tyler the house. She didn't want Tyler knowing her secrets.

"Sure."

Claire closed her eyes for a moment. **Think, think, think.** What would make Tyler forget her, make him less interested? What dish would turn his attention elsewhere? She didn't have time to make something specific.

She didn't need this. It was all she could do to deal with Sydney and Bay in her life, trying to ease them into her routine. And she did this knowing they were still going to leave. Sydney had hated everything about this house and this town. Even now she was trying to protect Bay from unnecessary strangeness, not explaining the garden or the apple tree to her, not telling her what being a Waverley meant in Bascom. It was only going to take one comment, one snub from someone, and Sydney would disappear again like smoke.

But Tyler was definitely something she could control in her life. She had to try to dissuade him in any way she could. Vehemently, rudely if necessary. There just wasn't any room for him. She was letting too many people in as it was.

Bay ran into the kitchen ahead of Sydney and Tyler. She hugged Claire, like it was the most natural thing in the world to give a hug for no discernible reason, and Claire held her tightly for a moment. Bay pulled away and ran to the kitchen table and sat.

Sydney walked in and Tyler followed. She noticed right away that he'd had his hair cut. It suited him, made him seem more focused. That, she decided when his eyes focused on her, was not a good thing. **You can't lose what you don't have,** she thought, and turned away.

"It must have been amazing, growing up in this house," Tyler said.

"It was interesting, all right," Sydney

said. "There's a step on the staircase, three steps up, that squeaks. When we were young, every time someone stepped on it, a mouse would stick his head out of the knothole on the step above to see what made the sound."

Claire looked at her sister, surprised. "You knew about that?"

"I'm not much of a Waverley, but I grew up here too." Sydney snagged a slice of bread as Claire made the sandwiches and put them on a plate. "Claire learned all these crazy recipes from our grandmother."

"This isn't a crazy recipe. This is soup and peanut butter and jelly sandwiches."

Sydney winked at Tyler. "Almond butter and ginger jelly sandwiches."

Claire's skin suddenly felt prickly. It came so easily to Sydney, and Claire used to hate her so much for it. Look how naturally she talked with Tyler, made it seem like it was no big deal to form connections when they were so easily broken.

"Were the two of you very close growing up?" Tyler asked.

"No," Sydney said, before Claire could.

Claire filled three bowls with soup and set them on the table with the plate of sandwiches. "Enjoy," she said, and left the kitchen and went out to the garden, Tyler, Sydney, and Bay watching her go.

About forty-five minutes later, Claire had finished digging a hole by the fence and was gathering up the apples that had fallen around the tree. It was humid, the air as thick as sorghum syrup, carrying a hint of the sticky summer to come.

"Stop it," she kept saying as the tree dropped apples around her, trying to vex her. "The more you drop, the more I bury. And you know it takes you a week to grow more."

It dropped a small apple on her head.

She looked up at the branches, which were twitching slightly though there was no wind. "I said stop it."

"Is that your secret?"

She turned to see Tyler standing on the grass. How long had he been there? She hadn't even heard him approach. The tree had been distracting her. Damn tree.

"My secret?" she asked warily.

"Your secret to this garden. You talk to the plants."

"Oh." She turned and gathered more apples in her arms. "Yes, that's it."

"Dinner was great."

"I'm glad you enjoyed it." When he didn't move, she said, "I'm a little busy."

"That's what Sydney said you'd say. And she said to come out anyway."

"Her confidence is attractive, I know, but I think she just needs a friend right now," Claire said, shocking herself. She never meant to say that. It sounded as if she **cared.** Sure, she wanted Tyler to turn his attention elsewhere. But not to Sydney. Claire closed her eyes. She thought she was past all that jealousy.

"What about you? Do you need a friend?"

She glanced over at him. He was so comfortable with himself, standing there in his loose jeans, his button-down shirt untucked. Just for a moment, she wanted to walk to him, into his arms, and let that sense of calm envelop her. What was the matter with her? "I don't need friends."

"Do you need something more?"

She didn't have a lot of experience with men, but she understood what he meant. She knew what those tiny purple snaps around him, the ones you could see only at night, meant. "I like what I have."

"I do too, Claire. You're beautiful," he said. "There, I said it. I couldn't keep it in any longer."

He wasn't afraid of getting hurt. He seemed to **welcome** it. One of them had to be sensible. "That thing about me being busy: I meant it."

"That thing about you being beautiful: I meant it too."

She walked over to the hole by the fence and dropped the apples in. "I'm going to be busy for a long, long time."

When she turned back around, Tyler was grinning. "Well, I'm not."

Feeling uneasy, she watched him as he walked away. Was he trying to tell her something? Was it a warning of some sort?

I have all the time in the world to wiggle my way in.

CHAPTER
5

The Matteson mansion looked the same as Sydney remembered. She could probably walk up to Hunter John's bedroom with her eyes closed, even now. When they spent time alone in the house, she used to pretend they lived there together. They would lie in bed and she would go on and on about their future.

But when he broke up with her at graduation, he said, "I thought you understood."

She didn't understand then, but she did now. She understood now that she'd loved him, and he was probably the only man she'd ever loved like that, with such hope. She understood now that she would always have left Bascom, whether or not it was with him. She understood now that he hadn't been able to accept her for what she was. She understood that part best of all, because even she hadn't been able to do that.

There was a small, remembered thrill to being somewhere she knew she really shouldn't be as Claire pulled around to the service entrance and they entered the kitchen. She shouldn't have come, but she couldn't help herself. Maybe it was the challenge, the way it used to be a challenge to sneak around boyfriends' houses while they were at work, stealing money from their secret hiding places before she left town. She was going to steal something here too. She was going to take memories that didn't belong to her anymore. And why was she doing it? Because the best time in her adolescence, her best memories of Bascom, were when she dated the biggest catch in town. Everyone had admired her. Everyone had accepted her. She needed those good memories, needed them more than the Mattesons did. They probably wouldn't even miss them. They probably forgot who she was a long time ago.

The housekeeper met them and introduced herself as Joanne. She was in her forties, and her black hair was so shiny and straight that it barely moved, which meant she hated mistakes.

"The flowers have already been delivered. I was told to wait to arrange them until you arrived," Joanne said. "When you finish unloading, I'll be on the patio. Do you know where that is?"

"Yes," Sydney said importantly as Joanne disappeared through the swinging door of the butler's pantry. "I liked Myrtle better."

"Who is Myrtle?" Claire asked.

"The old housekeeper."

"Oh" was all Claire said.

As soon as everything was in and the necessary things refrigerated, Sydney led Claire through the house to the patio. Mrs. Matteson had been proud of her antiques, which was why Sydney was surprised to find the house now was just so . . . pink. There was rose damask wallpaper in the dining room, and the chairs at the long dining-room table had pale-pink upholstery. The family room opened out of the dining room, and it was a riot of pink florals on the couch cushions and rugs.

The extensive patio was to the right, through a set of open French doors. A warm summer breeze glided in, carrying the scent of roses and chlorine. When they walked out, Sydney saw that there were round cast-iron tables and chairs set up around the pool, and an elaborate bar had been erected in a corner. The longer tables for the food were skirting the walls, and

that's where Joanne was standing, sur-
rounded by empty vases and buckets of
flowers.

Claire went to Joanne, but Sydney
couldn't move. She felt light-headed. It
was just the fantasy of it all—the white
linens on the buffet tables flapping in the
wind, the lights in the pool sending watery
shadows over the area, the starlights in
the shrubbery. She wanted this so much
when she was young, this prosperity, this
dream. Standing there, she could remember so clearly what it felt like to be a part of
it, to be a part of **something,** to know she
belonged somewhere.

Even if it had all been a lie.

She crossed her arms over her chest and
watched a maid put candles in tall glass
hurricane lamps on each of the tables.
Sydney listened distantly as Claire told
Joanne where the roses and the fuchsia and
the gladioli should be placed on the tables.
"Gladioli here," she said, "where the nutmeg stuffing in the squash blossoms and
the fennel chicken will be. Roses here,

where the rose-petal scones will go." It was all so intricate, a manipulative plan to make the guests feel something they might not feel otherwise. It didn't seem at all like Mrs. Matteson. Yet Claire had spent the better part of the evening on Monday discussing the menu on the phone with her. Sydney had made up an excuse to be in the kitchen and could hear Claire in the storeroom saying things like, "If it's love you want to portray, then roses." And, "Cinnamon and nutmeg mean prosperity."

After Claire had taken care of the nonedible-flower placement with Joanne, she started to walk back into the house but stopped when she realized Sydney wasn't following her.

"Are you all right?" Claire asked.

Sydney turned. "It's beautiful, isn't it?" she said, as if proud of it, as if it belonged to her. It did, for a while.

"It's very . . ." Claire hesitated a moment. "Deliberate. Come on, we don't want to get behind schedule."

A few hours later, in the kitchen,

Sydney said, "I see what you mean by deliberate. Why does everything have to be placed clockwise on the trays? We didn't have to do this at the botanists' luncheon."

"Those ladies only cared about the food, not what it meant."

"And what does this all mean?" Sydney asked.

"It means they want people to see them as madly in love and fabulously wealthy."

"That doesn't make any sense; everyone already knows that. Are Mr. and Mrs. Matteson having problems? They seemed so happy when I knew them."

"I don't question the motives. I just give people what they want. Are you ready?" Claire asked, carrying two trays to the swinging kitchen door. They'd set out the food before the guests arrived, but Joanne had just informed them that the trays needed refreshing.

Sydney wondered if she would recognize anyone out there. She'd tried to make out voices, sometimes stopping to crane her neck when she heard laughter, wondering if she'd heard that laugh before. Would Hunter John be out there? Did it matter? "As ready as I'll ever be," she said as she picked up her trays.

Parties made Emma feel enchanted, like she was a little girl playing dress up and this was a world all of her own making. Her mother had been the same way. "Leave the magic to the Waverleys," she used to say when Emma was little and she would watch her mother try on dress after dress before parties. "We have something better. We have fantasy."

Emma was standing by the bar because that's where Hunter John was, but it gave her an excellent view of everyone enjoying themselves. She loved parties, but she'd never had a party feel quite like this one, when every other sentence out of everyone's mouth was a compliment to her or an envious remark. It was **wonderful.**

Ariel walked over to Emma and kissed

her cheek. "Darling, you look wonderful. That red is perfect on you. Just perfect."

"This was a grand idea, Mama. Thank you for doing this. Who is the caterer? I'm getting compliments on the food. Not nearly as many comments as I'm getting on my dress, but still."

Ariel winked and turned Emma so that she faced the patio doors across the pool. "That, sugar, is my biggest gift to you this evening."

"What do you mean?"

"Wait. Watch. I'll show you."

Emma didn't understand, but she laughed with anticipation. "Mama, what did you do? Did you buy me something?"

"In a sense," Ariel said mysteriously.

"Mama, what is it? Tell me, tell me!"

The pitch of Emma's voice made Hunter John turn away from his conversation with some of his friends. "What's the matter, Emma?"

Emma grabbed Hunter John's hand and pulled him toward her. "Mama bought me a gift and won't tell me what it is."

"Ah, there it is," Ariel said, pointing with a glass of champagne in her hand.

"What?" Emma said excitedly. "Where?" Emma's eyes focused on two women coming out of the house, carrying trays. They were servers, obviously. She was just about to look away to find where her real gift was when she realized who one of the servers was. "Is that Claire Waverley? You hired **her** to cater my party?" It suddenly occurred to her in one terrible moment what her mother had done, and her eyes darted to the other woman with Claire. "Oh, my God."

"Is that Sydney Waverley?" Hunter John asked. He disengaged his hand from Emma's and left her standing there. He just **left**, walking toward Sydney as if he'd been roped.

Emma rounded on her mother. "Mama, what have you done?"

Ariel leaned in close and hissed, "Stop being a fool and go over there. Make people look at her. Make all her old friends look at her."

"I can't believe you did this."

"She's back, and you need to take control. Show her she doesn't belong here, that there's no chance of getting what she had back. And show your husband that you're better than she is. That you always were. You're the belle of the ball, and she's just the caterer. Now go."

It was the longest walk Emma had ever taken. Hunter John had already made his way over to Sydney and was staring at her while she arranged the new trays on the buffet tables. She hadn't looked up yet. Was she acting like she didn't know he was there? Was she just being coy? She was thinner and she looked older, but her face was still luminous and her hair was cut expertly. She always had the best hair. She never had to dye it or curl it like Emma had been doing since she was twelve.

Emma had nearly reached him when Hunter John finally cleared his throat and said, "Sydney Waverley, is that you?"

Several things happened at once. Sydney's head shot up and she locked eyes with Hunter John. Eliza Beaufort, who was standing at the next table, swiveled on her heel. And Claire stopped what she was doing to watch, her dark eyes sharply on them like a schoolteacher's.

"I've always said it, Emma," Eliza said as she sauntered over. "You throw the best parties. Carrie, come over here," Eliza called. "You have to see this."

Carrie Hartman, one of the old gang from high school, came forward. "Sydney Waverley," she said in a singsongy voice. Carrie had been the only girl in school who could even come close to Sydney's beauty.

Sydney looked cornered. Emma felt a hot rush of embarrassment for her.

"We all heard you were back in town," Eliza said. "You were away awhile. Where did you go?"

Sydney wiped her hands on her apron, then tucked her hair behind her ears. "I went everywhere," she said, her voice quivering slightly.

"Did you go to New York?" Hunter

John asked. "You always talked of going to New York."

"I lived there a year." Sydney's eyes darted around. "Um, where are your parents?"

"They moved to Florida two years ago. I took over the business."

"So **you** live here?"

"We live here," Emma said, hooking her arm in Hunter John's and leaning in to press her cleavage against him.

"Emma? You and Hunter John are . . . married?" Sydney said, and her shock was unsettling to Emma. How dare she be shocked that Hunter John chose her?

"We married the year we graduated. Right after you left. Sydney," she said, "I see two empty trays here." Emma tried to tell herself that Sydney had set herself up for this, that her humiliation was all her own doing. But it didn't make Emma feel any better. She didn't like making Sydney feel bad. Emma had won, after all. Right? But this is what Emma's mother would do, would say. And look how long she'd kept Emma's father.

Hunter John looked from Emma to Sydney and back. "I need to speak with you in private," he said, and led Emma through the crowd of guests into the house, Sydney's eyes following them.

"What's the matter, honey?" Emma asked when Hunter John led her into his study and closed the door. Emma had decorated this room for him, the butter-and-cocoa-colored walls, the framed photos of Hunter John's glory days on the high-school football field, the potted plants, and the huge walnut leather-top desk. She went to the desk and leaned against it provocatively. The reason she'd picked this particular desk was because it made a soft bed for when she surprised him with a quickie when he was working at home. She thought that's what he wanted now. Her mother was right again. Hunter John had seen Sydney and Emma together and known he'd made the right choice.

But Hunter John stood by the door, his glare as dark as charcoal. "You did this on purpose. You're humiliating Sydney on purpose."

She felt like she'd been given a gift on her birthday, sure it was the very thing she'd been asking for all year, only to find an ugly stone or a cracked mirror inside the box. "Since when do you care?"

"I care about how this looks. Why bring her here, into our home, for Christ's sake?"

"Shh, honey. Shh. Calm down. It's all right. I had nothing to do with it, I swear." She walked over to him and stood close, then she reached up and petted his lapels. Her hands slid down his jacket and rubbed against the front of his trousers.

His hands circled her wrists. "Emma, there are guests right outside."

"Then I'll just make this quick."

"No," he said for the first time in ten years, and he stepped away. "Not right now."

———

Claire felt nervous, and she hated the feeling. She hated when she didn't know what to do. She'd watched as Sydney's old friends converged on her like dust to static, and Claire just stood there. She hadn't known if Sydney wanted her to step in, or if Sydney would get mad if Claire pulled her away from the first time she'd seen her friends in ten years. Now Sydney's face was tight and her steps were sharp as Claire followed her back into the kitchen.

As soon as the door swung closed behind Claire, Sydney dropped her empty trays on the counter and said, "Why didn't you tell me Mr. and Mrs. Matteson were Hunter John and **Emma Clark**?"

Claire gathered Sydney's trays and stacked them on her own, then set them aside. "It didn't occur to me that you would think it was anyone else. Who did you think it was?"

"I thought it was Hunter John's parents! How on earth was I supposed to know Hunter John and Emma got married?"

"Because when you broke up with him, he and Emma started dating," Claire said, trying to keep a sensible tone to her voice, trying to keep her stomach from jumping, trying to keep her mind from saying, over and over, **This is bad. Something's wrong. This is bad.**

"How was I supposed to know that? I wasn't here!" Sydney said. "And I didn't break up with him. He broke up with me. Why do you think I left?"

Claire hesitated. "I thought you left because of me. I thought you left because I kept you from learning things, because I made you hate being a Waverley."

"You didn't make me hate being a Waverley. This whole town did," Sydney said impatiently. She shook her head like she was disappointed in Claire. "But if it makes you feel better, I'm leaving because of you now."

"Wait, Sydney, please."

"This was a setup! Didn't you see it? Emma Clark set me up to look like a . . .

like a servant in front of Hunter John and all my old high-school friends in their expensive dresses and their boob jobs. And how did she even know I was back in town? Why did you tell her?"

"I didn't tell her."

"Sure you didn't. How else would she have found out?"

"Maybe Eliza Beaufort told her," Claire said. "Her grandmother was one of the ladies at the luncheon in Hickory."

Sydney stared at Claire for a few long moments, her eyes shining with tears. Claire didn't think she'd ever seen Sydney cry. They'd both been stoic children. Neither had seemed too affected by their mother's abandonment, and neither had shed a tear. But for the first time Claire wondered what Sydney had been holding in all this time. "Why did you let me do this? Why did you let me go out there? Didn't you think it was unusual for Emma to be calling you to cater something meant to flaunt a lifestyle everyone else already knew about? The passion and the money. She did this so I would see it."

"She didn't arrange this, her mother did. I never even spoke to Emma. Maybe this was just a coincidence, Sydney. Maybe it doesn't mean anything."

"How can you, of all people, say that? To a Waverley, there's a meaning to everything! And how can you defend them? Are you actually this comfortable with people thinking the way they do about us? I saw you when we were kids, how no one wanted to be your friend, how no boys were ever interested in you. I thought that's why you retreated into all of this"—Sydney waved widely at the food and flowers on the countertops—"because you thought the house and Grandma were all you needed. I wanted more than that. I wanted those friends out there. I wanted all of this. I was devastated when Hunter John broke up with me, but you didn't even notice. And this hurt me tonight, Claire. Doesn't it matter at all to you?"

Claire didn't know what to say, which

seemed to make Sydney even more upset. Sydney turned with a hiss and went to the purse she'd set by the door. She took out a small piece of notebook paper, then went to the wall phone by the walk-in pantry.

"What are you doing?" Claire asked.

Sydney pointedly turned her back on her and dialed the number that was on the paper.

"Please, Sydney. Don't leave."

"Tyler?" Sydney said into the receiver. "It's Sydney Waverley. I'm stuck someplace and I need a ride." Pause. "Willow Springs Road, on the east side of town. Number thirty-two, a large Tudor home. Drive around back. Thank you so much."

Sydney took off her apron, dropped it to the floor. She grabbed her purse and walked out the door.

Claire helplessly watched her go. Her stomach was jumping so much she felt like she was going to be sick, and she had to bend over and put her hands on her knees. She couldn't lose what was left of her family, not so soon. She couldn't be the reason Sydney left again.

The past ten years weren't the only mystery surrounding Sydney. Claire realized she didn't even know her sister when they were kids. She didn't realize Sydney thought Hunter John was the one. She didn't realize it had hurt Sydney so much. But what Claire didn't know, those people out there on the patio did. And they **had** done this on purpose. Claire knew from the beginning that something had been off. Sydney was right. There was a meaning to everything, and Claire had ignored all the warning signs.

She took a deep breath, then straightened. She would fix this.

She went to the phone and pushed the redial button.

It took a few moments, but Tyler's voice finally came on the line, slightly breathless. "Hello?"

"Tyler?"

"Yes."

"This is Claire Waverley."

There was a definite pause of surprise. "Claire. This is strange. I just got a call from your sister. She sounded upset."

"She is. She's with me on a job. I need to . . . ask you for a favor."

"Anything," he said.

"I need you to go next door to my house before you pick Sydney up here. Will you bring me some things from the house and garden? I'll tell you where the keys are hidden."

About forty minutes later, there was a knock at the back door.

Claire opened the door and found Tyler there, carrying two cardboard boxes filled with flowers and ingredients from the house. "Where should I put this?"

"On the counter by the sink." When he passed her, she looked out to the service driveway, where Tyler's Jeep was parked with his lights still on. Sydney was sitting in the passenger seat, staring straight ahead.

"I saw you at work at Anna's, but I have to say, behind the scenes is even more impressive," Tyler said, taking a look around the kitchen as he set the boxes down.

Claire turned. While waiting for Tyler to bring the things she needed, Claire had lined up the food and flowers. Then she had written ingredient descriptions and a list of the flowers outside on index cards so she wouldn't confuse a recipe and cause mixed signals. This was too important. They wanted roses tonight to represent their love, but when you added sadness to love it caused regret. They wanted nutmeg because it represented their wealth, but when you added guilt to wealth it caused embarrassment.

"Thank you for doing this," she said, hoping he wouldn't ask what all this was for. But why would he? He wasn't from here. He didn't know the subversive nature of what she could do.

"No problem."

She lowered her eyes and noticed that

his jeans had dirt on the knees from the garden. "Sorry about the stains. I'll pay for a new pair."

"Sweetheart, I'm a painter. All my clothes look like this." He smiled, so warm, so calm. It almost took her breath. "Anything else I can do?"

"No," she said automatically, but then added, "Wait, yes. Will you ask Sydney not to leave tonight? Not until the night is over. I need to fix something."

"Did you two have a fight?"

"Sort of."

He smiled again. "I'll do my best."

When Claire got home, Sydney and Bay were already in bed. Sydney had obviously asked Tyler to pick Bay up at Evanelle's house on their way home.

At least they were going to stay the night, long enough for some things to be made right.

Claire stayed up late to make her regular order of six dozen cinnamon buns, which she delivered early to the Coffee House on the square every Sunday morning. Around midnight she sleepily made her way up to her room to set her alarm clock. She checked in on Bay, though she knew Sydney did it several times a night, then she walked down the hall.

She'd just passed Sydney's room when Sydney called out, "I had a lot of calls before you came home tonight."

Claire backed up a step and peered into Sydney's room. Sydney was awake, lying in bed with her arms behind her head. "Eliza Beaufort, Carrie, people at the party I didn't even know. They all said the same thing. That they were sorry. Eliza and Carrie even said they really liked me in high school and they wished things were different. What did you say to them?"

"I didn't say a word."

Sydney paused, and Claire knew by her next question that she was beginning to understand. "What did you give them?"

"I gave them lemon-balm sorbet in tulip cups. I put dandelion petals in the fruit salad, and mint leaves in the chocolate mousse."

"That wasn't on the dessert menu," Sydney said.

"I know."

"I noticed Emma Clark and her mother never called."

Claire leaned against the doorjamb. "They caught on to what I was doing. They wouldn't eat the dessert buffet. And I was ordered to leave."

"Did they pay you the remainder of your fee?"

"No. And I've had two cancelations tonight from acquaintances of theirs."

A rustle of sheets. Sydney turned in bed to face Claire. "I'm sorry."

"They officially canceled, but they'll call again when they need something. They'll just want me to keep it a secret."

"I've messed things up. I'm sorry."

"You didn't mess anything up," Claire

said. "Please don't leave, Sydney. I want you here. I may not act like it sometimes, but I do."

"I'm not leaving. I can't." Sydney sighed. "As crazy as this place is, the way people think, the sameness, is what makes it safe. Bay needs that. I'm her mother, I have to give that to her."

The words were left hanging in the air, and Claire could tell immediately that Sydney wanted to take them back. "Did you leave someplace that wasn't safe?" Claire had to ask.

But she should have known Sydney wouldn't answer. She shifted in her bed again, turning away. "I wish you'd do something about him," Sydney said, pointing to her open window. "It's hard to sleep with that."

There was a faint purple light filtering in. Curious, Claire entered Sydney's room and went to the window, which over-looked Tyler's house. She looked down and found Tyler walking around his front yard in pajama bottoms and nothing else, a cigarette in his hand. He was radiating those tiny purple snaps again. Occasionally he would stop and look over to the Waverley house, then he'd resume pacing.

"You can see it?" Claire asked, still looking down at Tyler.

"Of course."

"Then you're more of a Waverley than you give yourself credit for being."

Sydney snorted. "Oh, joy. So what are you going to do about him?"

Claire ignored the flutter like tiny birds' wings in her chest. She moved away from the window. "I'll take care of it."

"Just because no one expects you to do it doesn't mean you can't. Don't you ever want to prove people wrong?"

"I'm a Waverley," Claire said, walking back to the door. "There's nothing wrong with that."

"You're human. It's okay to date. It's okay to feel something. Go out with Tyler. Make people say, 'I can't believe she did that.'"

"You sound like Mom."

"Was that a compliment?"

Claire stopped at the door and gave a small laugh. "I'm not sure."

Sydney sat up in bed and punched her pillow a few times. "Wake me and I'll help you deliver the cinnamon buns in the morning," she said as she flopped back down.

"No, I can—" Claire stopped. "Thank you."

CHAPTER 6

Tuesday afternoon Claire announced she was going to the grocery store, and Sydney asked if she and Bay could ride along. Sydney wanted to get a newspaper to check out the want ads and, though it pained her to do so, she had to return the shirt Evanelle had given her. She'd put aside the money she made from working with Claire for emergencies, so she needed extra cash for toiletries, and Bay needed kid food. Claire was a great cook, but she'd looked at Bay blankly yesterday when Bay asked if she had any pizza rolls.

When they reached Fred's, Claire and Bay went into the grocery store and Sydney walked up the sidewalk. The square hadn't changed much, although now there was a university student's sculpture that looked like an oak leaf by the fountain on the green.

She returned the shirt at Maxine's and discovered that the shop had changed hands twice in the past ten years and was now run by a stylish woman in her fifties. She didn't have an opening in the store, but she took Sydney's number and said she would call if something came up. She recognized the Waverley name when Sydney wrote it down and asked Sydney if she was related to Claire. When Sydney said yes, the woman brightened and said Claire had made her daughter's wedding cake last year, and it had been the talk of all her friends from Atlanta. Then she said she would **definitely** call if she ever had an opening.

On her way back to the grocery store from Maxine's, Sydney passed the White Door Salon. Ten years ago it had been a trendy hair salon called Tangles, but now it was much more posh. A patron came out, and with her came the scent of chemicals cushioned by the fragrance of sweet shampoo. It was a smell that could almost lift Sydney up and make her float. Oh, how she missed that. It had been a long time since she'd been in a salon, and every time she passed one she felt like this, like she needed to go in and pick up her shears and get to work.

She started to get that prickly feeling she always got when she thought of being happy again. Like she shouldn't even bother. But she'd gone to beauty school under her real name, a name David didn't know. She had to remind herself that he wouldn't find them here. He wouldn't come just because she wanted to work again. The only reason David had found her in Boise was because she'd registered Bay under her real name. She didn't think she had a choice when the day care asked for Bay's birth certificate. She thought David would only be looking for Cindy Watkins, not Bay. She wasn't making that mistake again. Bay was a Waverley here.

She patted her hair, glad that she'd put it up in a clever twist and trimmed and shaped her bangs that morning.

Then she straightened her shoulders and walked in.

She was giddy when she met Claire and Bay at the van. She grinned as she helped them load the bags of groceries. She kept meeting Claire's eyes until Claire finally said, "Okay, what's with the grin?"

"Guess what?"

Claire smiled, obviously amused by Sydney's mood. "What?"

"I got a job! I told you I was staying. Getting a job is pretty clear, isn't it?"

Claire stopped what she was doing,

leaning halfway in the van. She looked genuinely perplexed. "But you already have a job."

"Claire, you do the work of three people. And you only need help occasionally. I'll still work when you need me." Sydney laughed. Nothing was going to ruin this mood. "Maybe not at Emma's house again . . . but, you know."

Claire straightened. "Where did you get the job?"

"At the White Door." It was going to take all her money, including the money from the shirt she'd just returned, to rent the booth and get supplies, but she had a wonderful feeling. She still had some of her equipment, and straightening out the state-to-state reciprocity licensing wouldn't take too long. She knew there'd been a reason she kept renewing her license. **This** was the reason. She would soon make the money to put back into the emergency fund, and people in Bascom would see that she was actually skilled at something. They would come to **her** like they came to Claire, because of what she could do.

"You're a hairstylist?" Claire asked.

"Yep."

"I didn't know that."

Claire was getting too close to asking again about where she and Bay had been, and Sydney still wasn't ready to tell her. "Listen, Bay will be starting kindergarten in the fall, but it will be a while before I can afford day care. Will you look after her? I'll ask Evanelle too."

She could tell that Claire knew what Sydney was doing, avoiding the obvious questions, but Claire didn't press her. Maybe one day she'd tell her sister about the past ten years, one day when there was enough trust between them to warrant such a revelation, when she knew the entire town wouldn't find out, but Sydney secretly hoped it all would just disappear as if it never happened, like a photograph fading to nothing.

"Of course I will," Claire finally said.

They started loading the bags again.

Sydney looked in a bag and asked, "What is all this stuff?"

"I'm going to make pizza rolls," Claire said.

"You can buy them frozen, you know."

"I knew that," Claire said. Then she whispered to Bay, "Is that true?"

Bay laughed.

"What about this stuff?" Sydney asked, nosing around some more in the bags. "Blueberries? Water chestnuts?"

Claire shooed her away and closed the back of the van. "I'm going to make a few dishes for Tyler," Claire said.

"Are you, now? I thought you didn't want anything to do with him."

"I don't. These are special dishes."

"A love potion?"

"There's no such thing as a love potion."

"You're not going to poison him, are you?"

"Of course not. But the flowers in our garden . . ." Claire paused. "Maybe I can make him less interested."

That made Sydney laugh, but she didn't say a word. She knew a lot about men, but making them less interested had never been her specialty. Leave it to Claire to make it hers.

Bay stretched out on the grass, the sun on her face. The things that happened even a week ago were fading in her mind, like the way the color pink faded until it was almost white and you couldn't believe it was ever pink once. What color were her father's eyes? How many steps were there from their old house to the sidewalk? She couldn't remember.

Bay knew all along that they were going to leave Seattle. She never told her mother this, because it was too hard to explain and she didn't understand it fully herself. They just didn't belong there, and Bay knew where things belonged. Sometimes, when her mother would put things away at their old house, Bay would sneak in later and put the things where she knew her father wanted them to be. Her mother would put his socks in his sock drawer, but Bay would know that when he got home he would want them in the closet with his shoes. Or when her mother would put the socks with his shoes, Bay would know when that would make him mad, and she'd put them in the drawer. But sometimes his desires changed so quickly that Bay couldn't keep up with them, and he'd yell and do bad things to her mother. It had been exhausting, and she was glad to be someplace it was clear where things belonged. Utensils were always in the drawer to the left of the sink. Linens were always put in the closet at the top of the stairs. Claire never changed her mind about where things went.

Bay had dreamed of this place a long time ago. She'd known they were coming here. But today Bay was lying in the garden trying to figure out what was missing. In the dream she was stretched out on the grass in this garden, by this apple tree.

The grass was soft like in her dream. And the scent of the herbs and flowers was exactly like in the dream. But in her dream there were rainbows and tiny specks of light on her face, like something sparkling above her. And there was supposed to be the sound of something like paper flapping in the wind, but the only sound around was the rustling of the leaves on the apple tree as it dropped apples around her.

An apple hit her leg, and Bay opened one eye to look up at the tree. It kept dropping apples on her, almost like it wanted to play.

She sat up suddenly when she heard Claire call her name. This was Sydney's first day at work and Claire's first day of watching Bay. Sydney hadn't allowed Bay into the garden, but Claire said it was okay to be out here as long as she didn't pick any of the flowers. Bay had been so excited to finally see the garden. She hoped she hadn't done anything wrong.

"I'm right here," Bay called as she stood. She saw Claire standing at the other end of the garden by the gate. "I didn't pick any flowers."

Claire held up a casserole dish covered with aluminum foil. "I'm going over to Tyler's to take him this. Come with me."

Bay ran down the gravel pathway to Claire, glad that she was going to see Tyler again. When she and her mother had visited last time, he let her draw on an easel, and when she showed him what she'd drawn, he hung it on his refrigerator.

Claire closed and locked the gate behind them, and they walked around the house to Tyler's yard. Bay walked close to Claire. She liked the way Claire smelled, comfortable, like kitchen soap and garden herbs. "Aunt Claire, why does the apple tree keep dropping apples on me?"

"It wants you to eat one," Claire said.

"But I don't like apples."

"It knows that."

"Why do you bury the apples?"

"So no one else will eat them."

"Why don't you want people to eat them?"

Claire hesitated a moment. "Because if you eat an apple from that tree, you'll see what the biggest event in your life will be. If it's good, you'll suddenly know that everything else you do will never make you as happy. And if it's bad, you'll have to live the rest of your life knowing something bad is going to happen. It's something no one should know."

"But some people want to know?"

"Yes. But as long as the tree is in our yard, we get a say-so."

They reached Tyler's steps. "You mean it's my yard too?"

"It's very definitely your yard too," Claire said, smiling. Just for a moment, Claire was Bay's age, looking at her with the same happiness Bay felt, that happiness at simply belonging in a way she'd never belonged before.

"This is a pleasant surprise," Tyler said when he opened the door. Claire had taken a deep breath before she knocked, and when she saw him she forgot to let it out. He was in a paint-splattered T-shirt and jeans. Sometimes her very skin felt so jumpy that she wanted to crawl out of her body. She wondered what a kiss from him would do. Help? Make it worse? He smiled, not looking at all put out that she'd shown up unannounced. That's how she would feel. But he was, quite obviously, nothing like her. "Come in."

"I made you a casserole," she said breathlessly as she handed it to him.

"It smells delicious. Please, come in." He stood back for them to enter, which was the last thing Claire wanted to do.

Bay looked at her curiously. She thought something was wrong. Claire smiled at her and entered so she wouldn't worry.

Tyler led them through a living room with a few pieces of comfortable furniture and a lot of boxes, into a white kitchen with glass-front cabinets. There was a very large breakfast nook—another room, really—off the kitchen, with floor-to-ceiling windows. The floor of the nook was covered with a tarp, and there were paint supplies littered across a long huntboard. Two easels were set up.

"That's the reason I bought this house. All that beautiful light," Tyler said as he put the casserole dish on the kitchen counter.

"Can I draw, Tyler?" Bay asked.

"Sure, kiddo. Your easel is right over there. Let me put some paper on it."

While Tyler adjusted the easel to her height, Bay went to the refrigerator and pointed to a colored drawing of an apple tree. "Look, Claire, I did that."

It wasn't that Tyler had put Bay's drawing on his refrigerator that Claire appreciated; it was that he'd left it there. "It's beautiful."

As soon as Bay was settled, Tyler walked back to Claire, smiling.

Claire's eyes went to the dish worriedly. It was a chicken and water chestnut casserole made with the oil from snapdragon seeds. Snapdragons were meant to ward off the undue influences of others, hexes and spells and the like, and Tyler needed to free himself of her influence over him. "Aren't you going to eat it?" she prompted.

"Right now?"

"Yes."

He shrugged. "Well, okay. Why not. Will you join me?"

"No, thank you. I've already eaten."

"Then sit while I eat." He took a clear glass plate from the cabinet and spooned some of the casserole onto it. He led Claire to two stools at the counter. "So, how are you and Bay getting along with Sydney at work?" he asked as they took their seats. "She stopped by yesterday and told me about her new job. She has a gift with hair. A real passion for it."

"We're doing fine," Claire said, watching Tyler as he brought a forkful of the casserole to his mouth. He chewed and swallowed, and she thought for a moment that maybe she shouldn't be watching. It was almost sensual, his full lips, the bob of his Adam's apple. She shouldn't feel this way about a man who was going to be free of her in a few seconds.

"Ever thought of having kids?" he asked.

"No," she answered, still staring.

"Never?"

She took her mind off his mouth and thought about it. "Not until you just asked me."

He took another bite, then pointed to his plate with his fork. "This is wonderful. I don't think I've ever eaten as well as I have since I met you."

Maybe it just took a few minutes to kick in. "Next you're going to tell me I remind you of your mother. I expect more creativity from you. Eat."

"No, you're nothing like my mother. Her free spirit doesn't include anything to do with the kitchen." She raised her brows at this bit of information. He smiled at her and took another bite. "Go on, you know you want to ask."

She hesitated a moment, then gave in and asked. "How was she a free spirit?"

"They're potters, my parents. I grew up in an artists' colony in Connecticut. You didn't want to wear clothes? You didn't have to. You didn't want to wash the dishes? You broke them and made some more. Do a little pot and sleep with your best friend's husband. It was all okay. It wasn't for me, though. I can't help my artistic nature, but security and routine mean more to me than they do to my parents. I just wish I was better at it."

You're looking at an expert, she thought, but didn't say it out loud. He would probably like that about her.

Two more bites and he'd cleaned his plate.

She looked at him expectantly. "Did you like it? How do you feel?"

He met her eyes, and she almost fell off her stool from the force of his desire. It was like a hard gust of autumn wind that blew

fallen leaves around so fast they could cut
you. Desire was dangerous to thin-skinned
people. "Like I want to ask you on a date."

Claire sighed and her shoulders
dropped. "Damn."

"There's music on the quad at Orion
every Saturday night in the summer.
Come with me this Saturday."

"No, I'll be busy."

"Doing what?"

"Making you another casserole."

Sydney's third day at work was the third
day she went without a single walk-in
wanting her to cut their hair, and not a
single regular White Door patron wanting
her to do their shampoo when their own
stylist was running behind.

And that was the high point.

At lunchtime, since she didn't have anything else to do and she had already eaten
the olive sandwich and sweet-potato chips
Claire had packed for her, Sydney offered
to fetch the other stylists' lunches. They
were a nice bunch, and they were encour-

aging and kept telling Sydney it would get better. But that didn't extend to sharing their clients. Sydney had to find some way to get how good she was out there, to start bringing people in.

At the Coffee House and at the Brown Bag Café, Sydney chatted up the workers and offered them discounts if they wanted to come to the White Door and let Sydney cut their hair. None seemed too enthusiastic, but it was a start. She walked back to the salon and put the bags of lunches in the break room, then she placed the lattes and iced coffees at the stations where some stylists were still working.

The last station she went to was Terri's. Sydney smiled and put her soy latte on the counter.

"Thanks, Sydney," Terri said, elbow deep in highlighting her client's blond hair.

The client's head shot up, and Sydney saw that it was Ariel Clark.

Despite her initial desire to demand an apology for what Ariel had put her and

Claire through that Saturday night, Sydney held her tongue and walked away without a word. She wanted to salvage what was left of her day.

Ariel Clark, however, had other ideas.

Later, Sydney was sweeping around a station at the other end of the salon when Ariel walked up to her. Emma looked a lot like her mother, the same ice-blond hair, the same blue eyes, the same confident swagger. Even back when Sydney and Emma were friends, Ariel had always been standoffish toward Sydney. When Sydney spent nights at the Clark house, Ariel had always been polite, but there was something about her that made Sydney feel like being there was charity, not acceptance.

When Ariel didn't move from the only spot left to sweep, Sydney finally stopped.

She managed a polite smile, even though she was choking the broom handle. If she was going to make a success out of this venture, she couldn't whack White Door clients over the head with a broom, no matter how much they deserved it.

"Hello, Mrs. Clark. How are you? I saw you at the party. I'm sorry we didn't get to say hello."

"Understandable, sugar. You were working. It would have been inappropriate." Her eyes slid down the broom to the sad pile of hair Sydney had swept up. "You're working here, I gather."

"Yes."

"You don't actually . . . cut hair, do you?" she asked, as if appalled by the thought. A fine beginning, Sydney thought, if everyone in town who knew her was going to react to the news this way.

"Yes, I do actually cut hair."

"Don't you need some sort of degree to do that, sugar?"

Her fingertips were going numb and turning white from gripping the broom handle so tightly. "Yes."

"Hmm," Ariel said. "So I hear you have a daughter. And who is her father?"

Sydney knew enough not to let Ariel see her vulnerable spots. Once some people knew how to hurt you, they would do it again and again. Sydney had a lot of experience with that. "No one you know."

"Oh, I'm certain of that."

"Anything else, Mrs. Clark?"

"My daughter is very happy. She makes her husband very happy."

"She's a Clark, after all," Sydney said.

"Exactly. I don't know what you hoped, coming back here. But you can't have him."

That's what this was all about? "I know this is going to come as a surprise, but I didn't come back to get him."

"So you say. You Waverleys have your tricks. Don't think I don't know." As she walked away, she flipped her cell phone out of her purse and started dialing. "Emma darling, I have the most delicious news," she said.

Around five o'clock that afternoon, Sydney was going to give up for the day and leave. That's when she saw a man in a nice gray suit at the reception desk, and she got a sinking feeling.

This day was never going to end.

Hunter John asked the receptionist something and she turned and pointed at Sydney.

He walked across the salon to her. She should have walked away to the break room, avoided him entirely, but memories kept her there. At twenty-eight, his sandy hair was thinning. A better cut would hide it. His hair was still beautiful and shiny, which meant he still had what he had when he was young, but he was losing it. He was turning into someone else.

"I heard you were working here," Hunter John said when he reached her.

"Yes, I imagine you did." She crossed her arms over her chest. "You have lipstick on your neck."

He rubbed his neck sheepishly. "Emma came to tell me at work."

"So you took over your family's business."

"Yes."

Matteson Enterprises was a group of mobile-home manufacturing plants about twenty minutes outside of Bascom. Sydney had worked as a receptionist in the front office the same summers Hunter John had interned there. They used to meet in his father's office when he went to lunch, and they'd make out. Sometimes Emma would drive out when things were slow, and the three of them would sit on the stacks of lumber outside the warehouse and smoke.

What was his life like now? Did he really love Emma, or had she just gotten him with sex, as Clark women were wont to do? It was Emma, after all, who told Sydney how to give the perfect blow job. It was only years later that a man finally told Sydney she'd been doing it wrong. It suddenly occurred to Sydney that Emma had told her the wrong way to do it on purpose. Sydney had no idea Emma even liked Hunter John. And Hunter John had always said Emma was a little too high-strung for him. Sydney had never put the two together in her mind. But, then, she'd been oblivious to a lot of things back then.

"Can I have a seat?" Hunter John asked.

"Do you want me to cut your hair? I'm great at it."

"No, I just don't want it to look like I only stopped by to talk," he said as he sat.

She rolled her eyes. "Heaven forbid."

"I wanted to say a few things to you, to clear the air. It's the right thing to do." Hunter John always did the right thing. That's what he'd been known for. The golden boy. The good son. "That night at the party, I didn't know you'd be there. And neither did Emma. We were as surprised as you. Ariel hired Claire. No one knew you were working for her."

"Don't be naive, Hunter John. If Eliza Beaufort knew, everyone knew."

Hunter John looked disappointed. "I'm sorry for the way it happened, but it was for the best. As you saw, I'm happily married now."

"Good Lord," Sydney said, "does everyone think I came back just for you?"

"Why **did** you come back, then?"

"Is this not my home, Hunter John? Is this not where I grew up?"

"Yes, but you never liked who you were here."

"Neither did you."

Hunter John sighed. Who was this person? She didn't know him at all anymore. "I love my wife and kids. I have a great life, and I wouldn't trade it for the world. I did love you once, Sydney. Breaking up with you was one of the hardest things I've ever done."

"So hard that you sought comfort in marrying Emma?"

"We married so soon because she got pregnant. Emma and I just grew close after you left. Complete serendipity."

Sydney had to laugh. "You're being naive again, Hunter John."

She could tell he didn't like hearing that. "She is the best thing that ever happened to me."

He was saying that because he gave up Sydney his life was great. **She** didn't like hearing that. "Did you go to Notre Dame? Did you travel around Europe like you wanted to?"

"No. Those are old dreams."

"Seems to me you gave up a lot of dreams."

"I'm a Matteson. I had to do what's best for my name."

"And I'm a Waverley, so I get to curse you for it."

He gave a little start, like she meant it, and it gave Sydney a curious sensation of power. But then Hunter John smiled. "Come on, you hate being a Waverley."

"You should go," Sydney said. Hunter John stood and reached for his wallet. "And don't you dare leave money for a pretend haircut."

"I'm sorry, Sydney. I can't help who I am. Obviously, neither can you."

As he walked away, she thought what a sad thing it was to say about herself, that she'd only ever loved one man. And that man had to be **that** man, one who had from the beginning relegated her to a youthful indiscretion, when she thought it would be forever.

She wished she really did know a curse.

———

"I was getting worried," Claire said when Sydney came into the kitchen that evening. "Bay's upstairs."

Sydney opened the refrigerator and took out a bottle of water. "I stayed late."

"How was your day?"

"It was fine." She walked over to the sink where Claire was rinsing a bowl of blueberries. "So, what are you making? Something to take to Tyler again?"

"Yes."

Sydney picked up the bouquet of blue flowers laying on the counter by the sink and put them to her nose. "What are these?"

"Bachelor's buttons. I'm going to sprinkle the blueberry tarts with their petals."

"And what do they mean?"

"Bachelor's buttons make people see sharper, helpful for finding things like misplaced keys and hidden agendas," Claire said easily. The power came so naturally to her.

"So you're trying to make Tyler realize you're not what he's looking for?"

Claire smiled slightly. "No comment."

Sydney watched Claire work for a while. "I wonder why I didn't inherit it," she said absently.

"Inherit what?"

"That mysterious Waverley sensibility you and Evanelle have. Grandma had it too. Did Mom?"

Claire turned off the spigot and reached for a hand towel to dry her hands. "It was hard to tell. She hated the garden, I remember that much. She wouldn't go near it."

"I don't mind the garden, but I guess I'm more like Mom than anyone in the family." Sydney grabbed a few blueberries and popped them in her mouth. "I don't have a special thing like Mom, and Mom moved back here so you had a stable place to live and go to school, just like I did for Bay."

"Mom didn't move back because of

me," Claire said, as if surprised Sydney thought that. "She moved back so you could be born here."

"She left when I was six," Sydney said as she went to the open door to the sunroom porch and looked out. "If it weren't for those photographs of Mom Grandma gave me, I wouldn't even remember what she looked like. If I meant something to her, she wouldn't have left."

"What did you do with those photos?" Claire asked. "I'd forgotten about them."

One moment Sydney was tilting her head and taking a deep breath of the herbs drying on the porch, the next moment she was blown out the door, transported on the wind back to Seattle. She landed in the living room of the town house, staring at the couch. She walked to it and lifted one side. There under the couch was an envelope marked **Mom.** It had been so long since she'd felt like looking at the photos that she'd forgotten they were there. These were photos of Lorelei's life on the road, a life Sydney had tried to emulate for so long. She took the envelope and leafed through the stack of photos, and she found one that made her head want to explode with fear. There was her mother, maybe eighteen years old, standing in front of the Alamo. She was smiling and holding a handmade sign that read **No More Bascom! North Carolina Stinks!** When Sydney was a teenager, she thought it was the funniest thing. But what if David found the envelope? What if he figured it out? She heard him at the front door. She put the envelope back under the couch quickly. He was coming in. He was going to find her there.

"Sydney?"

Sydney opened her eyes with a start. She was back in Bascom. Claire was beside her, shaking her arm.

"Sydney?"

"I forgot to take them with me," Sydney said. "The photos. I left them."

"Are you all right?"

Sydney nodded, trying to get a hold of herself. But she had a bad feeling that

David would know she'd been there. He'd know she'd been thinking about something she left behind. She'd opened a door. Even now she thought she could smell his cologne near her, as if she'd brought him back with her. "I'm fine. I was just thinking of Mom." Sydney shrugged, trying to get rid of the tension in her shoulders. David didn't know where the photos were.

He wouldn't find them.

That evening Evanelle put on a short-sleeved robe over her nightgown and walked into her kitchen. She had to step around boxes full of Band-Aids and matches, rubber bands and Christmas ornament hooks. Once in the kitchen, she went searching for microwave popcorn. She pushed aside toasters in their original boxes and aspirin she'd bought in bulk.

She didn't want any of this stuff, she didn't even particularly like having it around. She tried to keep it all in corners and unused rooms, but some of it always managed to spill out. One day someone was going to need it, so it was better to have it around than to go looking for it at three in the morning at the all-night Wal-Mart.

She turned when she heard a knock.

Someone was at her door.

Now, this was a surprise. She didn't get many visitors. She lived in a small neighborhood of old arts and crafts houses, an area that had become a little more fancy than when she and her husband, who had worked for the phone company, moved there. Her neighbors were mostly couples in their thirties and forties without children and commuter jobs that brought them home after dark. She'd never even spoken to her next-door neighbors, the Hansons, who moved in three years ago. But the fact that they'd told their lawn man to "keep their neighbor's lawn neat too, for the sake of the neighborhood" spoke volumes.

But it got her lawn mowed for free, so who was she to complain.

She turned on the porch light, then

opened the door. A short, square, middle-aged man with sharply cut dark-blond hair stood there. His slacks and shirt were wrinkle-free and his shoes shone like fire-crackers. He had a small suitcase at his feet. "Fred!"

"Hello, Evanelle."

"What on earth are you doing here?"

His face was drawn, but he tried to smile. "I . . . need a place to stay. You were the first person I thought of."

"Well, I can see why. I'm old and you're gay."

"Sounds like a perfect relationship." He was trying to be upbeat, but in the glow of the porch light he was as shiny as glass, and one small shove and he'd break into a thousand tiny pieces.

"Come in."

Fred picked up his suitcase and entered, then stood in the living room looking like a little boy who had run away from home. Evanelle had known Fred all his life. He won the county spelling bee two years in a row, then he lost to Lorelei Waverley in the fourth grade. Evanelle had come to see Lorelei compete, and afterward she found Fred crying outside the gymnasium. She'd given him a hug, and he made her promise not to tell his father that he was so upset. His father told him he should never cry in front of other people. What would they think of him?

"Shelly came in early today. She caught me in my pajamas in my office. It's been easier just to stay at work. I know what to do there," Fred said. "But word is probably out now, and I can't stay in a motel. I don't want to give James that kind of satisfaction. Hell, I don't even know if he's noticed I haven't been there. He hasn't called to ask where I've been. Nothing. I don't know what to do."

"Have you talked at all?"

"I tried. Like you said. After that first night I slept at the store, I called him. He was at work. He said he didn't want to talk about it, that just because I finally noticed something was wrong didn't mean I could make it right now. I told him about the wine I bought from Claire. He said I was crazy, crazy for wanting things the way they were when we were first together. I don't understand what happened. One moment we were fine. Six months later I suddenly realize I can't remember the last time we had a regular conversation. It's like he's been leaving me by degrees, and I didn't even notice. How does a person not notice that?"

"Well, you can stay here as long as you like. But if anyone asks, I get to say my undeniable womanliness turned you straight."

"I make terrific Belgian waffles, with a wonderful peach compote. Just tell me what you want me to cook and I'll cook it."

She patted his cheek. "Not that anyone will believe me."

She showed him to the guest bedroom down the hall. There were a few boxes of first-aid kits and three kerosene heaters in the room, but she'd been keeping this room mostly clear and the bed made with fresh sheets every week for over thirty years. There was a void—which still existed, just better concealed these days—left in her home after Evanelle's husband died. During those sad days following his death, Lorelei would spend the night with Evanelle, but she stopped as she got older and wilder. Then Claire would stay the night sometimes when she was young, but she liked to stay at home mostly. Evanelle never imagined Fred would be staying here one day. But surprises were nothing new to her. Like opening a can of mushroom soup and finding tomato instead; be grateful and eat it anyway.

Fred put his suitcase on the bed and looked around.

"I was going to make some popcorn and watch the news. Want to join me?"

"Sure," Fred said, following her, as if glad to be told what to do. "Thank you."

Well, isn't this nice, Evanelle thought as they sat on the couch with a bowl of popcorn. They watched the eleven o'clock news together, and then Fred washed the popcorn bowl.

"I'll see you in the morning," Evanelle said as she took a can of Coke from the refrigerator. She liked to open it and leave it on her bedside table and then drink it flat first thing in the morning. "The bathroom's down the hall."

"Wait."

Evanelle turned around.

"Is it true that you once gave my father a spoon when you were kids? And that he used it to dig a quarter out of the dirt when he saw something shiny? And he used the quarter to go to the movies? And that's where he met my mother?"

"It's true that I gave him a spoon. I don't have the power to make things all better, Fred."

"Oh, I understand," he said quickly, looking down and folding the dish towel in his hands. "I was just asking."

Evanelle suddenly realized the real reason he was there.

Most people tried to avoid her because she gave them things.

Fred wanted to move in to be closer, on the off chance she was going to produce something that would make sense out of everything happening with James, that spoon that was going to help him dig out of this.

Sydney, Bay, and Claire sat on the porch that Sunday, eating extra cinnamon buns that Claire had made from her regular Sunday order to the Coffee House. It was hot and things were out of whack. Doorknobs that everyone swore were on the right side of the doors were actually on the left. Butter melted in the refrigerator. Things weren't being said and were left to stew in the air.

"There's Evanelle," Sydney said, and Claire turned to see her coming up the sidewalk.

Evanelle walked up the steps, smiling. "Your mother had two beautiful girls. I'll give her that. But you two don't look so chipper."

"It's the first heat wave. It makes everyone cranky," Claire said as she poured Evanelle a glass of iced tea from the pitcher she'd brought outside. "How have you been? I haven't seen you in a couple of days."

Evanelle took the glass and sat in the wicker rocker by Claire. "I've had a guest."

"Who?"

"Fred Walker is staying with me."

"Oh," Claire said, surprised. "Are you okay with that?"

"I'm fine with it."

"I guess the rose geranium wine didn't work."

Evanelle shrugged and sipped her tea. "He never used it."

Claire glanced over to the house next door. "Do you think Fred would let me buy it back?"

"I don't see why not. Got another customer for it?"

"No."

Sydney piped in and said, "She probably wants to use it on Tyler."

Claire gave her a look, but it was only halfhearted. She was right, after all.

Evanelle put her tea down and rooted through her tote bag. "I came because I had to give you this," she said, finally bringing out a white headband and handing it to Claire. "Fred tried to talk me out of giving it to you. He said you use combs, not headbands, that headbands were for people with short hair. He doesn't understand. **This** is what I had to give you. It's been a while since I've lived with a man. I forgot how stubborn they can be. They smell right nice, though."

Sydney and Claire exchanged glances. "Evanelle, you do know Fred is gay, don't you?" Claire asked gently.

"Of course," she said, laughing, looking happier and lighter than Claire had seen her in ages. "But it's nice to know that you two aren't the only ones who like having me around. So tell me, Sydney, how is work?"

Sydney and Bay were sitting on the porch swing, and Sydney was using one bare foot to gently rock them back and forth. "I have you to thank for it. If you hadn't given me that shirt I returned, I never would have gone into the White Door to see if they had an open booth."

"Fred said he saw you a couple of times last week, getting lunch for the girls. And once he saw you sweeping up."

"That's all I'm good for right now."

"What's the matter?" Claire asked, aware that Sydney had been mopey lately. She'd been so excited about her job at the White Door at first, but as the days wore on she came home earlier and earlier, smiling less and less. Claire had mixed feelings about Sydney's new job. Claire liked working with Sydney, liked having her around. But Sydney had a light to her when she talked of hair. She left every morning with so much hope.

"The clientele at the White Door all seem to know the Clarks and the Mattesons. I had a visit from Hunter John

my third day. Apparently some people—
and I'm not naming names—aren't happy
with that and spread the word. Not that I
was busy before, but there seems to be a
reason for it now."

"Did you cut his hair?"

"No, he wouldn't let me. It's a shame,
because I do great men's cuts," Sydney
said. "I was the one who cut Tyler's hair."

"You were?"

"Uh-huh. And Bay's and my own."

"So . . . so people have been snubbing
you?" Claire asked. "Not even giving you a
chance?"

"If this keeps up, I'm not going to be
able to keep the booth. But maybe it's just
as well," Sydney said, putting her arm
around Bay. "I'll get to spend more time
with Bay. And I'll be free to help you any-
time you want."

Claire had been in a hair salon three times
in her adult life, only when her hair would
get too long to control and she needed a
couple of inches taken off. She went to

Mavis Adler's Salon of Style on the highway. Mavis used to make special house calls to cut Claire's grandmother's hair, and if Mavis was good enough for her grandmother, she was good enough for Claire.

Claire didn't consider herself a rube, and she'd passed by the White Door countless times, but when she walked in and found leather couches and original artwork and a gaggle of some of the more wealthy women in town, some of whom she'd catered brunches, lunches, and teas for, she suddenly felt frighteningly out of place.

She spotted Sydney in the back, sweeping hair from around another stylist's chair, looking beautiful and self-contained. She looked so alone, which was all well and good for Claire, but not for Sydney.

Sydney saw her and immediately walked to the reception area. "Claire, what's wrong? Where's Bay? Is she okay?"

"She's fine. I asked Evanelle to watch her for an hour or two."

"Why?"

"Because I want you to cut my hair."

A crowd of stylists and patrons gathered around Sydney and Claire. Rebecca, the owner of the White Door, stood like an instructor, waiting for Sydney to begin. Whispers of Claire's beautiful long hair and Sydney's untested abilities floated around like dust motes.

"Do you trust me?" Sydney asked as she pumped up the chair after she'd washed Claire's hair.

Claire met her sister's eyes in the mirror. "Yes," she said.

Sydney turned her around, away from the mirror.

Over the next few minutes, Claire's hair felt lighter and lighter as wet chunks of dark hair fell onto the smock she was wearing, looking like thin strips of molasses candy. Every so often, Rebecca would ask Sydney a question and Sydney would answer confidently, using words like **beveled**

cut and **wisps of bangs.** Claire didn't understand what it meant. It made her think of bevel-cut crystal bowls and wisps of steam rising from curried rice.

When Sydney finally turned the chair back around, the people around her applauded.

Claire couldn't believe what she saw. Sydney had taken off at least twelve inches of length. The cut angled down so that it was longer in the front, but high and full in the back. The thin bangs made Claire's eyes look beautiful and sparkling, not flat and judgmental. There in the mirror was someone who looked like Claire had always wanted to be.

Sydney didn't ask her if she liked it. There was no question. It was a transformation performed by a master. Everyone was looking at Sydney with such awe, and Sydney was shining like polished silver.

Claire felt tears come to her eyes, a joy of birth, of redemption. Somewhere deep inside her, Claire had always known. It had been the source of all her jealousy when they were kids. Sydney had been born here. That was a gift, and this had always been inside Sydney, just waiting for her to embrace it.

"You can't deny it anymore," Claire said.

"Deny what?" Sydney asked.

"**This** is your Waverley magic."

PART TWO

Insight

CHAPTER
7

Lester Hopkins sat in an aluminum lawn chair under the chestnut tree in his front yard. A ribbon of dust followed a car in the distance, coming up the long driveway to the house next to the dairy.

Lester had come back from his stroke last year with a limp and a corner of his mouth that

wouldn't quite turn up, so he kept a hand-
kerchief handy to wipe away the spittle
that collected there. Didn't want to offend
the ladies. He spent a lot of time sitting
these days, which he didn't mind so much.
It gave him time to think. Truth be told,
he had always looked forward to this time
in his life. When he was a boy, his grandfather lived the life of Reilly, his days full of
big breakfasts, hunting when he felt like it,
sleeping in the afternoons, and picking the
banjo in the evenings. That, Lester
thought, was the way to live. You even got
money in the mail every month, like
clockwork. So Lester decided early on that
he wanted to grow up and be retired.

But there were a few glitches along the
way. He had to work harder than he imagined after his father died when Lester was
seventeen, which left him to run the dairy
by himself. And he and his wife were
blessed with only one son. But his son
married a hardworking woman and they
all lived there in the house, and his son
had a son and everything was all right. But

then Lester's wife got the cancer and his son died in a car accident two years later. Lost and grieving, his daughter-in-law wanted to move to Tuscaloosa, where her sister lived. But Henry, Lester's grandson, then eleven years old, wanted to stay.

So Lester had known only two things of constant faith: his farm, and Henry.

As the car came closer, Lester heard the screen door bang shut. He turned to see that Henry had come out of the front of the house to see who it was. It was too late for business. The sun was nearly set.

Henry called out, "Are you expecting something, Pap?"

"My ship to come in. But that ain't it."

Henry walked down to the chestnut tree and stood beside Lester. Lester looked over at him. He was a handsome boy, but like all Hopkins men, he was born old and would spend his whole life waiting for his body to catch up. This was the reason all Hopkins men married older women. Henry was taking his time, though, and Lester had taken to helping him along a little. Lester would tell Henry to lead the elementary-school tours of the dairy if the teachers were the right age and unmarried. And the decorating committee at church consisted of mostly divorced women, so Lester let them come out to collect hay in the fall and holly in the winter, and he always made Henry go out to help them. But nothing ever took. Solid and sure of himself, hardworking and kindhearted, Henry was quite a catch, if only he wasn't so happy with himself.

But that's what happens when you're born old.

The car came to a stop. Lester didn't recognize the driver, but he did recognize the woman getting out of the passenger seat.

He cackled. He always liked for Evanelle Franklin to come by. It was like finding a robin in the winter. "Looks like Evanelle needs to give us something."

The man stayed in the car as Evanelle crossed the yard. "Lester," she said, stopping in front of him and putting her hands on her hips, "you look better every time I see you."

"They have a cure for cataracts now, you know," he teased.

She smiled. "Devil man."

"What brings you out this way?"

"I needed to give you this." She reached into her bag of goodies and handed him a jar of maraschino cherries.

Lester looked over to Henry, who was trying to hide his smile. "Well, I haven't had these in a long time. Thank you, Evanelle."

"You're welcome."

"Say, who's that who brought you?"

"That's Fred, from the grocery store. He's been staying with me. It's been real nice."

"Would you two like to stay for dinner?" Henry asked. "Yvonne made potato cakes."

Yvonne was their housekeeper. Henry had hired her after Lester's stroke last year. She was married, of course. Lester would have hired someone single.

"No, thank you, I have to get along," Evanelle said. "I'll see you at the Fourth of July celebration?"

"We'll be there," Lester said, and he and Henry watched her walk away.

"She gave me a ball of yarn once," Henry said. "I was probably fourteen and we were on a school field trip downtown. I was so embarrassed. I threw it away. But the very next week I needed it when I was working on a school project."

"Men in this town learn their lesson young when it comes to Waverley women," Lester said, reaching for the cane he'd rested against the tree. He slowly stood. "Whenever there's one around, sit up and pay attention."

The next afternoon Claire heard Sydney's voice upstairs. "Where is everyone?"

"I'm down here," Claire called to her.

Soon she heard the creak of the dusty stairs as Sydney walked down to the basement. It was cool and dry, and sometimes grown men who had too much to do would knock on the front door and ask to go sit in the Waverley basement for a while because it cleared their thoughts and brought back their equilibrium.

Sydney's footsteps drew closer as she followed the racks deeper into the basement, toward the shine of Claire's flashlight. The lightbulbs in the basement had all burned out in 1939, and what had started out as someone too tired to replace them had turned into a family tradition of keeping the basement in the dark. No one knew why they did it now, just that this was the way it had always been done.

"Where is Bay?" Sydney asked. "Isn't she down here with you?"

"No, she likes to stay in the garden most of the time. She's okay. The tree stopped tossing apples at her when she started throwing them back at it." Claire handed Sydney the flashlight. "Help me with this, will you? Shine here."

"Honeysuckle wine?"

"The Fourth of July celebration is next week. I'm counting the bottles to see how many we have to bring."

"I saw a bottle on the kitchen table when I came in," Sydney said as Claire counted.

"That's the rose geranium wine Fred gave back to me. He wouldn't let me return his money. I think it might be a bribe to keep quiet," Claire said, then clapped her hands together to get rid of the dust. "Thirty-four bottles. I thought I made forty last year. No matter. This should be enough."

"Are you going to give it to Tyler?"

Claire took back the flashlight. "Am I going to give what to Tyler?"

"The rose geranium wine."

"Oh," Claire said, walking away. Sydney was soon on her heels. "Actually, I was sort of hoping you would take it to him for me."

"He's teaching his summer-session classes," Sydney said. "He won't be around much."

"Oh." Claire was glad Sydney couldn't see her, see her confusion. She sometimes thought she was going crazy. Her first thought when she woke up was always how to get him out of her thoughts. And she would keep watch, hoping to see him next door, while plotting ways to never have to see him again. It made no sense.

They reached the kitchen, and Claire closed and locked the basement door behind them. "He's a good guy, Claire," Sydney said. "I know. Surprised the hell out of me too. Imagine that. Men can be good. Who would've thought?"

Claire took the flashlight back to the storeroom and put it on the shelf where she kept candles and battery-powered lanterns. The electricity from her frustration caused the portable radio on the shelf to crackle to life as she passed it, and she jumped in surprise. She immediately turned it off, then leaned against the wall. This couldn't go on. "He's not a constant," Claire said from the storeroom. "The apple tree is a constant. Honeysuckle wine is a constant. This house is a constant. Tyler Hughes is not a constant."

"I'm not a constant, am I?" Sydney asked, but Claire didn't answer. Was Sydney a constant? Had she really found her niche in Bascom, or would she leave again, maybe when Bay was grown or if she fell in love? Claire didn't want to think about it. The only thing Claire could control was not being the reason Sydney left, giving her reasons to stay. She would focus only on that.

Claire took a deep breath and walked back out to the kitchen. "So how's work?" she asked brightly.

"Oh, my God, so busy. Thanks to you."

"I didn't do anything. You did."

Sydney shook her head. "People look at me now like I'm a teacher or something. I don't understand it."

"You've just learned the secret to my success," Claire said. "When people believe you have something to give, something no one else has, they'll go to great lengths and pay a lot of money for it."

Sydney laughed. "So you're saying, if we're going to be strange anyway, we might as well get paid for it?"

"We're not strange." Claire paused. "But exactly."

"You have cobwebs in your hair from the basement," Sydney said, walking over to her and sweeping them away with her fingertips. Territorial about Claire's hair now, Sydney had taken to simply walking up to her and tucking some strands behind Claire's ear, finger-combing the bangs across her forehead, or fluffing up the back. It was nice, like she was playing, like something they would have done as girls, if they'd been close.

"Where did you cut hair before?" Claire asked, watching Sydney's face close up as she smoothed out Claire's hair. She'd grown up so much while she was away.

Sydney stepped back and tried to get the cobwebs off her fingertips, where they were sticking like tape. "It's been a few years. But in Boise, for a while." She gave up on the cobwebs and turned away. She grabbed the rose geranium wine off the table and hurried out the back door, a curious smell of men's cologne trailing after her. "I'm going to say hi to Bay, then I'll just take this over to Tyler."

Ever since that day Sydney mentally returned to the town house in Seattle when she remembered she'd left the photos of her mother there, the scent of David's cologne would appear around her without warning. Ceiling fans downstairs would turn on by themselves when the scent was particularly strong, as if to chase it away. When it hovered in the upstairs hallway at night, away from fans and night breezes, it paced, hot with anger. Those nights Bay would crawl into bed with Sydney and they would whisper about what they'd left behind. They'd talk in code, saying how happy they were to be away from there, how nice it was to be free. When they said this, they would cross their thumbs and make butterfly shadow puppets on the wall in the purple light coming through the window from Tyler's yard.

Claire still wanted to know about where Sydney had been and what she'd done while she was away. Sydney knew she should tell her now, especially since sometimes even Claire would smell cologne in the house and wonder aloud where it had come from. But the cologne made Sydney realize what kind of danger she'd put her sister in by coming here, and she was doubly ashamed to admit her mistakes. Claire was doing so much for her.

When Sydney walked outside, the scent of cologne faded in the garden, pummeled by the fragrance of apples and sage and earth. Sydney sat with Bay under the tree and they talked about her day and about the Fourth of July celebration and about how one day they were going to walk over to the elementary school so Bay could see where it was. Ever since Claire had said it was okay for Bay to go into the garden, Bay spent several hours every day lying on the grass by the apple tree. When Sydney asked her why, she said she was just trying to figure something out. Sydney didn't press, and so much had happened that it was natural that Bay needed time to figure it out.

After talking to Bay, Sydney walked over to Tyler's. She found him in his back-yard, bringing a lawn mower out of his small shed.

"I don't know, Tyler, are you emotion-ally ready for all that cut grass again?" she called to him.

He turned and laughed. "If I don't cut it soon, small neighborhood dogs are going to get lost in it. Even now, when Mrs. Kranowski can't find Edward, she comes over and beats the grass with a stick, look-ing for him."

"I come bearing a gift from Claire." She held up the wine bottle.

Tyler hesitated, as if silently squelching the first thing he wanted to say. "You know, I'm having no luck figuring out your sister. She gives me gifts when she clearly doesn't like me. Is this a Southern thing?"

"Oh, she likes you. That's why she's giving you this stuff. Do you mind if I have some of this? I'm a little shaky right now."

"Sure, come on." They walked into his kitchen through the back, and Tyler took two wineglasses out of his cabinet.

As soon as he poured her a glass, she took a long drink of it.

"What's wrong?" he asked.

"My mind went somewhere it shouldn't have a while back. It still spooks me."

"Anything you want to talk about?"

"No."

He nodded. "Okay. So, what is this?" Tyler poured himself a glass and lifted it to his nose.

"Rose geranium wine. It's supposed to bring back good memories."

He lifted his glass to her. "Here's to good memories."

Before he could drink it, Sydney blurted out, "She's hoping this will make you remember someone else and forget her. Like the casserole with the snap-dragon oil and the tarts with the bachelor's buttons."

He lowered his glass. "I don't understand."

"The flowers grown in our backyard are special. Or maybe it's the way the dishes made from them are prepared that makes them so special. They can affect the eater. You're obviously immune. Or maybe she's trying too hard, maybe that changes the way it works. I don't know."

Tyler looked at her incredulously. "She's trying to make me not interested in her?"

"Which means you're in already. Let me tell you something about Claire. She likes things that don't go away. So don't go away."

Tyler leaned against the counter, as if for support, as if someone had pushed him there. For a moment Sydney wondered if she should have revealed something so personal about her sister. Claire obviously didn't want him to know. But then Tyler smiled, and she knew she'd done the right thing. It had just been such a long time since she'd brought anyone any real happiness that she'd forgotten what it was like. Claire was doing so much for her. This was something she could give Claire. She could show her she could have happiness outside of what she knew. Happiness with Tyler. "I'm not going anywhere," he said.

"Good." Sydney looked away. The words of a good man could bring tears to a woman's eyes. She envied Claire for this, for Tyler. She'd known a lot of men after she left Bascom, none of them good. She didn't even think she'd know what to do with a good man now. "Drink up," she said, turning away and walking around the kitchen.

Tyler lifted his glass to his lips and took a sip. "This is good. Unusual, but good."

"Welcome to Claire's world."

"So what are your good memories?" he asked.

She walked to his nook, past the easels, and looked out the windows. "It's so strange. My good memories are of this week. Everything in all my years of living, and this week has been the best week of my life. You?"

"It's good wine, but I'm not getting anything. I'm just thinking of Claire."

She smiled and drank some more. "You're hopeless."

CHAPTER
8

Bascom's Fourth of July celebration was held every year on the square downtown. On the green by the fountain, families and church groups set up tables and canopies and brought food so everyone could sample delicacies, like a big potluck, before the fireworks display. Waverleys always brought honeysuckle wine so people could see in the dark, but, whether or not the town knew it, the wine also brought about a few revelations every Fourth of July. A side effect of being able to see in the dark, after all, is being aware of things you weren't aware of before.

The Waverleys had a table off to the side—a most popular table, to be sure, but set apart from everyone else. Sydney fidgeted in her seat. Bay was over in the supervised children's area, making paper hats and getting her face painted, so it was just Sydney and Claire and the honeysuckle hooch. People would quietly come by for small paper cups of honeysuckle wine, like it was somehow hallowed, and every once in a while the sheriff would stroll by and ask, "Now, this is nonalcoholic, right?"

And Claire would answer, straight-faced, as every Waverley had, "Of course."

When Sydney was a teenager, the Fourth of July always meant spending the day at a friend's pool, then showing up on the green just in time for the fireworks. She felt older than other people her age now, people like her old high-school friends, most of whom had obviously come from backyard barbecues or pool parties and had tans and bathing-suit straps peeking out from under their shirts. Emma was at the Presbyterian church's table, talking with Eliza Beaufort. Knowing what she knew now, Sydney didn't envy that life of privilege anymore. Curious then, that she felt sad for losing something she never had. Maybe she just missed friendship in general, the camaraderie of people her own age.

Sydney looked away. "I can't remember the last time I sat here at the Waverley table," she said to Claire.

"It has been a while."

She took a deep breath. "It feels okay."

"Why are you so uncomfortable? No one is going to throw rotten tomatoes at us."

"Right," Sydney said. She could be like Claire and not care what anyone thought. She was even starting to dress like Claire— crisp sleeveless button-downs, khaki pants,

234 Sarah Addison Allen

madras shorts, flowy sundresses. What Claire had said that day at the salon, that she had Waverley magic, changed her mind-set completely. She felt like a Waverley. But right now it was a little like living in a country where she didn't speak the language yet. She could dress like the natives, and it was nice, but a little lonely. "It's okay to be strange. I can get used to this."

"We're not strange. We are who we are. Hello, Evanelle!"

Evanelle had walked up to them and taken a cup of wine. "Whew, I need this," she said, throwing back the wine like a shot. "There's so much to do. I need to give something to Bay." She set the cup down and brought a truly gaudy brooch out of her tote bag. Faintly 1950s, the brooch was made of clear but yellowing crystal in a starburst pattern.

"She's getting her face painted right now," Sydney said.

"Okay, I'll stop by there. Fred is helping me organize my house. He's been a real help. I found this in an old jewelry box we came across, and when I saw it I knew I had to give it to Bay."

Claire leaned forward in her seat. "Fred has been helping you?"

"He's come up with a system for all the stuff I have. He created something called a spreadsheet."

"I've been offering to help you do that for years, Evanelle," Claire said. Sydney turned to her curiously. Claire seemed hurt.

"I know. I didn't want to bother you with it. But since Fred is living with me—"

"Living with you?" Claire exclaimed. "I thought he was just staying with you for a while."

"Well, we figured he might as well be comfortable while he's there. He's turning the attic into his own little apartment and making some improvements around the house. It's been real handy having him around."

"You know if you ever need me, I'm here for you," Claire said.

"I know. You're a good girl." She put the brooch back in her tote bag. "After Bay, I have to take some nails to Reverend McQuail and a mirror to MaryBeth Clancy, then that will be it and I'll meet Fred by the fountain. I hate big crowds, always so much to do. I'll see you later."

"Bye, Evanelle. Call me if you need me!"

Sydney snorted. "Oh, yeah. We're strange."

"We are not," Claire said, distracted. "What do you think of Fred staying with Evanelle?"

"I think it's sad that he and James are having problems." Sydney shrugged. "But Evanelle seems to like having him there."

"Hmm."

A few minutes and another walk-by from the sheriff later, Sydney nudged Claire. "In case you haven't noticed, Tyler keeps looking at you."

Claire snuck a glance, then groaned. "Damn. You had to go and make eye contact. Now he's coming over."

"Oh, heaven forbid."

"Yeah, well, I'm not the only one who's being stared down. You've got one too." Claire indicated a canopy across the green with HOPKINS DAIRY written on it. There was a handsome man there, blond and lean and tan, scooping ice cream out of electric ice-cream makers to put on paper cones. He was solid, as if made to withstand wind. He kept looking over to the Waverley table.

"Does he think we need some ice cream? Maybe we look hot."

"That's Henry Hopkins," Claire said.

"Henry!" From a distance Sydney couldn't make out his features, but now that she thought about it, there was something familiar about his hair, his deliberate movements. "I'd almost forgotten him."

"I didn't realize you knew him." Claire started to stand, but Sydney caught her arm. "Let go. I forgot something in the van."

"You didn't forget anything. You're trying to avoid Tyler. And, yes, I knew Henry. We were . . . friends, I guess. In elementary school. We grew apart after that."

"Why?" Claire asked, tugging against Sydney's hand, her eyes darting to Tyler as he got closer.

"Because I was a blind ass in high school," Sydney said.

"You were not."

"Was so."

"Were not."

"Hello, ladies. Need a referee?"

Sydney released Claire's arm now that her work was done. "Hi, Tyler."

"Claire, your hair," Tyler said, and Claire's hand went to her hair self-consciously. She was wearing the white headband Evanelle had given her, which made her look as young and innocent as she pretended not to be. "It's beautiful. I had a dream . . . I dreamed your hair was like this once. I'm sorry, there was really no way for that not to sound stupid." He laughed, then rubbed his hands together. "So, everyone keeps telling me I need to drink some of the Waverleys' honeysuckle wine. Either it's a town tradition, or everyone is in on this Claire-trying-to-make-me-not-interested-in-her game."

"What?"

"Sydney told me what you were trying to do with the dishes you were giving me."

Claire turned to Sydney, who tried to look sheepish but felt otherwise unrepentant.

"Honeysuckle wine helps you see in the dark," Claire said stiffly. "Have it or don't have it. Walk into a tree when it gets dark. Fall over a curb. I don't care."

Tyler picked up a paper cup and smiled at her. "This means I'll be able to see **you** in the dark."

"I haven't worked out all the glitches in the recipe yet."

Tyler drank the wine, not taking his eyes off her as he did so. Sydney just sat back and smiled. It was like watching a dance when only one of the dancers knew the steps.

When Tyler walked away, Claire rounded on her sister. "You told him?"

"Why are you so surprised? You should have known. I'm predictable like that."

"You are not."

"I am so."

"Oh, go socialize and stop feeling your Waverley oats," Claire said, shaking her head. But there it was, a hint of a smile, the beginning of something new and close between them.

It felt good.

Henry Hopkins could still remember the day he and Sydney Waverley became friends. Sydney was sitting alone inside the dome of the monkey bars during recess. He'd never understood why other kids didn't want to play with her, but he went along because that's what everyone else did. But that day there was something about her, she seemed so sad, so he went over to her and started climbing the bars above her. He wasn't actually going to talk to her, but he thought she might feel better having someone around. She watched him awhile before she asked him, "Henry, do you remember your mother?"

He'd laughed at her. "Of course I do. I saw her this morning. Don't you remember yours?"

"She left last year. I'm starting to forget her. When I grow up, I'm never leaving my kids. I'm going to see them every day and not let them forget me."

Henry remembered feeling ashamed, a feeling so intense he actually fell off the monkey bars. And from that day forward, he stuck like glue to Sydney at school. For four years, they played and ate lunch together and compared homework answers and buddied up on class projects.

He had no reason to expect that, on their first day of middle school after summer break, things would be any different. But then he walked into their homeroom and there she was. She'd grown in ways that made his pubescent head spin. She looked like autumn, when leaves turned and fruit ripened. She smiled at him and he immediately turned around and left the room. He spent the rest of homeroom in the bathroom. Every time she tried to speak to him that day, he felt like fainting and he ran away. After a while, she stopped trying.

It was so unexpected, that attraction, and it made him miserable. He wanted things back the way they were. Sydney was fun and bright and could tell things about people just by the way they wore their hair, which he thought was absolutely amazing. He told his grandfather about it, about how there was this girl who was just a friend but suddenly things changed and he didn't know what to do. His grandfather said that things happened the way they were supposed to, and it was no use trying to predict what was going to come next. People liked to think otherwise, but what you thought had no practical influence on what eventually happened. You can't think yourself well. You can't make yourself fall out of love.

He was sure Sydney thought he had abandoned her, like her mother, or that he didn't want to be her friend, like the other kids. He felt terrible. In the end, Hunter

John Matteson fell hard for her and did what Henry couldn't—he actually told her. Henry watched while Hunter John's friends became her friends and she began to act like them, laughing at people in the hallways, even Henry.

That was so long ago. He'd heard she was back in town, but he didn't think much of it. Just like before, he had no reason to expect that her coming back would make things any different.

Then he saw her, and the whole thing started over again, that curious wanting, that sensation of seeing her again for the first time. Hopkins men always married older women, so he wondered if seeing her change, get older, made him feel like this. Like when she grew up over the summer before sixth grade. Like coming back after ten years looking wiser, more experienced.

"You're staring so hard you're going to knock her over."

Henry turned to his grandfather, who was sitting in his aluminum lawn chair behind the tables. He was holding his cane and every once in a while called out to passersby like a carnival barker. "I was staring?"

"For the past thirty minutes," Lester said. "You haven't heard a word I've said."

"Sorry."

"Heads up. She's on the move."

Henry turned and saw that Sydney had left the Waverley table and was walking to the children's area. Her hair shone in the sun, bright like honey. She went to her daughter and laughed when her daughter put a paper hat on her head. Sydney said something to her, her daughter nodded, and together they walked hand in hand toward him.

They were walking toward him.

He wanted to run to the bathroom, just like he did in middle school.

When they approached the table, Sydney smiled. "Hi, Henry."

Henry was afraid to move for fear he would explode from the riot going on in his body.

"Do you remember me?" Sydney asked.

He nodded.

"This is my daughter, Bay."

He nodded again.

Sydney looked disappointed but shrugged it off and discussed the choices of ice cream with her daughter. There was chocolate mint, strawberry rhubarb, caramel peach, and vanilla coffee. It was his grandfather's idea. Give people something they don't know they like yet. They'll always remember you for it. The wives of some of the dairy workers were helping that day. Henry did some scooping, but it was clear the women were in charge.

"Could we have two chocolate mint, please?" Sydney finally asked.

Henry immediately scooped out small balls of ice cream and put them on the paper cones. Sydney watched him while he did it, her eyes on his hands, then traveling up his forearms, then finally to his face.

She studied him as he handed them the cones. Still, he didn't say a word. He couldn't even smile.

"It's nice to see you again, Henry.

You look good." She and her daughter turned and walked away. Halfway across the green, she looked over her shoulder at him.

"That was the most pitiful display I've ever seen," Lester finally said, cackling. "I was shocked by a milking machine once when I was a boy. Knocked me off my feet. You look like I felt."

"I can't believe I didn't say anything," Henry said.

"Zap! That machine got me. Couldn't say a word. I just opened and closed my mouth like a fish," Lester said, and laughed some more. He lifted his cane and poked Henry in the leg. **"Zzzzzzzppppp!"**

Henry jumped in surprise. "Very funny," he said, and started to laugh.

Evanelle and Fred sat on the rock bench circling the fountain. They waved as Sydney and Bay passed, eating ice cream. Bay had the ugly brooch Evanelle had given her pinned to her pink T-shirt, and

Evanelle felt guilty. Bay was so conscientious and concerned for others' feelings that she felt she had to wear the pin just because Evanelle gave it to her. But that wasn't a pin for a little girl. Why on earth did Evanelle need to give her such a thing? She sighed. She might never know.

"I'm nervous," Fred finally said, rubbing his hands on his neatly pressed shorts.

Evanelle turned to him. "You look it."

Fred stood and paced. Evanelle stayed where she was, in the shade of the oak-leaf sculpture. Fred was hot and bothered enough for the both of them. "He said he'd be here to talk. In public. What does he think I'm going to do if we're alone, shoot him?"

"Men. You can't live with them, you can't shoot them."

"How can you be so calm? How would you feel if your husband said he'd show up and didn't?"

"Given that he's dead, Fred, I wouldn't be real surprised."

Fred sat back down. "I'm sorry."

Evanelle patted his knee. It had been nearly a month since Fred had asked for sanctuary in her home, and he had become an unexpected bright spot to her days. The whole arrangement was supposed to be temporary, but slowly, surely, Fred was moving in. He and Evanelle had spent days going through all her old things in the attic, and Fred seemed to enjoy the stories she told. He was footing the bill to renovate the attic space, and workers with nice posteriors started showing up, which Evanelle enjoyed so much she shoved a chair to the base of the stairs just so she could sit and watch them walk up.

It all had a nice ring of domesticity to it, and Fred would say he knew he deserved better than the way James was treating him. But sometimes, when Evanelle would pass him the butter at dinner, or hand him a hammer to hold while she hung a picture on the wall, he would look at what she'd given him, then look back at her with such expectation that her heart would crack like dry wood for him. Even with all his brave words, he still secretly harbored the belief that one day Evanelle was going to give him something that would make everything all right with James.

"It's getting late," Fred said. "People are already putting out blankets. Maybe I missed him."

Evanelle saw James approach before Fred did. James was a tall, handsome man. He'd always been very thin, the way moody, creative poets with long fingers and soulful eyes were thin in days of old. Evanelle had never had a bad word to say about James. No one did, really. He worked for an investment firm in Hickory and kept to himself. Fred had been his one and only confidant for over thirty years, but suddenly that had changed, and neither Fred nor anyone else in town could figure out why.

But Evanelle had her suspicions. You stick around long enough in this life and you start to understand its ebbs and flows.

There was a type of craziness caused by

long-term complacency. All the Burgess
women in town, who never had less than
six children each, walked around in a fog
until their children left home. When their
youngest finally left the nest, they always
did something crazy, like burn all their re-
spectable high-neck dresses and wear too
much perfume. And anyone who had been
married for more than a year could testify
to the surprise of coming home one day
and finding that your husband had torn
down a wall to make a room bigger or your
wife had dyed her hair just to make you
look at her differently. There were midlife
crises and hot flashes. There were bad decisions. There were affairs. There was a certain point when sometimes someone said,
I've just had enough.

Fred went still when he finally saw
James approach.

"I'm sorry I'm late. I almost didn't make
it." James was a little out of breath, and a
fine sheen of perspiration dotted his forehead. "I was just at the house. I took a few
things, but the rest is yours. I wanted to

tell you that I have an apartment in Hickory now."

Ah, Evanelle thought. That was the reason James wanted Fred to meet him here, so James would know when Fred wasn't going to be in the house and he could take things out without having to discuss it first with Fred. One look at Fred, and Evanelle knew he'd figured that out too.

"I'm taking early retirement next year, and I'll probably move to Florida. Or maybe Arizona. I haven't decided yet."

"So that's it?" Fred asked, and Evanelle could tell there were too many things he wanted to say, all fighting to get out. Ultimately, the only thing that escaped was "That's really it?"

"For months, I was angry. Now I'm just tired," James said, and he leaned forward and put his elbows on his knees. "I'm tired of trying to show you the way. I dropped out of school for you, I came here to live with you because you didn't know what to do. I had to tell you that it was all right for people to know you were gay. I had to drag you out of the house to show you. I had to plan the meals and what we did with our free time. I thought I was doing the right thing. I fell in love with your vulnerability in college, and when your father died and you had to leave, I was terrified you wouldn't be able to make it on your own. It's taken me a long time to realize that I did you a great disservice, Fred. And myself also. By trying to make you happy, I prevented you from knowing how to figure it out on your own. By trying to give you happiness, I lost my own."

"I can do better. Just tell me—" Fred stopped, and in one terrible moment he realized that everything James said was true.

James squeezed his eyes shut for a moment, then he stood. "I should be going."

"James, please don't," Fred whispered, and grabbed James's hand.

"I can't do this anymore. I can't keep telling you how to live. I've almost forgotten how to do it myself." James hesitated. "Listen, that culinary instructor at

Orion—Steve, the one who comes into your store and talks recipes with you—you should get to know him better. He likes you."

Fred let his hand drop, and he looked as if he'd been punched in the stomach.

Without another word, James walked slowly away, so tall and thin and stiff-legged that he looked like a circus performer on stilts.

Fred was left to watch him go. "I used to overhear the checkout girls in the break room," Fred finally said softly, to no one in particular. Evanelle wondered if he even remembered she was there. "I used to think they were such silly teenagers, believing the worst hurt in the world was when you couldn't let go of someone who had stopped loving you. They always wanted to know **why. Why** didn't the boy love them anymore? They said it with such anguish."

Without another word, Fred turned and walked away.

Sydney sat alone on one of Grandma Waverley's old quilts. Bay had made a few friends in the children's area, and Sydney had spread a quilt near their families so Bay could play with the kids in the violet-blue dusk.

Emma was sitting in a cushioned lawn chair with some other people Sydney didn't know. Hunter John was nowhere to be seen. Emma would sneak glances at Sydney every once in a while but otherwise made no attempt to communicate with her. It felt strange to be so close to her onetime friends, only to find them strangers now. Sydney was making new friends at the salon, but new friendships took time. History took time.

Sydney watched Bay run around the green with a sparkler, but she turned when she saw someone approach from the right.

Henry Hopkins walked to the edge of her quilt and stopped. He'd grown up to be a handsome man, lots of blond hair cut close and practical, and tight muscles in his arms. The last she clearly remembered of Henry was laughing at him with her friends when he tripped and fell in the hallway in high school. He'd been a gangly mess in his youth, but he had a quiet dignity that she appreciated so much when they were little kids. They grew apart as they grew up, and she didn't know exactly why. She just knew she'd been horrible to him once she got everything she thought she wanted in high school. She didn't blame him for not wanting to talk to her when she went to the Hopkinses' table that afternoon.

"Hi," Henry said.

Sydney couldn't help but smile. "He speaks."

"Do you mind if I sit here with you?"

"As if I could refuse a man who gives me free ice cream," Sydney said, and Henry lowered himself beside her.

"I'm sorry about before," Henry said. "I was surprised to see you."

"I thought you were mad at me."

Henry looked genuinely confused. "Why would I be mad?"

"I wasn't very nice to you in high school. I'm sorry. We were such good friends when we were little."

"I was never mad at you. Even today, I can't pass a set of monkey bars and not think of you."

"Ah, yes," Sydney said. "I've had many men tell me that."

He laughed. She laughed. All was right. He met her eyes after they'd quieted, then said, "So, you're back."

"I'm back."

"I'm glad."

Sydney shook her head. This was an unexpected turn to her day. "You are, quite possibly, the first person to actually say that to me."

"Well, the best things are worth waiting for."

"You don't stay for the fireworks?" Tyler asked as Claire was boxing up the empty wine bottles. He'd come up behind her, but she didn't turn around. She was too embarrassed to. If she turned around, she would become that deeply disturbed woman who couldn't handle a man being interested in her. As long as she kept her back to him she was the old Claire, the self-contained one, the one she knew before Tyler introduced himself and Sydney moved in.

Sydney and Bay had already spread out a quilt, waiting for it to finally get dark enough for the fireworks. Claire noticed earlier that Henry Hopkins had joined them, and she was still trying to get her mind around it. Henry Hopkins liked her sister.

Why did it bother her? Why did Fred helping Evanelle bother her?

Her edges were crumbling like border walls, and she was feeling terribly unprotected. The worst possible time to deal with Tyler.

"I've seen this show before," she said, her back still to him. "It ends with a bang."

"Now you've ruined it for me. Can I help you?"

She stacked the boxes and took two of them, planning to get the other two on her second trip. "No."

"Right," Tyler said, picking up the boxes. "So I'll just grab this."

He followed her across the green to her van, which she'd parked on the street. She could feel his stare on the back of her neck. She never realized how vulnerable short hair could make a person. It exposed places that were hidden before, her neck, the slope of her shoulders, the rise of her breasts.

"What are you afraid of, Claire?" he asked softly.

"I don't know what you're talking about."

When they reached the van, she unlocked the back and put her boxes in. Tyler came up beside her and set his boxes beside hers. "Are you afraid of me?"

"Of course I'm not afraid of you," she scoffed.

"Are you afraid of love?"

"Oh, the arrogance," she said as she

strapped the boxes in to keep the bottles from breaking as she drove. "I refuse your advances so it must be because I'm afraid of love."

"Are you afraid of a kiss?"

"No one in their right mind is afraid of a kiss." She closed the back of the van and turned around, finding him closer than she expected. Too close. "Don't even think about it," she said, sucking in her breath, her back plastered against the van as he stepped closer still.

"It's just a kiss," he said, moving in, and she didn't think it was possible for him to be so close and not actually touch her. "Nothing to be afraid of, right?"

He put one hand on the van, near her shoulder, leaning in. She could leave, of course. Just scoot away and turn her back on him again. But then he lowered his head, and up close she could see the tiny spiderweb lines around his eyes, and it looked as if his ear had been pierced at one time. Those things told stories about him, storyteller's stories, spinning yarns, lulling her into listening. She didn't want to know so much about him, but one tiny bit of curiosity and she was done for.

Slowly his lips touched hers, and there was a tingling, warm, like cinnamon oil. So this was all there was to it? This wasn't so bad. Then his head tilted slightly and there was this **friction.** It came out of nowhere, streaking through her body. Her lips parted when she gasped in surprise, and that's when things really got out of control. He deepened his kiss, his tongue darting into her mouth, and a million crazy images raced through her mind. They didn't come from her, they were images from him— nakedness and legs twining, holding hands, having breakfast, growing old. What was this mad magic? Oh, God, but it felt so good. Her hands were suddenly everywhere, touching, grabbing, pulling him closer. He was pressing her against the van, the force of his body nearly suspending her in air. It was too much, she was surely going to die, yet the thought of stopping, of actually breaking contact with this man, this beautiful man, was heartbreaking.

She'd wondered what a kiss from him would feel like, if her jumpiness, her restlessness, would fade away, or would he make it worse? What she found was that he actually absorbed it, like energy, and then he radiated it like a firestone, warming her. What a revelation.

The whistles slowly invaded her senses, and she pulled back to see some teenagers walk by on the sidewalk, sucking their teeth and smiling at them.

Claire watched them walk away, over Tyler's shoulder. He wasn't moving. He was breathing heavily, each breath pressing against her breasts, which were suddenly so sensitive it was almost painful.

"Let go of me," she said.

"I don't think I can."

She pushed at him and slid out from between him and the van. He fell forward against the van, as if he had no strength to stand. She understood why when she tried to walk to the driver's side and nearly didn't make it. She was weak, like she hadn't eaten in days, like she hadn't walked in years.

"All this from one kiss. If we ever make love, I'm going to need a week to recover."

He talked of the future so easily. The images from him were so vivid. But she couldn't start this, because then it would end. Stories like this always ended. She couldn't take this pleasure, because she would spend the rest of her life missing it, hurting from it.

"Leave me alone, Tyler," she said as he pushed himself away from the van, his chest still rising and falling rapidly. "This never should have happened. And it's not going to happen again."

She got in the van and sped away, jumping curbs and running stop signs all the way home.

CHAPTER
9

More than a century ago, Waverleys were wealthy, respected people in town. When they lost their money on a series of bad investments, the Clarks were secretly overjoyed. The Clarks were wealthy landowners, with acres full of the best cotton and the sweetest peaches. The Waverleys weren't nearly as wealthy, but they were mysterious old money from down in Charleston who built a showy house in Bascom and always held themselves better than the Clarks thought they should.

When news of the Waverleys' poverty reached them, the Clark women danced a little dance in the secretive light of the half-moon. Then, thinking themselves quite charitable, they brought the Waverleys woolen scarves riddled with moth holes and tasteless cakes made without sugar. They secretly just wanted to see how badly the floor needed polishing without the servants and how empty the rooms looked with most of the furniture gone.

It was Emma Clark's great-great-great-aunt Reecey who took the apples from the backyard, and that started the whole thing. The Waverley women, their clothing mended and their hair messy from trying to put it up without maids, wanted to show the Clarks their flowers, because tending the garden was the only thing they really had any success doing themselves. It made Reecey Clark jealous, because the Clarks' garden could never compare. There were many apples around the garden, shiny and perfect, so she secretly filled her pockets and her reticule. She even stuffed some down her jacket. Why should the Waverleys have so many beautiful apples, apples they didn't even eat? And it was almost as if the apple tree wanted her to have them, the way they would roll to a stop at her feet.

When she got home, she took the apples to the cook and told her to make apple butter. For weeks after, every single one of the Clark women saw such wonderful and erotic things that they began to get up earlier and earlier each morning just for breakfast. The biggest events in the lives of Clark women, it turned out, always involved sex, which could have come as no surprise to their frequently exhausted husbands, who spent and forgave too much because of this.

But then, quite suddenly, all the apple

butter was gone and with it the erotic breakfasts. More was made, but it wasn't the same. Reecey knew then that it had been **those** apples. The Waverley apples. She became insanely jealous, thinking the tree gave erotic visions to everyone who ate them. No wonder the Waverleys always seemed so happy with themselves. It wasn't fair. It simply wasn't fair that they got to have such a tree and the Clarks didn't.

She couldn't tell her parents what she'd done. For anyone to know she'd actually stolen something, much less from a family so recently poor, would be mortifying. So she got out of bed in the middle of the night and crept to the Waverley house. She managed to pull herself up the fence, but her skirt got caught on the finials and she fell. She ended up hanging upside down on the fence for the rest of the night, where she was discovered the next morning by the Waverleys. Her family was summoned, and with the help of Phineas Young, the strongest man in town, she was helped down and immediately sent away to live with her strict aunt Edna in Asheville.

It was there, two months later, that she had the most wonderful passionate night of her life with one of the stable hands. It was exactly what she'd seen when she'd eaten the apple butter. She thought it was fate. She was even willing to put up with her unlikable aunt Edna to keep up the incredible affair. But weeks later she was caught in the stables with him and she was quickly married off to a stern old man. She was never happy, or sexually satisfied, again.

She decided it was all the Waverleys' fault, and when she was an old woman, she made a point of visiting Bascom every summer just so she could tell all the Clark children how horrible and selfish the Waverleys were, to keep that magical tree all to themselves.

And that resentment stuck in the Clark family, long after the reason faded away.

The day after the Fourth of July, Emma Clark Matteson tried to use the time-honored Clark way of getting what she wanted. She and Hunter John made love that morning, pillows knocked off the bed, sheets pulled from their corners. Had the radio not been on, the kids would surely have heard. He was exhausted and slap-happy afterward, so naturally Emma tried to get him to talk about Sydney. She wanted him to think about how sexy Emma was compared to how old Sydney looked in her plaid shorts yesterday, which she had de-scribed to him in detail. But Hunter John refused to talk about Sydney at all, say-ing she had nothing to do with their lives anymore.

He got up and went to the bathroom to shower, and Emma bit her lip tearily. She was distraught, so she did the only thing she could think of.

She called her mother and cried.

"You did what I said and you kept Hunter John away from the Fourth of July celebration. That was good," Ariel told her. "Your mistake was in bringing Sydney up with Hunter John this morning."

"But you said to make him compare us," Emma said, lying in bed and hugging a pillow after Hunter John had gone to work. "How can I do that without bringing her up?"

"You're not paying attention, sugar. I set that up so he could compare Sydney to you when Sydney was serving and you were the hostess. Just that once. Don't keep doing it, for heaven's sake."

Emma's head was spinning. She'd never doubted her mother's considerable knowledge in the ways of men, but this seemed so complicated. How could she keep this up? At some point, Hunter John was going to suspect something.

"You haven't let Hunter John anywhere near Sydney since he went to see her at the White Door, have you? That was another big mistake."

"No, Mama. But I can't keep track of him all the time. When do I trust him? When do I know?"

"Men are the most untrustworthy creatures on God's green earth," Ariel said.

"This is entirely up to you. You have to work to keep him. Buy something new and skimpy, just for him. Surprise him."

"Yes, Mama."

"Clark women don't lose their men. We keep them happy."

"Yes, Mama."

"Where is Bay?" Sydney asked, walking into the kitchen on the first Monday since the Fourth of July. It was her day off. "I thought she was helping you."

"She was, but she heard a plane overhead and ran out to the garden. Happens every time."

Sydney laughed. "I don't understand it. She was never this crazy about planes before."

Claire was at the kitchen island making chocolate cupcakes for the Havershams, who lived four doors down. They were hosting their grandson's pirate-themed tenth birthday. Instead of a cake, they wanted six dozen cupcakes with something baked inside, a child-size ring or a coin or a charm. Claire had made candy strips from thin shoots of angelica from the garden and was going to make a tiny X on the frosting of each cupcake, like the sign on a treasure map; then she was going to put tiny cards on toothpicks with riddles as to what was buried within.

Sydney watched Claire with the frosting. "So when is this gig?"

"The Havershams' birthday party? Tomorrow."

"I'll be glad to take off work to help you."

Claire smiled, touched by Sydney's offer. "I've got this one covered. Thanks."

Bay came in at that moment, and Sydney laughed. "Oh, honey, you don't have to wear that brooch Evanelle gave you every day. She doesn't expect you to."

Bay looked down at the brooch she'd pinned to her shirt. "But I might need it."

"Ready to go for our walk to see the school?"

"Will you be okay without me, Aunt Claire?" Bay asked.

"You were a great help today. Thank you. But I think I can finish up," Claire said. She was going to be sad when Bay started school in the fall. But then there would be afternoons to look forward to, when Bay got home from school and Sydney got home from work and they'd all be together. She was happy having Sydney and Bay there with her. She wanted to focus only on that, not on how long it would last.

She wasn't quite up to admitting that she still thought about how it was going to end. She thought about it every single day.

"We won't be gone long," Sydney said.

"Okay." Claire suddenly felt prickly, and she looked at the hair on her arms standing on end. Damn. "Tyler's about to come to the front door. Please tell him I don't want to see him."

Sydney laughed as soon as there was a knock. "How did you know that?"

"I just knew."

"You know, Claire, if you ever want to talk . . ."

Still so many secrets. **I'll tell you mine if you tell me yours.** "Ditto."

Tyler and Bay waited together on the front-porch swing. Tyler used his long legs to swing them high, and Bay laughed because it was so Tyler. He was easily distracted and ready to have fun. But Bay's mom said if he was ever concentrating on something not to bother him, that it was like not asking a person a question at dinner until they finished chewing.

As they swung, Bay thought about her dream, the one of her in the garden. Things here weren't going to be perfect until she could replicate it exactly. But she couldn't figure out how to make sparkles on her face in the sun and, even though she'd taken notebooks out to the garden and held paper up to the wind, she could never quite get the sound of paper flapping right either.

"Tyler?" Bay said.

"Yes?"

"What kinds of things would make

sparkles on your face? Like if you were lying outside in the sun? Sometimes I see
planes go by and they're shiny and sometimes the sun makes sparkles on them, but
when I try lying in the yard when planes
pass overhead, they don't make sparkles
on me."

"You mean like light reflecting and making sparkles?"

"Yes."

He thought about it for a moment.
"Well, when a mirror catches the sun, it
causes flashes. Metal or crystal wind
chimes outside in the sun, when the wind
blows, might have reflections coming off
them. And water in the sun has sparkles."

Bay nodded, eager to try them out.
"Those are good ideas! Thank you."

He smiled. "You're welcome."

Sydney walked out at that moment,
and Tyler stopped the swing so suddenly
that Bay had to hold on to the chain to
keep from falling off. Her mother and
Aunt Claire had that effect on people.

"Hi, Tyler," Sydney said, standing in

front of the screen door. She looked back into the house, unsure. "Um, Claire said she didn't want to see you."

Tyler stood, which set Bay swinging again. "I knew it. I scared her."

"What did you do?" Sydney demanded in the voice she used when Bay tried to cut her own hair once.

Tyler looked down at his feet. "I kissed her."

Sydney suddenly laughed, but then covered her mouth with her hand when Tyler's head shot up. "I'm sorry. But that's all?" Sydney walked over and patted his arm. "Let me talk to her, okay? If you knock, she won't answer. Let her act like Queen Elizabeth for a while. It'll make her feel better." Sydney gestured for Bay to get off the swing and they all walked down the steps together. "A kiss, huh?"

"It was some kiss."

Sydney put her arm around Bay. "I didn't know she had it in her."

Tyler said good-bye to them when they reached his house. "I did."

"Is Claire upset about something?" Bay asked as they turned the corner. "She forgot where to put the everyday silverware this morning. I had to show her." It worried her a little, Claire not knowing where things went. If only Bay could get the dream just right. Then everything would be fine.

"She's not upset, honey. She just doesn't like when she can't control things. Some people don't know how to fall in love, like not knowing how to swim. They panic first when they jump in. Then they figure it out."

"Do you?" Bay plucked a blade of grass out of a crack in the sidewalk and tried to blow on it through her fingers to make it whistle like her new friend Dakota had shown her on the Fourth of July.

"Do I know how to fall in love?" Sydney asked, and Bay nodded. "Yes, I suppose I do."

"I've already fallen in love."

"You have, have you?"

"Yes, with our house."

"You get more like Claire every day," Sydney said as they finally stopped in front of a long red brick building. "Well, there it is. Your aunt Claire and I went here. My grandmother never liked to leave the house much, but she would walk me to school every day. I remember that. It's a good place."

Bay looked at the building. She knew where her classroom was going to be, through the door and down the hall, the third door on the left. She even knew what it smelled like, like construction paper and carpet cleaner. She nodded. "It's the right place."

"Yes," Sydney said. "Yes, it is. So, are you excited about school?"

"It's going to be good. Dakota belongs in my class."

"Who's Dakota?"

"A boy I met on the Fourth of July."

"Oh. Well, I'm glad you're making friends. That's one thing I wish now that Claire had done," Sydney said. Sydney talked a lot about Claire these days, and there were times when Sydney and Claire were together that Bay could see, in just the right light, them turn into little girls again. Like they were living life over.

"You should make friends too, Mommy."

"Don't worry about me, honey." Sydney put her arm around Bay's shoulder and pulled her close as the scent of David's cologne floated by on the wind. It made Bay afraid for a moment, not for herself but for her mother. It was never Bay her father wanted, anyway. "We're close to downtown. Let's go by Fred's and get some Pop-Tarts!" Sydney said brightly, in that voice adults always used to try to distract kids from what was really going on. "And you know what I'd really like? Cheetos. I haven't had Cheetos in a long time. Don't tell Claire, though. She'll try to make some herself."

Bay didn't argue. Pop-Tarts were good, after all. And she liked them better than her father.

When they reached Fred's, they walked

in and Sydney took a basket by the door. They had just passed the produce section when there was a crash. Suddenly there were hundreds of oranges rolling everywhere, into the bread section, under people's carts, and Bay could almost hear them laughing, like they were suddenly struck with the joy of freedom. The produce man and a couple of bag boys appeared like the ball catchers at tennis games, as if they'd been crouching nearby, waiting for such a thing to happen.

The culprit was standing by the now-empty orange display, not looking at what he had done but staring straight at Sydney.

It was Henry Hopkins, the man who'd given them ice cream, then sat on their blanket on the Fourth. Bay liked him. He was still, like Claire. Steadfast. Not taking his eyes off Sydney, he walked over to her.

"Hi, Sydney. Hi, Bay," he said.

Sydney pointed to the oranges. "You know, we impress easily. You didn't have to do this to get our attention."

"Here's a secret about men. Our foolishness is always unintentional. But it's usually for a good reason." He shook his head. "I sound like my granddad. It's all **Don't take any wooden nickels** from here."

Sydney laughed. "Bay and I are on a Pop-Tart run."

"It must be a sweet tooth kind of day. A couple of weeks ago Evanelle brought my granddad a jar of maraschino cherries. He saw them yesterday and said, 'Why not make more ice cream and have banana splits?' The only thing we were lacking was the hot fudge. So I took off early today to get it."

"Sweet stuff is definitely worth the extra trip," Sydney said.

"Why don't you come out? Are you busy? There'll be plenty of banana splits. And I could show Bay around. She could see the cows."

Bay's mind cleared, like the sun peeking through clouds. "Let's go see the cows!" Bay said enthusiastically, trying to get her mother in on it. "Cows are great!"

Sydney looked at her, puzzled. "First planes and now cows. Since when did you get to be such a cow lover?"

"Don't you like cows?" Bay asked.

"I'm indifferent to cows," Sydney said, then turned to Henry. "We walked here. We don't have a way out there."

"I can take you," Henry offered.

Bay tugged on her mother's shirt. Didn't she see, didn't she see how calm she was around him, how their hearts were beating in rhythm? The pulses at their throats were in sync. "Please, Mommy?"

Sydney looked from Bay to Henry. "Looks like I'm outnumbered."

"Great! I'll meet you at the checkout," Henry said, and walked away.

"Okay, dairy queen, what gives?" Sydney asked.

"Don't you see it?" Bay said, excited.

"See what?"

"He likes you. Like Tyler likes Claire."

"Maybe not quite that way, honey. He's my friend."

Bay frowned. This was going to be

harder than she thought. Usually, things fell into place a lot easier when Bay pointed out where they belonged. She really had to figure out how to reproduce her dream exactly in real life. Nothing was going to be exactly right until she did. It was even now keeping her mother from realizing what was perfect for her.

They met Henry in front and he showed them to his cool silver truck. It was a king cab and Bay got to sit in the back, which she liked because it was so improbable to be sitting in the backseat of a truck without actually being in the bed.

The day turned out to be absolutely wonderful. Henry and his grandfather seemed more like brothers, and Bay liked their calm sense of themselves. Sydney liked it too, Bay could tell. Old Mr. Hopkins, upon first seeing Sydney, asked her when her birthday was. When he discovered that she was exactly five months and fifteen days older than Henry, he laughed and clapped his grandson on his back and said, "Oh, well, that's all right, then."

The more Bay saw and the more she knew of Henry and his grandfather, the more she was certain. This was the place. This was where her mother belonged.

But Sydney didn't know it.

Her mother, she realized, had always had a problem knowing where she went.

Lucky for her, that was Bay's specialty.

As Sydney carried Bay up the front steps late that evening, she felt good.

While Lester and Bay manned the electric ice-cream maker by the chestnut tree in the front yard that afternoon, Sydney and Henry had walked around the field and talked, mostly of old things, elementary school and former teachers.

Henry drove them home after dark and Bay fell asleep in the back. When Henry pulled in front of the house, he cut the engine and they talked some more. About new things this time, where they wanted to go with their lives, what they thought the future might be like. Sydney didn't tell Henry anything about the stealing she'd done, or about David. It was almost as if they didn't exist. She liked that feeling. Denial was a luxury, especially with that memory of David floating around, his cloying cologne not letting her forget. But she could forget with Henry.

She talked herself hoarse, sitting there in his truck.

Before she knew it, it was midnight.

She'd just entered the house, Bay in her arms, when Claire appeared in her night-gown. "Where have you been?"

"We met Henry Hopkins at the grocery store. He invited us to his place for banana splits," Sydney said. She took a good look at Claire, and her heart suddenly lurched in fright. Claire's face was pinched and her hands were clasped tightly in front of her as if she had terrible news. Oh, God. It was David. David had found them. She took a deep breath, trying to smell him. "Why? What happened? What's wrong?"

"Nothing's wrong." Claire wrung her hands for a moment, then she turned and headed to the kitchen. "You just should have called me to let me know."

Sydney followed, clutching Bay to her now. By the time she caught up with her, Claire had already walked through the kitchen and was in the sunroom, putting on her gardening clogs. "That's all?" Sydney said breathlessly. "That's it?"

"I was worried. I thought . . ."

"What? What did you think happened?" Sydney asked, scared because she'd never seen Claire like this. It had to be something horrible.

"I thought you left," Claire said softly.

Sydney couldn't quite get her mind around it. "You're upset because you thought we left? You mean for good?"

"If you need me, I'll be in the garden."

"I . . . I'm sorry I worried you. I should have called. I was wrong." Sydney was nearly out of breath with all the oxygen Claire's frustration was consuming in the enclosed sunroom. "Claire, I told you. We're not going anywhere. I'm sorry."

"It's okay," Claire said, pushing open the sunroom door and leaving a smoldering brown imprint of her hand on the casing.

Sydney watched Claire cross the driveway and unlock the garden gate. When she disappeared into the garden, Sydney turned and went back into the kitchen. There were cupcakes spread out over the countertops. They each had X-marks-the-spot symbols and tiny cards with riddles printed on them, held up by toothpicks. Sydney walked closer to read them.

You think there's nothing, but no cause for alarm. Dig deep and you will find your charm.

Who knows what the future brings? Maybe a broken heart, maybe a diamond ring.

Have no money in order to join? Dig right here and you'll find a coin.

And for the ones that didn't have anything inside, she'd written a very telling riddle:

No gift, no luck, no play, no toys. Don't dig here, you'll find a void.

Sydney was thoughtful for a moment, then she went to the storeroom and sat at Claire's desk with Bay cuddled in her lap.

She reached for the phone.

CHAPTER
10

Like every person who had ever fallen in love, Tyler Hughes wondered what in the hell was wrong with him.

Claire had all this energy, this frustration, and it came out of her and surged through him when they kissed. Every time he thought of it now, he had to sit down and put his head between his legs, and when he finally caught his breath he had to drink two full glasses of water to cool his fever.

But what made him light-headed and changed the color of every room he entered to bright, fantastic red had scared Claire to tears. What was wrong with him that he could take so much pleasure from the same thing that caused her so much pain?

He was doing what he'd always done, making up his own agenda under the guise of it being romantic, carrying it through, and all the while losing track of what was real. Claire was real. And Claire was scared. What did he really know about her, anyway? What did anyone really know about Claire Waverley?

That afternoon he had been sitting at his desk in Kingsly Hall during office hours before his night class, thinking of that very thing, when he saw Anna Chapel, the head of the department, pass by.

He called to her, and she popped her head in.

"How well do you know Claire Waverley?" he'd asked.

"Claire?" Anna shrugged and leaned against the doorjamb. "Let's see. I've known her for about five years now. She caters all our department parties."

"I mean personally how well do you know her?"

Anna smiled in understanding. "Ah. Well, personally I don't know her well. You've been here a year, I'm sure you've noticed certain . . . peculiarities in this town."

Tyler leaned forward, curious to know where this was going. "I've noticed."

"Local legend is important here, as it is with most small towns. Ursula Harris in the English department teaches a course on this." Anna walked farther in and took a seat opposite him. "For example, I was sitting in the movie theater last year and two elderly ladies came in and sat behind me. They were talking about someone named Phineas Young and how he was the strongest man in town and he was going to tear down a rock wall at the back of their property for them. I'd been looking for someone to remove some stumps in my backyard, so I turned around and asked them if I could have his number. They told me he had a waiting list and he might not live long enough to get to me. It turns out that the strongest man in town is ninety-one years old. But local legend has it that in every generation of Youngs, there's always one named Phineas, who is born with superior strength, and that's who you want to help you with hard labor."

"What does this have to do with Claire?"

"Locals believe that what's grown in the Waverleys' garden has certain powers. And the Waverleys have an apple tree that is talked about in almost mythic proportions around here. But it's just a garden, and it's just an apple tree. Claire is mysterious because all her ancestors were mysterious. She's really just like you and me. She's probably even more savvy than the average person. After all, she was smart enough to turn that local legend into a lucrative business."

There was probably some truth to what Anna was saying. But Tyler couldn't help but remember how, when he was young, every year on January 17 it snowed on their colony in Connecticut. There was no meteorological explanation, but legend had it that a beautiful Indian maid, a daughter of winter, had died on that day, and every year since, the sky wept cold snowy tears for her. And as a boy it was a fact that if you caught exactly twenty fireflies in a jar, then let them all out before you went to bed, you'd sleep through the night without bad dreams. Some things couldn't be explained. Some things could. Sometimes you liked the explanation. Sometimes you didn't. That's when you called it myth.

"I get the feeling this isn't what you wanted to know," Anna said.

Tyler smiled. "Not exactly."

"Well, I know she's not married. And I know she has a half-sister."

"**Half**-sister?" Tyler said with interest.

"They have different fathers, from what I've heard. Their mother was a little wild. She left town, had kids, brought the kids here, then left again. I take it you're interested in Claire?"

"Yes," Tyler said.

"Well, good luck," Anna said as she stood. "But don't mess it up. I don't want to have to find someone else to work our department parties just because you broke our caterer's heart."

At home late that night, Tyler sat on his couch in his shorts and a short-sleeved button-down shirt, trying to focus on the class line-drawing assignments, but he kept thinking about Claire. Anna didn't know Claire. No one really knew Claire. As a matter of fact, Sydney was probably the only person who could give him any insight into the woman who wouldn't leave his thoughts since the moment he first spoke to her.

Sydney said she'd talk to Claire, so he'd wait to hear from her.

Or maybe he would call Sydney in the morning and talk about Claire.

Or stop by the White Door tomorrow.

The phone rang, and he reached over to where he'd set the portable on the coffee table.

"Hello?"

"Tyler, it's Sydney."

"Whoa," Tyler said, sitting back on the couch. "I was just hoping you'd call."

"It's Claire," Sydney said in a soft voice. "She's out in the garden. The gate is unlocked. You might want to come over."

"She doesn't want me over there." He hesitated. "Does she?"

"But I think she might need you. I've never seen her like this."

"Like what?"

"She's like a live wire. She's actually singeing things."

He remembered the feeling. "I'll be right over."

He walked across the yard and around the Waverley home to the back garden.

Like Sydney said, the gate was unlocked, and he pushed it open.

He was immediately met with the scent of warm mint and rosemary, as if he'd walked into a kitchen with herbs simmering on the stove.

The footpath lamps looked like small runway lights, and they cast a yellowy glow over the garden. The apple tree was a dim figure at the back of the lot, shivering slightly, like the way a cat's fur crawls in its sleep. He found Claire in the herb patch, and the image stopped him short. Her short hair was pulled back with that white headband. She was on her knees in a long white nightgown that had straps over the shoulders and a ruffle at the hem. He could make out the sway of her breasts as she picked at the ground with a hand rake. All of a sudden he had to bend over and put his hands on his knees, taking deep breaths.

Sydney was right. He was hopeless.

When he finally felt he could stand

without passing out, he slowly walked over to Claire, not wanting to startle her. He was almost next to her when she finally stopped raking around the plants. The leaves of some were dark, as if burned. More still looked wilted, as if they'd been exposed to something hot. She turned her head and looked up at him. Her eyes were red.

Good God, she was crying?

Tears did him in. All his students knew it. All it took was one tear from a freshman who had too much homework and couldn't complete her assignment for him, and he was giving her an extension and offering to talk to her other professors for her.

She winced when she saw him and looked away. "Go away, Tyler."

"What's wrong?"

"Nothing is wrong," she said tersely, clawing the dirt with her hand rake again.

"Please don't cry."

"What does it matter to you? This has nothing to do with you."

"I'm making it something to do with me."

"I hit my thumb. It hurt. Ouch."

"Sydney wouldn't have called me if this was just about a sore thumb."

That did it. That pushed a button. Her head jerked around. **"She called you?"**

"She said you were upset."

She seemed to struggle with the words at first. But she got over that pretty quickly. "I can't believe she called you! Will it ease her conscience if she knows you'll be here for me when she goes? You'll leave too. Doesn't she know that? No, she doesn't know that, because she always does the leaving. She never gets left."

"She's leaving?" Tyler asked, confused. "I'm leaving?"

Claire's lips were trembling. "You all leave. My mother, my grandmother, Sydney. Even Evanelle has someone else now."

"First of all, I'm not going anywhere. Second, where is Sydney going?"

Claire turned away again. "I don't know. I'm just afraid she is."

She likes things that don't go away. Sydney had told him that. This woman had been abandoned too many times to let anyone in again. The epiphany brought him to his knees. His legs literally gave out from under him. So many things about her made sense now. He'd lived next door to the Waverley house long enough to know that maybe there was some merit to local legend, but Anna was right about one thing. Claire was like everyone else. She hurt just like everyone else. "Oh, Claire."

He was beside her now, both on their knees. "Don't look at me like that."

"I can't help it," he said, reaching out to touch her hair. He expected her to pull away, but to his surprise, she leaned into his hand slightly, her eyes closed, looking so vulnerable.

He inched forward, lifting his other hand to her hair, now cupping her head. Their knees touched and she leaned forward to rest her head on his shoulder. Her hair was so soft. He ran his fingers through it, then he touched her shoulders. She was soft everywhere. He rubbed her back, trying to give her some comfort but not knowing exactly what she needed.

After a moment Claire pulled back and looked at him. Her eyes were still wet with tears, and he used his thumbs to wipe her cheeks. She lifted her hands to his face, touching him like he touched her. Her fingers outlined his lips and he could only watch, as if he were outside himself, as she leaned in to kiss him. This would be a stupid time to faint, he told himself. Then she ended the kiss, and he returned to his body and thought, **No!** He followed her as she pulled back, his lips finding hers. Minutes passed like this, hearts beating harder, their hands going everywhere. At one point he had to tell himself this was about her, not him, about her pain, not his pleasure. But she wasn't exactly complaining, he thought on a wince as she bit his bottom lip.

"Tell me to stop," he said.

"Don't stop," she whispered back, kissing down his neck. "Make it better."

She worked at the buttons on his shirt, her fingers shaking, clumsy. Finally she had his shirt open and her hands touched his chest, sliding around to his back. She hugged him, putting her cheek over his heart. His skin tightened and air hissed through his teeth at the contact. It almost hurt, but it felt so good, that energy, that hot frustration seeping through his skin. There was too much of it, though, and he couldn't absorb it all.

This was probably going to kill me, he thought drunkenly. But it was a hell of a way to die.

He shrugged out of his shirt, but she didn't let go. He finally pulled her up so he could kiss her again. She pushed and he fell on his back to the ground, but they never broke the kiss. He was lying on some herb, thyme maybe, and his weight was crushing it, its scent exploding around them. This all was faintly familiar to him somehow, but he couldn't quite place it.

Claire finally pulled up for a breath. She was straddling him, her hands flat against his chest, sending erotic pulses into him. Tears were still running down her cheeks.

"God, please don't cry. Please. I'll do anything."

"Anything?" she asked.

"Yes."

"Will you not remember this tomorrow? Will you forget everything tomorrow?"

He hesitated. "Are you asking me to?"

"Yes."

"Then yes."

She pulled her gown over her head, and suddenly it was hard to breathe again. His hands went up to touch her breasts, and she cried out at the surge the contact caused.

He immediately pulled back. He felt like a teenager again. "I don't know what to do," he whispered.

She lowered herself to his chest, flattening her breasts against him. "Just don't let go."

He wound his arms around her and reversed their positions, rolling her over onto some sage. Again, it was so familiar. He kissed her hard, and she grabbed his hair and wound her legs around him. He couldn't make love to her, not right now. She wasn't thinking straight, and she didn't want consequences tomorrow. That's why she wanted him to forget.

"No, don't stop," she said when he broke the kiss.

"I'm not stopping," he said, kissing her neck as his thumbs hooked into the sides of her plain white underwear. Her abdominal muscles jumped nervously as he pulled them down. He kissed her breasts, took one nipple in his mouth. He could almost remember doing this to her once, but he didn't understand. He'd never been with Claire before.

Then he remembered.

It was that dream.

He'd dreamed this all before.

He knew exactly what was going to happen, the smell around them, how she would taste.

Everything about Claire screamed fate. And everything that had brought him here to Bascom, following dreams that never came true, led him to this.

The one dream that did.

The next morning, Claire felt a swish of air and heard a thud echo in her ear, coming from the ground beside her.

She opened her eyes, and there was a small apple about six inches from her face. Another thud, and another apple appeared beside it.

She'd fallen asleep outside again. She'd done it so many times before that she didn't even think. She just sat up, shaking dirt out of her hair, and automatically reached for her gardening tools.

But something wasn't right. First of all, the ground she used to leverage herself up was soft and warm. And the air seemed to feel a little cooler on her skin. She felt a little . . .

She looked down and gasped.

She was naked!

And that soft warm ground beside her was Tyler!

His eyes were open, and he was smiling. "Good morning."

Everything came back to her, every humiliating, cathartic, erotic thing he'd done to her. But then she realized she was sitting there naked, staring at him like an idiot. She slapped an arm over her bare breasts and looked around for her nightgown. Tyler was lying on it. She tugged on it and he sat up.

She pulled the gown over her head, relishing the brief time she could hide her face behind the fabric. Oh, God. Where was her underwear? She saw them by her feet and snatched them up. "Don't say anything," she said as she stood. "You promised me you would forget everything. Don't say a word about this."

He rubbed at his eyes sleepily, still smiling. "Okay."

She stared at him again. He had dirt and thyme in his hair. He still had on his shorts, but his chest was bare. He had red splotches all over his skin, burn marks from her, and yet he didn't seem to mind. Not then, not now. How could he do that, all that last night, for no pleasure on his part, just for her?

She turned and started walking down the pathway, but stopped when he said, "You're welcome."

For some reason, that made her feel better. He was being an asshole. He expected her to thank him. She turned around. "Excuse me?"

He pointed to the ground beside him. "You wrote it, here."

Curious, she walked back to him and looked. There on the ground were the words **Thank You,** raised in the dirt, as if written from underneath.

She let out a growl of frustration and picked up one of the apples. She threw it as hard as she could at the tree.

"I didn't write that," she said, and stormed away. Fat raindrops began to fall as she ran out of the garden. By the time she'd reached the house, the sky had opened up and it was pouring.

Fred drove home in the rain that evening, thinking about James. He was always alone when he let himself think of him, afraid that someone might see him and know what he was doing.

Fred had always known he was gay, but when he met James his freshman year at Chapel Hill University, he thought he finally understood why. Because he was meant to be with James. Fred's mother had died in her bed when he was fifteen; his father died at the kitchen table when Fred was in college. That's when Fred had to drop out and leave James, to come home and take over the store. He thought it was his father's final punch, to take Fred away from something that finally brought him joy regardless of what people thought.

But after a tearful good-bye at school, to Fred's surprise, James showed up in Bascom three weeks later.

Eventually, with time on his hands, James took classes at Orion while Fred ran the store. He got his degree in finance and a commuter job in Hickory. Over the years he encouraged Fred to get rid of everything that reminded Fred of his father and his cruelly withheld approval. It was James who said, "Let's go out to eat. Let's go to the movies. Let's dare the people of this town to say something."

And what was once youthful indiscretion, two twenty-one-year-olds quitting school and moving in together, finally answerable to no one, turned into more than thirty years of companionship. To Fred, those years seemed to pass like quickly skimming a book and then finding the ending wasn't what he expected. He wished he had paid more attention to the story.

He wished he'd paid more attention to the storyteller.

He drove to Evanelle's house. He'd forgotten his umbrella, so he had to run to the porch in the rain. He stopped at the door to take off his wet jacket and shoes. He didn't want to get water all over her nice floors.

When he walked in, he didn't see Evanelle anywhere, so he called out her name.

"I'm up here," she said, and he followed her voice to the attic.

Evanelle was trying to sweep the sawdust that the workers had produced that day, but it was like trying to sweep tiny birds who flew away in a flurry when you touched them. She was wearing a white face mask, because every sweep of her broom sent the sawdust birds into the air, making the entire space beige and smoky.

"Please don't do this. I don't want you to wear yourself out," Fred said, walking over to her and taking her broom. Being left makes you doubt your ability to keep people, even friends. He wanted Evanelle to be happy he was there, to do all he could for her. He couldn't bear to lose her too. "The workers will clean up when they're done."

Evanelle still had on the mask, but the skin around her eyes crinkled in a smile. "It's coming along real nice up here, don't you think?"

"It looks great," he said. "It's going to be great." As soon as he moved his things in, that is. But that involved going back to his house, something he'd been avoiding.

"What's the matter?" Evanelle asked, sliding the mask up and resting it on the top of her head like a beanie.

"I had some bag boys drop off boxes at my house today. I'm finally going over there to do some packing. I was thinking of renting out the house. What do you think?" he asked, eager for her opinion.

She nodded. "I think it's a fine idea. You know you can stay here with me as long as you want. I love having you."

He let out a wet laugh, full of sudden tears in the back of his throat. "You love having a fool with a broken heart around?"

"Some of the best people I know are fools," Evanelle said. "The strongest people I know."

"I don't know how strong I'm being."

"Trust me. Even Phineas Young would be in awe. Want me to go with you to your house?"

He nodded. He wanted that more than he could say.

It was the first time since James had taken his things out that Fred had been in the house. He looked around the living room. It felt strange to be here now, and he didn't want to linger. This place wasn't home without James, it was just a lot of bad memories of Fred's father.

Evanelle walked into the living room behind him, her shoes squeaking on the hardwood floors. "Whoa," she said. "This place sure looks better than the last time I saw it. It was right after your mother died. God rest her soul, she sure did like her pictures of Jesus." She reached over and rubbed the back of the soft leather reading chair. "You've got some nice stuff."

"I'm sorry I never invited you here, Evanelle. I left that all up to James."

"Don't worry. I don't get invited places. It's just a fact."

"You should," Fred said, looking at her curiously. "You're a good person."

"Nothing I can do about it now. It all started in 1953. I tried to fight it, but you have to understand, when I have to give someone something, **I have to do it.** Drives me crazy if I don't."

"What happened?"

"I had to give Luanna Clark condoms. And you couldn't get condoms in Bascom in 1953. I had to go all the way to Raleigh to get them. My husband drove me there, and he kept telling me it was a bad idea. I couldn't help it, though."

Fred found himself laughing. "Even in 1953, giving someone condoms wasn't so bad, was it?"

"It wasn't the what, it was the who. I told Luanna that I had something to give her in church the next day. I was trying to do it private. She was with her friends and said, real uppity-like, 'Well, give it to me, Evanelle.' Like it was her due. You know

Clarks and Waverleys have never gotten along. Anyway, I gave them to her, right there in front of her friends. Oh, I'm leaving out the most important part. Luanna's husband lost his private parts in the war. My name was Mud, but it got even worse when Luanna got pregnant a year later. She should have used those condoms. After that, everyone got this look when I was around them, like I was going to tell their secrets. Not the sort you invite to dinner. I didn't really mind so much, until my husband died."

This old woman was his hero, no doubt about it. You are who you are, whether you like it or not, so why not like it? Fred walked up to her and extended his elbow. "I would be honored, Evanelle, to make you dinner tonight. An invitation-only affair."

With a laugh she put her arm in his. "Well, aren't you the one."

chapter 11

If you need us, Bay and Henry and I are going to be at Lunsford's Reservoir. His housekeeper stays with his grandfather until only five o'clock, so he'll be dropping us off before then. No later than five o'clock," Sydney said, as if trying to calm Claire down. "We'll be back."

Claire closed the lid to the picnic basket, raised the handles, and handed it to Sydney. She must have really scared Sydney that night a week ago. But as long as Claire pretended it was all okay, maybe it really was. Sydney and Henry had spent a lot of time together this past week, dinners with Bay, mostly. On Sunday they went to the movies. Claire tried to tell herself that it was a good thing. She used that time alone to can and weed the garden and catch up on paperwork, all secure and routine things. She needed that. Those were her constants.

"Will you be okay there?" Claire asked, following Sydney out of the kitchen.

"Of course. Why wouldn't we be?"

"It's pretty far out and you'll be all alone."

Sydney laughed and set the basket by the front door. "We'll be lucky if we find a place to eat our lunch. The reservoir is always crowded in the summer."

"Even on a Monday?"

"Even on a Monday."

"Oh," Claire said, embarrassed. "I didn't know. I've never been there."

"So come with us!" Sydney said, just as she'd said every time she went out this past week.

"What? No."

"Yes!" Sydney grabbed Claire's hands. "Please? You have to stop saying no to me. It will be fun. You've lived here most all your life and you've never been to the reservoir. Everyone goes to the reservoir at some point. Come on. Please?"

"I don't think so."

"I really want you to come," Sydney said, squeezing Claire's hands hopefully.

Claire felt a familiar anxiousness, or maybe it was a learned anxiousness. It was how her grandmother always acted at the thought of doing something purely social, as if she wanted to curl up like a cutworm until the threat passed. Work was fine. Claire didn't socialize when she worked— she communicated. She said what needed to be said or she didn't say anything at all. Unfortunately, this didn't translate well into a social setting. It made her seem rude and standoffish, when it was only a sincere and desperate effort not to do or say anything foolish. "I'm sure you and Henry want this time together."

"No, we don't," Sydney said, suddenly serious. "We're just friends. We've always been friends. That's what I like about him. This is for Bay. You packed the picnic, at least come eat it. Hurry, go change."

Claire couldn't believe she was actually considering it. She looked down at her white capris and sleeveless shirt. "Change into what?"

"Shorts. Or a swimsuit if you want to go swimming."

"I don't know how to swim."

Sydney smiled, like she already knew that. "Want me to teach you?"

"No!" Claire said immediately. "I mean, no, thank you. I'm not a fan of large bodies of water. Does Bay know how to swim?"

Sydney went into the sitting room, where she'd left two quilts and a beach bag full of towels. She carried them to the foyer and set them by the picnic basket. "Yes, she had lessons in Seattle."

Claire instantly perked up. "Seattle?"

Sydney took a deep breath and nodded. That tidbit of information hadn't just slipped out. Sydney had told her on purpose. A first step. "Seattle. That's where Bay was born."

So far she'd mentioned New York and Boise and Seattle. They were cities farther north than the ones their mother had traveled to. Lorelei had gone due west after leaving Bascom. Claire herself had been born in Shawnee, Oklahoma. Maybe bad things had happened to Sydney and Bay, bad things Sydney still didn't want to tell Claire about, but Bay's welfare had been, and still was, a priority to Sydney. She had signed Bay up for swimming lessons, after all. That alone made Sydney a better mother than Lorelei had ever been.

There was a honk outside and Sydney called, "Come on, Bay!"

Bay came running down the stairs. She

was wearing a bathing suit under a yellow sundress. "Finally!" she said as she shot out the door.

"Okay, don't change." Sydney took a pink canvas sun hat out of her bag and put it on Claire's head. "Perfect. Let's go."

She dragged Claire out of the house. Henry took Claire's addition to their party gracefully. Sydney said that they were just friends, but Claire wasn't sure if Henry felt the same way. There were times when he looked at her sister and his whole body seemed to go transparent, losing himself in her.

He had it bad.

Claire and Bay had climbed into the backseat of the king cab and Sydney was about to lift herself into the front seat when Claire heard her sister call, "Hi, Tyler!"

Claire immediately turned in her seat to see Tyler getting out of his Jeep in front of his house. He was wearing cargo shorts and a crazy Hawaiian shirt. This was the first time since the garden that she'd seen him, and her breath caught. How did people act after something like that? How on earth did people live and function after intimacy? It was like telling a secret to someone, then immediately regretting that they knew. The thought of actually talking to him now made her face chili-pepper hot.

"We're going to the reservoir for a picnic; want to come?" Sydney asked him.

"Sydney, what are you doing?" Claire demanded, and Henry looked at her in the rearview mirror curiously. She felt a little ashamed that he could be so gracious about inviting people along and she couldn't.

"I'm teaching you to swim," Sydney answered cryptically.

"I have a night class tonight," Tyler called.

"We'll be back in time."

"Then sure. I'm in," Tyler said, and walked toward them.

When Claire saw that Sydney was going to open the back door, she nearly hurt herself climbing over Bay so Bay would be in the middle, a kiddie buffer between her and Tyler. But she felt ridiculous when Tyler started to climb in and saw her.

"Claire!" he said, stopping short. "I didn't know you were going too."

When she finally got the nerve to meet his eyes, she didn't find anything hidden there, no telltale sign that he was thinking of her secret. He was just Tyler. Should that be a relief, or should that make her more worried?

As soon as they were off, Tyler asked Claire, "So what's this reservoir?"

Claire tried to think of something normal to say. She couldn't casually mention that she'd been there before. She couldn't even say that she'd ever been to a picnic that she didn't cater. But Claire not knowing what she was doing could come as no surprise to him, of all the people in the truck. She'd been nothing but a contradiction since she met him—go away, come closer; I know enough, I know so little; I can handle anything, look how easily

I break. "I've never been there," she finally admitted. "Ask Sydney, our social director."

Sydney turned in her seat. "It's a popular swimming hole. Lots of teenagers and families with young kids go there in the summer. And at night it's something of a lovers' lane."

"And how do **you** know that?" Tyler asked.

Sydney grinned and wagged her eyebrows.

"You went out there at night?" Claire asked. "Did Grandma know what you were doing?"

"Are you kidding? She said she used to go out there at night all the time when she was a teenager."

"She never told me that."

"She probably worried about all the flies zooming into your wide-open mouth."

Claire snapped her mouth shut. "I didn't think she did things like that."

"Everyone does something like that at least once in their lives." Sydney shrugged. "She was young once."

Claire snuck a look at Tyler. He was smiling. He'd been young once too.

Claire had always wondered what that felt like.

Lunsford's Reservoir was located in the ninety acres of thick woods passed down through a long line of lazy Lunsfords. It was too much trouble to try to keep people away from the reservoir, and the maintenance would be too much hassle if they turned it into a park. And this was the rural South, so they'd be damned if they sold their family land or, worse, gave it to the government. So they posted NO TRESPASSING signs everyone ignored, and left it at that.

There was a trail about a half mile long from the gravel parking lot to the reservoir. Tyler walked behind Claire all the way there, and she felt very conscious of her body, of what he knew of it, things about her no one else knew. She thought she could feel his eyes on her, but when she looked over her shoulder, his eyes were always elsewhere. Maybe she felt them there because she wanted them there. Maybe **this** was how people coped after intimacy. When you tell a secret to someone, embarrassing or not, it forms a connection. That person means something to you simply by virtue of what he knows.

Finally, the path opened and the noise swelled. The reservoir itself was a forest lake with a natural beach on one side and a high promontory of southern yellow pines on the other side that kids climbed up in order to dive into the water. It was indeed as crowded as Sydney said it would be, but they found a place toward the back of the beach and spread the quilts.

Claire had made avocado and chicken wraps and fried peach pies, and Sydney had packed Cheetos and Coke. They sat and ate and chatted, and a surprising number of people came by to say hello. Clients of Sydney's mostly, who came by to tell Sydney that their new haircuts gave them more confidence, that their husbands noticed them more, and their mechanics were unable to shyste them on their car repairs. Claire was unspeakably proud of her.

As soon as Bay was finished eating, she wanted to go swimming, so Henry and Sydney walked with her to the water.

Which left Claire and Tyler alone.

"All right, get ready. I'm going to tell you a story," Tyler said, stretching back on the quilt and putting his hands behind his head.

Claire was sitting on a separate quilt, but she was close enough to be able to look down at him. This was a secret she knew about **him,** she realized. She knew what he looked like under her. "What makes you think I want to hear a story?"

"It's either that or talk to me. I'm guessing you would rather hear the story."

"Tyler, it's just that—"

"Here's the story. When I was a teenager, going to the local pool was a big deal, particularly to the kids in the colony, because we were a good ten miles from town and pretty secluded. There was a girl I knew from school named Gina Paretti. When she developed, the boys were never the same. She would pass us in the hallways and literally take our words. We couldn't talk for days. Gina spent every day at the pool in the summer, so when I was sixteen I went every day I could, just to stare at her in her bikini. It was toward the end of the summer when I decided to go for it. I couldn't take it anymore. I'd fantasized about her for months. I couldn't eat. I couldn't sleep. I had to talk to her. I jumped into the pool and did some laps in front of her, manly stuff, before I got out and walked over to her. So there I was, standing in front of her, deliberately blocking out the sun and dripping on her, because I was still young enough to think that annoying a girl was a legitimate way of telling her I liked her. She finally opened her eyes and looked up at me . . . **and screamed.** It seems my shorts had fallen waaaaay past my hips when I had pulled myself out of the water. So I was standing there, flashing her. I was almost arrested."

Claire wasn't expecting that, and she laughed. It felt good to laugh—strange, but good. "That must have been horrible."

"Not really. Three days later, she asked me out. Come to think of it, after that I received a lot of attention from girls who had been at the pool that day," he said, preening.

"Is that true?"

He winked at her. "Does it matter?"

She laughed again. "Thank you for that."

"My humiliations are yours for the asking."

"Humiliating or not, it was a normal thing. You were a normal teenager. You spent your summers at a pool. You've probably even been to a lovers' lane. You and Sydney would have gotten along."

"You weren't a normal teenager?"

"No," she said simply, and it couldn't

have come as a surprise to him. "Henry was the same way. We were the kids who embraced our legacies young."

Tyler sat up on his elbows, his eyes going to the edge of the water where Henry and Sydney were watching Bay. Someone on the beach called to Sydney. Sydney said something to Henry and he nodded, then she walked to a nearby gathering of women to talk. "Do you mind your sister dating him?"

"She's not dating him. But why would I mind?" She said this almost defensively, not wanting him to know how much she was still struggling with Sydney spending so much time with Henry. That night in the garden was weakness. She was stronger than that.

"I guess I just don't want you to be disappointed. It's a difficult position, being interested in someone not interested in you."

"Oh," Claire said, realizing she'd misunderstood what he meant. "I'm not interested in Henry."

"Good," he said, standing up and kicking off his shoes. "I think I'll go for a swim."

"But you still have your clothes on."

"I love a lot of things about you, Claire," he said, reaching his hands over his head and grabbing his shirt at his shoulders and pulling it off, "but you think too much."

He ran to the water and dived in. Wait a minute. Did he mean that? **He loved her?** Or was that just one of those things people said? She wished she understood these games. Maybe she could play if she did. Maybe she could do something with these feelings for Tyler that alternately pinched and stroked her, feeling so painful and so good at the same time.

Henry was still watching Bay, so Sydney walked back to the quilts and sat beside Claire. "Was that Tyler?"

"Yes," Claire said, watching his head emerge from the water. He shook his head and his dark hair flung around and stuck to his face in wet ropes. Bay was laughing at him, so he swam over to her and splashed her. She splashed back. Henry, at the edge of the water, said something to them and they paused for a moment, looked at each other, then they splashed Henry. Hesitating only a moment, Henry took off his shoes, pulled his shirt over his head, and jumped in after them.

"Wow," Sydney said. "Milk, it does a body good."

"There's a reason I am the way I am, you know," Claire blurted out, because she had to explain it to someone.

Sydney grabbed a can of Coke and turned to her curiously.

"We didn't have a home, Mom and I, the first six years of my life. We slept in cars and homeless shelters. She did a lot of stealing, and a lot of sleeping around. You never knew that, did you?" Claire asked. Sydney had the Coke can halfway to her mouth, frozen. She slowly shook her head and lowered the can. "Sometimes I got the feeling you romanticized what her life was like before she came back to Bascom. I don't know if she ever intended to stay, but when we came here, I knew I was never going to leave again. The house and Grandma Waverley were permanent things, and when I was young, that's all I ever dreamed of. But then you were born, and I was so jealous of you. You were given that security from the moment you entered the world. It's my fault, our relationship as kids. I made it contentious because you were from here and I wasn't. I'm sorry. I'm sorry I'm not good at being a sister. I'm sorry I'm not good with Tyler. I know you want me to be. But I can't seem to help it. I can't help but think how temporary everything is, and I'm scared of that kind of temporary. I'm scared of people leaving me."

"Life is about experience, Claire," Sydney finally said. "You can't hold on to everything."

Claire shook her head. "I think it might be too late for me."

"No, it's not." Sydney suddenly slapped the quilt beside her angrily. "How could

Mom ever think that was the kind of life for a child? It's inexcusable. I'm ashamed of myself for envying her, and there are times I think I've turned out just like her, but I'm not leaving you. Never. Look at me, Claire. I'm not leaving."

"Sometimes I wonder what her reason was. She was a smart woman. Evanelle told me she was a crackerjack student before she dropped out. Something had to have happened."

"Whatever the reason, there's no excuse for her messing up our lives like she did. We can get past this, Claire. We can't let her win. Okay?"

Words were easier said than implemented, so Claire said, "Okay." Then she wondered how in the world she was going to get past something that had taken her decades to perfect.

They stared at the water for a while. Bay had grown tired of the splashing game, and she swam back to the beach and walked over to Claire and Sydney. Henry and Tyler were still splashing at each other, each trying to make the biggest splash with his hand.

"Look at those two," Sydney said. "Boys, the both of them."

"This is nice," Claire said.

Sydney put her arm around her. "Yes, it is."

At the same time Sydney and Claire were enjoying the reservoir, Emma Clark Matteson was getting ready to spend some **quality** time with her husband.

Hunter John's desk in his office at work wasn't as comfortable as his desk in his office at home. The dark paneling on the walls and the ugly metal desk had been there since Hunter John's father ran the business. Emma found herself laughing at the thought of Hunter John's mother, Lillian, coming to the plant and greeting John Senior this way.

Lillian definitely would have changed the desk if she had. The metal was damn uncomfortable on one's bare bottom.

Hunter John's receptionist said that he

was giving a tour of one of the plants and would be back in a few minutes. Perfect. It gave Emma enough time to undress and drape herself across his desk, wearing only stockings, garters, and a pink ribbon tied around her neck.

She'd never surprised him at his office like this. Oh, she'd come by to bring him lunch and they'd neck a little sometimes, but they'd never actually had sex at work. There were very few places she and Hunter John hadn't done it. It was a lot of work trying to keep things interesting, trying to keep Hunter John's attention focused only on her so he wouldn't think of Sydney or maybe how his life hadn't turned out quite like he wanted. Emma would never tire of trying to make her husband happy. She liked sex, after all. No, she loved sex. It was just difficult sometimes to keep going when she didn't know if this was really what he wanted. She wanted Hunter John to love her. But in the end, if he didn't, she didn't want to know. She would take this over not having him at all. She wondered if her mother settled like this. She wondered if love mattered to Ariel at all.

She heard Hunter John's voice approaching his office and opened her legs a little wider.

And in walked Hunter John's father.

"Whoa Nelly," John Senior said.

Emma screamed and rolled off the far side of the desk.

"What's wrong?" She heard Hunter John enter the office as she scooted into the recess of the desk and hugged her knees to her chest.

"I think I'll just leave you and your wife alone for a while," John Senior said.

"My wife? Where is she?"

"Under the desk. Her clothes, however, are over there on the chair. Really, son, this is no way to run my business."

Emma heard the door close. Then Hunter John's footsteps approached, and he knelt facing her. "Damn it, Emma, what are you doing here?"

"I wanted to surprise you."

"You never come here for this. Why

now? Why, on the day my father decides to show up without warning for a tour to see if I'm running the place right? My father just saw you naked! I can't believe this."

She crawled out from under the desk. What his father thought meant the world to Hunter John. And she'd just embarrassed them both. How did things go so wrong so fast?

Everything had been fine—at least, things were pushed under the rug, where no one thought of them—until Sydney came back. Why couldn't she have stayed away? "I'm sorry," she said, going over to her clothes and starting to dress.

"What has gotten into you lately? You are all over me. You never want to go out together. You call me sixteen times a day. Now you show up here like this."

She pulled her dress over her head and slid her feet into her heels. "I need to know . . ." She hesitated. **That you love me.**

"Need to know what?"

"That you're going to stay with me."

Hunter John shook his head. "What are you talking about?"

"I've been worried. Ever since Sydney came back . . ."

"You've got to be kidding me," Hunter John said. "You have **got** to be kidding me. This is about Sydney? Go home, Emma." He went to the door without another look at her. "I have to catch up with my dad and try to explain this to him."

"Do you know what I heard today from Eliza Beaufort?" Emma said brightly at dinner that night. "Sydney and Claire Waverley went on a double date to Lunsford's Reservoir. What does Sydney think she's doing? No one our age goes out there. And Claire! Can you imagine Claire at the reservoir?"

Hunter John didn't look up from his dessert. It was his favorite chocolate cake with buttercream frosting. Emma had ordered it especially for him.

Instead of answering her, Hunter John

wiped his mouth and put down his nap-
kin. "Come on, boys," he said, and pushed
back his chair. "Let's go toss a football."

Josh and Payton immediately jumped
up. They loved when their dad played with
them, and Hunter John always made time
for his boys.

"I'll come with you," Emma said.
"Wait for me, okay?"

Emma rushed upstairs and changed
into her red bikini, the one Hunter John
liked, but when she came back down, they
hadn't waited. The pool was right off the
tiled family room, so she walked out and
to the balustrade that looked over the lawn
below. Hunter John and the boys were
playing in the yard, their hair already wet
with sweat. It was seven-thirty in the
evening but still light and still sweltering.
Summer was a lady who didn't give up her
spotlight easily. Emma understood that.
She liked summer. The boys were home,
and there was so much daylight that there
was still time to do things with Hunter
John when he got home from work.

There was no sense in getting her hair wet if Hunter John wasn't going to watch her swim, so she put on a sarong and cheered on the boys from the patio. She couldn't wait for football season. Going to the high-school games, sitting in front of the television on Sunday afternoons and Monday nights. It was something they did together as a family, something that Sydney had never done with Hunter John. Sydney had gone to football games when Hunter John played, but she didn't really like the game. Emma loved it. She loved it because he loved it. But Hunter John gave up the game when he didn't go to Notre Dame. He gave it up because of her.

When the sun began to set, Emma brought out a pitcher of lemonade. Soon, the boys and Hunter John made their way up to the pool.

"Lemona—" she said, but before she could finish, the boys had jumped in the pool to cool off.

Emma shook her head indulgently.

Hunter John was walking toward her. She smiled and held a glass out. "Lemona—"

She didn't even get the word out before he passed her and walked into the house. He hadn't said a word to her since the incident in his office that afternoon.

She didn't want the boys to know anything was wrong, so she waited for them to play in the water awhile, then got them towels and made them get out. She shooed them to their rooms to change and watch television, then she went to find Hunter John.

He was in their steam shower, so Emma lifted herself to sit on the bathroom counter facing the stall and waited for him to come out.

When the door opened and he emerged, her breath caught. He could still do this to her. He was so beautiful. He had just washed his hair, and she could see how much it was thinning, but that didn't matter to her. She loved him so much.

"We need to talk," she said. "I need to

know why you never want to discuss Sydney."

He looked up, startled to find her there. He grabbed a towel and dried his hair vigorously. "I think the more important question is why are you so obsessed with her? Have you noticed that Sydney isn't actually in our lives? Has it escaped your attention that she hasn't actually done anything to us?"

"She's done plenty, just by being back," she said, and his movements stopped. His face was still hidden by the towel. "You won't talk about her. How do I know you're not talking about her because you still have feelings for her? How do I know you didn't take one look at her and remember all the choices you had before I got pregnant? How do I know, if you went back, you would do the same thing? Would you sleep with me? Marry me?"

He slid the towel off his head. His expression was tight as he walked up close to her, which made her heart beat faster with both fear, because he looked so angry, and with anticipation, because he was so damn sexy. "How do you know?" he repeated incredulously, his voice low and vibrating. **"How do you know?"**

"She's been places. You always wanted to travel."

"What have you been thinking these past ten years, Emma? The sex and the boob job and the sexy clothes. The perfect dinners and the football games. Was all of that because you thought I didn't want to be here? Was any of that because you loved me at all? Or have you been competing with Sydney all this time?"

"I don't know, Hunter John. Have I?"

"That was the wrong answer, Emma," he said, and walked out.

"Claire, are you awake?" Sydney said from the doorway of Claire's bedroom that night.

She wasn't surprised to hear Claire say, "Yes."

Claire never slept much when they were young. She used to stay out in the garden until their grandmother called her in. And Sydney remembered that Claire would clean the house or make bread while everyone else slept. This was the first and only place she'd felt any real security, and Sydney understood now that Claire had either been trying to make it her own or had been trying to earn her keep so she could stay. Either way, it hurt to think about how Sydney had thought Claire was just anal and odd, how she didn't understand what Claire had been through.

She walked into Claire's room, the turret bedroom that had once been their grandmother's. Grandma Waverley had covered the walls with her quilt hangings, but Claire had replaced them with framed black-and-white photos and a couple of old family prints. The walls were pastel yellow and the floors were covered with calico-colored throw rugs. Sydney's eyes went right away to the place where Claire obviously spent most of her time in the room, the comfortable window seat. There were stacks of books on the floor beside it.

Sydney went to the bed and looped her arm around one of the bottom posts. "I need to tell you something."

Claire sat up on her pillows.

"About the past ten years."

"Okay," Claire said quietly.

There had been a chance, on the quilts at the beach, to tell Claire this, but she hadn't been able to do it. She didn't know it then, but she was waiting for night, because it was the sort of thing that needed darkness to tell. There wasn't a doubt in her mind now that Claire would understand. And she owed it to Claire to tell her. David wasn't going away. "I went to New York first, you know that. But after that, it was Chicago. Then San Francisco, Vegas . . . then Seattle. I've known a lot of men. And I did a lot of stealing. I changed my name to Cindy Watkins, an identity I stole."

"Mom did that too," Claire said.

"Do you think she did it for the thrill? Because it was thrilling, but it was exhausting too. Then Bay came along." Sydney moved to sit at Claire's feet, just to feel her near, to be able to touch her if Sydney got too scared. "Bay's father lives in Seattle. That's where I met him. David Leoni." She swallowed, frightened by saying his name out loud. "Leoni is Bay's real last name, but not mine. We never married. David was a scary man when I met him, but I'd known scary men before and I thought I could handle him. I was getting ready to leave him—that's what I always did when things got too intense—but then I found out I was pregnant. I didn't realize how having a baby could make you so vulnerable. David started hitting me, and he got more and more violent. When Bay turned one, I left him. I took Bay to Boise, went to beauty school, got a job. Everything seemed to be going so well. Then David found us. I lost a tooth and couldn't see out of my left eye for weeks after his payback. What good would I be to Bay dead? So I went back with him, and he made my world smaller and smaller and more and more hellish until the only three things I knew were Bay, David, and his anger. Sometimes I used to think it was punishment for living the way I did before I met him. But then I met a woman at the park David let me take Bay to three times a week. She knew what was going on just by looking at me. She got me that car and helped me escape. David doesn't know my real name, and he thinks I'm from New York, so this was the only place I knew to go, the only place he wouldn't find me."

Claire sat up straighter and straighter the longer Sydney talked. It was dark, but she felt Claire's assessing gaze.

"I guess I just want you to know that I understand how you felt when you came here when you were six. I took everything I had here for granted. But I've come to realize this is the only security I've ever known. I want that for Bay. I want to erase everything she's seen, everything she's known because of me. Do you think that's possible?"

Claire hesitated, and that was all the answer Sydney needed. No, it wasn't possible. Claire never forgot.

"So, those are my secrets." Sydney sighed. "They don't seem as big as I thought they were."

"Secrets never are. Do you smell that?" Claire suddenly asked. "I've smelled it before. It's like cologne."

"It's him," Sydney whispered, as if he would hear her. "I brought that memory with me."

"Quick, get in bed," Claire said, and threw back the sheet. Sydney darted in and Claire tucked the sheet around her. It was a humid night and all the upstairs windows were open, but Sydney was suddenly cold and she snuggled against her sister. Claire put her arm around her and held her close. "It's okay," Claire whispered, resting her cheek on the top of Sydney's head. "Everything's going to be okay."

"Mommy?"

Sydney turned quickly to see Bay in the doorway. "Hurry, honey, get in bed with me and Claire," Sydney said, throwing back the sheet as Claire had done.

They held on to each other as thoughts of David drifted out the window.

The next morning dawned bright and sweet, like ribbon candy. Claire opened her eyes and stared at the bedroom ceiling, the same ceiling her grandmother had woken up to and stared at every day of her life.

She turned her head and saw Sydney and Bay, fast asleep, turned into each other. Sydney had been through and done more than Claire could ever imagine. That much experience, that much change, would devastate Claire.

Or maybe, even as extraordinary as it was, it was life. Everyone had stories to tell.

She looked back up at the ceiling.

Even her grandmother.

Sydney said that Grandma Waverley had gone to Lunsford's Reservoir. As shocking as that was, Claire assumed she had gone there with her husband-to-be. But then Claire began to wonder about those old photos of her grandmother before she married her husband, when she was a pretty young woman with a joyful smile and hair that seemed perpetually in motion, as if she'd been followed around by a lovesick breeze. The photos were of her with several different boys, all with the same looks of admiration on their faces. On the backs of the photos her grandmother had written **In the garden with Tom** and **At homecoming with Josiah.** Then there was the one with just the name **Karl.**

Her grandmother had a life, a life Claire hadn't known about or even imagined. She had tried so hard to know everything about Grandma Waverley, to be everything she was. But Grandma Waverley must have sensed something in Sydney, a kindred soul, with Sydney's brightness and popularity. She gave Claire the wisdom of her old age, but she gave Sydney the secrets of her youth.

Claire didn't have a single photograph that someone years from now would see and think, **That boy loved her.**

She got out of bed and made breakfast for Sydney and Bay. It was a nice morning, lots of chatter and good feelings, no scent of anything bad in the air. Sydney left for work by the back door, calling over her shoulder as she left, "There's a whole bunch of apples out here!"

So Claire took a box from the storeroom and she and Bay gathered the apples the tree had thrown at the back door.

"Why did it do this?" Bay asked as they walked to the garden gate in the bright, wavy morning light.

"That tree has a hard time minding its own business," Claire said as she unlocked the gate. "We were all together last night, and it wanted to be a part of it."

The tree fluffed itself up when they entered the garden.

"It must be kind of lonely."

Claire shook her head and went to the shed for a shovel. "It's cranky and selfish,

Bay. Don't forget that. It wants to tell people things they shouldn't know."

She dug a hole by the fence while Bay stood under the tree and laughed as it shed little green leaves all around her. "Look, Claire. It's raining!"

Claire had never seen the tree so affectionate. Bay was just innocent enough to be able to overlook the pall it cast. "It's a good thing you don't like apples."

"I hate them," Bay said. "But I like the tree."

As soon as Claire finished, she and Bay went back to the house.

"So," Claire said, as casually as possible as they walked. "Does Tyler have a night class tonight, like last night?"

"No. Monday and Wednesday are his night classes. Why?"

"Just wondering. You know what we're going to do today? We're going to go through some old photos!" Claire said enthusiastically. "I want to show you what your great-grandmother looked like. She was a wonderful lady."

"Do you have any photos of your and Mommy's mother?"

"No, I'm afraid not." Claire thought about what Sydney had said some time ago, about leaving the photos of their mother behind. Did she leave them in Seattle? She had seemed so panicked at the time, when she remembered that she had left them.

Claire made a mental note to ask Sydney about it.

Was a dress too much? Claire looked at herself in her bedroom mirror. Did it look like she was trying too hard? She'd never tried at all before, so she had no idea. The white dress she was wearing was the same dress she'd worn the night she met Tyler, the one Evanelle said made her look like Sophia Loren. She put a hand to her bare neck. Her hair had been longer then.

Was this stupid? She was thirty-four years old. It wasn't as if she was sixteen, but she certainly felt that way. Probably for the first time in her life.

As she walked down the stairs that evening, her shoes made unnaturally loud clicks on the hardwood. She had almost reached the bottom when she stopped. She heard voices. Sydney and Bay were in the sitting room. She was going to have to walk past them. Okay, so what? This was a perfectly normal thing to do.

She straightened her shoulders and walked down the remaining steps. Sydney and Bay were painting their toenails. Claire was so nervous she didn't even tell them to be careful not to get polish on the furniture or the floor.

When they didn't look up, Claire cleared her throat. "I'm going over to Tyler's," she said from the archway. "I may be a while."

"Okay," Sydney said, still not looking up from Bay's toes.

"Do I look okay?"

"Yes, you always—" Sydney finally looked up and saw what Claire was wearing, the way her hair was styled, the makeup on her face, the fact that she didn't have a dish in her hands. **"Oh,"** she said, smiling. "Keep your feet out, Bay. I'll be right back."

Sydney duck-walked with her wet toe-nails into the foyer. "This is certainly a sur-prise."

"What do I do?" Claire asked.

Sydney finger-combed Claire's hair and tucked some strands behind one ear. "It's been a long time since I've seduced a man, honestly. Come to think of it, I don't think I've ever seduced a man honestly. Huh. But we're talking about Tyler here, the man who has turned my bedroom walls purple from all his midnight romps around his yard, thinking of you. It won't be hard to do. He's already there, he's just waiting for you."

"I don't know how to do temporary."

"Then don't. Believe it's permanent. Either it will be or it won't."

Claire sucked in a small, deep breath, like just before a shot at the doctor's office. "That will hurt."

"Love always hurts. That's one thing I know you know," Sydney said. "But it's worth it. That's what you don't know. Yet."

"Okay," Claire said. "Here I go."

Sydney opened the front door, but Claire just stood there, looking out into the darkening evening.

"Well," Sydney said when Claire didn't move, "I suggest you walk, since floating isn't working."

One foot in front of the other, Claire walked out the door and down the steps. She rarely wore heels, but she did that night, sandals with long thin heels, so she had to go to the sidewalk instead of walking across the yards.

When she reached his front door, she was cheered by the warm light and the soft music undulating from his open windows. He was listening to something lyrical, classical. She could imagine him relaxing, maybe with a glass of wine. What if he didn't have wine? She should have brought wine.

She looked over at her house. If she

went back there, she wouldn't have the courage to come back. She straightened her dress and knocked on the door.

He didn't answer.

She frowned and turned to make sure she did see his Jeep parked on the street. She had her back to the door when she felt it open. It stirred the hem of her dress and she turned back around.

"Hi, Tyler."

He stood there, as if so shocked he couldn't move. If he was going to leave this all up to her, they were both in trouble. **Break it down into steps,** she told herself, **like a recipe. Take one man and one woman, put them in a bowl.**

She really sucked at this.

"Can I come in?" she asked.

He hesitated and looked over his shoulder. "Well, sure. Of course," he said, stepping back to let her enter. She walked past him, almost touching him, letting him feel the static. This was obviously the last thing he expected, because the first thing he asked was, "What's wrong?"

"Nothing's wrong," she said, then she saw her.

There was a woman, a petite redhead, sitting cross-legged on the floor, two bottles of beer on the coffee table next to her. She either meant something to Tyler or clearly wanted to. Her shoes were off and nowhere to be seen, and she was leaning forward so that the flowy V-neck of her shirt fell away from her chest slightly. She was wearing a peach-colored bra. It seemed Tyler had two females ready to seduce him that night.

How could she be so stupid? Did she really think he was just sitting here **waiting** on her? "Oh. You have company." She started backing away and backed right into him. She whirled around. "I didn't know. I'm so sorry."

"There's nothing to be sorry about. Rachel is an old friend, passing through on her way to Boston from Florida. She's staying with me a few days. Rachel, this is Claire, my next-door neighbor. She's a caterer specializing in edible flowers. She's incredible." Tyler took Claire by the arm and tried to lead her farther into the living room. After a couple of seconds he had to pull his hand away quickly, flipping it back and forth as if burned. He met her eyes with a dawning understanding.

"I'm sorry. I really have to go. I didn't mean to bother you."

"You weren't—" Tyler said, but she was already out the door.

"Claire?" Sydney called. She was halfway up the staircase before Sydney made it out of the sitting room. "Claire?"

She stopped and turned. **"Rachel."**

Sydney looked up at her, confused. "What?"

"He was with **Rachel,**" Claire said. "They have history. They have a bond. She's staying with him. She was looking me over like competition. I've seen it before. Women do it to you all the time."

Sydney looked flabbergasted and indignant, which, when Claire thought about it later after she had calmed down, was nice.

Her sister was mad on her behalf. **"He had another woman over there?"**

Claire thought of those photographs of her grandmother with a series of smitten boys. "I don't need a photo of a man looking at me as if he loves me. I'm fine. Aren't I fine?"

"You really want me to answer that right now?"

Claire put her hand to her forehead. She was still so hot. This was unbearable. "I don't know how to do this. Maybe I'll just go out to the garden and every once in a while he can come by and we won't talk about it afterward but the apple tree will thank him, like last time."

"You've lost me."

Claire let her hand fall to her side. "I feel like a fool."

"That, dear sister, is step one."

"Do you think you could write it down? I have the recipe all wrong," she said, and turned to walk up the steps. "I'm going to take a bath."

"You just took one this afternoon."

"I smell like desperation."

Sydney chuckled. "You'll be fine."

Claire changed out of her dress and put on her old seersucker robe. She was looking for her slippers when her bedroom door opened.

She could only stare, dumbfounded, as Tyler entered and ominously closed the door behind him. She grabbed the lapels of her robe, which was ridiculous, considering what she'd just gone over to his house to do.

"Why did you change out of that dress? I love that dress. But I like the robe too." His eyes slid down her body. "Why did you come to see me tonight, Claire?"

"Please forget it."

He shook his head. "I'm through forgetting. I remember everything about you. I can't help it."

They stared at each other. Take one man and one foolish woman and put them in a bowl. This wasn't going to work.

"You're thinking too much again," Tyler

said. "So this is your bedroom. I've wondered which one was yours. I should have guessed it was the turret room." He walked around, and she had to force herself to stay where she was, not to run to him and take the photo he'd lifted from the bureau, not to tell him to leave the books stacked by the window seat alone, that she had a particular order to them. She'd been about to share her body with this man, and she couldn't even share her room? Maybe with some preparation, time to shove her shoes under the bed, to take the stained coffee cup off the nightstand.

"Isn't Rachel waiting for you?" she asked anxiously when he peered into her open closet.

He turned to face her. She was across the room, in the corner where she'd last kicked her slippers. "Rachel is just a friend."

"You have history."

"We used to be a couple, when I first moved to Florida to teach. It lasted about a year. We didn't work out as lovers, but we remained friends."

"How is that possible? After all you've been through?"

"I don't know. It just is." He walked toward her. She could have sworn chairs and rugs moved out of his way to make his path easier. "Did you want to talk? Did you want to ask me to dinner or a movie?"

She was literally backed into a corner. He came up close to her, doing that not-quite-touching thing he was so good at, like she was able to feel him without actually feeling him, like she was imagining him somehow. "If I have to say it, I will die," she whispered. "Right here. I'll fall to the floor, dead from embarrassment."

"The garden?"

She nodded.

His hands went to her shoulders, and his fingers snaked in under the collar. "Not so easy to forget, is it?"

"No."

The robe slid off her shoulders and

would have fallen off completely had she not still had a hold of the lapels. "Your skin is hot," he whispered. "You could have blown me over with a whistle when I felt how hot you were at my house."

He kissed her and pulled her away from the corner. He then backed her toward her bed, devouring her. Take one man, one foolish woman, put them in a bowl and **stir.** Her head was spinning, her thoughts dizzy. She felt like she was falling, then she actually was. The back of her knees hit the bed and she fell back. Her robe opened and Tyler was there, breaking the kiss only long enough to take off his shirt so that their bare chests touched.

He knew. He remembered how she needed that kind of body-to-body touch, how she needed someone to absorb what she had too much of.

"We can't do this here," she whispered. "Not with Sydney and Bay downstairs."

He kissed her hard. "Give me ten minutes to get rid of Rachel."

"You can't get rid of Rachel."

"But she's going to be here three days." They stared at each other, and he finally took a deep breath and rolled beside her. She was going to close her robe, because how could she just lie there with her robe open? But he stopped her by sliding his hand over her chest and cupping one of her breasts. It felt so secure, so right. **Mine.** "Expectation can be nice too, I guess," he said. "Three whole days of expectation."

"Three whole days," she repeated.

"What changed your mind?" he said, moving to his side and dipping his head, putting his mouth where his hand had been.

She grabbed his hair in one hand and squeezed her eyes shut. How could she want something this much, something she didn't even understand? "I should let people in. If they leave, they leave. If I break, I break. It happens to everyone. Right?"

He lifted his head to look in her eyes. "You think I'm going to leave?"

"There can't be this forever."

"Why do you think that?"

"No one I know has ever had this forever."

"I think of the future all the time. All my life I've chased dreams of what could be. For the first time in my life, I've actually caught one." He kissed her again before grabbing his shirt and standing. "I'll give you one day at a time, Claire. But remember, I'm thousands of days ahead already."

It was Fred's first night in the attic, and Evanelle could hear him moving around upstairs. It was nice, knowing someone was around, making small busy noises like mice. The thing about ghosts was that they didn't make a sound. And she'd been living with the silent ghost of her husband for long enough to know.

She wondered if she was being hypocritical, encouraging Fred to move on. It wasn't as if Evanelle had moved on, really. Maybe it was different when the one you loved died, as opposed to the one you loved simply leaving you. Or maybe it was the same thing. It probably felt like the same thing, anyway.

All of a sudden, Evanelle sat up.

Damn.

She needed to give someone something. She thought about it a moment. It was Fred. She had to give Fred something.

She turned on the light by her bed and reached for her robe. She walked into the hall, then paused, figuring out where to go. The two other bedrooms downstairs were now neatly organized with filing cabinets and nice wooden storage shelves for all her things.

Left.

The second bedroom.

She flipped the switch, went to the filing cabinets, and opened the drawer marked **G.** In the drawer she found gloves, a geode, and grass seeds neatly categorized under their proper headings. Under the heading **Gadget,** there was a reference note Fred had put there that said, **See also Tools.** It was trouble he needn't have gone to. If she needed a tool, she went right to the tool. But Fred still hadn't gotten his mind around how exactly it worked. Well, hell, neither had she.

Under **Gadget,** she found what she needed. It was a gizmo still in its store packaging, a kitchen instrument called a mango splitter, purportedly making cutting around the seed of a mango easier.

She wondered how he was going to take this. He had initially moved in because he'd hoped she would give him something that would help him with James. Was he disappointed in her for not producing that hallowed thing? Now, after all this time, she was going to give him something, and it had nothing to do with James. Maybe it was for the best. Maybe he would take it as a sign that he was doing the right thing, moving on.

Or maybe he would think he just needed to eat more mangoes.

She heard the soft chirp of Fred's cell phone upstairs. He had said he didn't want to use her phone, in case she needed to call someone to tell them that she was coming over with something they needed, which made her feel good, like he thought of her as a superhero.

She knocked once on the door to the attic, then walked up the stairs. When she reached the top step, she saw Fred in his leather reading chair near the corner cupboard that housed his television. An antiques magazine was on the leather ottoman in front of him. The area still smelled like fresh paint.

"Right, right," he was saying into the phone. He saw her and waved her in. "Do the best you can. Thanks for calling." He hung up.

"Did I interrupt something?"

"No. It was just business. A delayed order." He put the phone down and stood. "What brings you up here? Are you all right? Can't sleep? Do you want me to cook something for you?"

"No, I'm fine." She held out the package. "I needed to give this to you."

CHAPTER
12

Sometimes Henry wished he could fly, because he couldn't run fast enough. A couple of nights a week, Henry would get out of bed, quietly so he wouldn't wake his grandfather, and he would simply run. On the night he turned twenty-one he ran all the way to the base of the Appalachians, heading into

Asheville. Being that age suddenly gave him a burst of energy, and he knew he had to do something with it or else he would explode. It took him six hours to get back home. His grandfather had been waiting on the porch for him that morning, and Henry told him that he'd been sleepwalking. He doubted his grandfather would understand. There were times when Henry couldn't wait to be old, like his grandfather, but there were times also that his body was alive and jumping with youth, and he didn't know what to do with it.

He didn't tell Claire that day they all went to the reservoir, but he'd never been there before either. He'd never done those things other kids his age had done. He was too busy with the dairy and dating older women who knew what they wanted. Being with Sydney made him feel young, but it also made him feel a little sick, like he'd eaten too much and he could never run enough to make the feeling go away.

Tonight he stopped by the edge of the field, his feet wet and his ankles scratched from the thorns of the wild roses that bloomed in the bramble next to the highway. The lights of a car came at him from the road and he ducked into the grass as it passed, not wanting anyone to see that he was out there at two in the morning in only his boxer shorts.

He didn't get up, even after the sound of the car disappeared. He stared up at the moon, which looked like a giant hole in the sky, letting light through from the other side. He took deep breaths of the wet grass and warm roses and the black pavement from the highway that was still so hot from the summer sun that it melted at the edges and smelled like fire.

He imagined himself kissing Sydney, putting his hands in her hair. She always smelled mysteriously female, like the salon where she worked. He liked that smell. He always had. Women were amazing creatures. Amber, the receptionist where Sydney worked, was pretty and smelled the same way. She was interested in him too, but Sydney always stopped just short of encouraging him to go out with her when he sometimes met Sydney at the White Door. Sydney didn't feel passion for him, but maybe she did feel a little possessive of him. He wondered if there was any shame to hoping she would grow to love him. He could feel this lust enough for them both.

He stood and ran back toward the house, a faint purple light trailing behind him like the tail of a comet.

From his bedroom window, Lester watched his grandson run. All Hopkins men were like that. Lester had been like that. It was a common misconception that being old meant you couldn't feel passion. They all felt passion. They all had run that same stretch of field. Long ago, when Lester first met his wife, he'd set trees on fire just by standing under them at night. He wished for Henry the same thing he had with his dear Alma. And running at night like you were on fire was the first part of getting there. Eventually, if Sydney was the one, Henry would stop running to nowhere and start running to her.

Claire discovered that expectation was nice for some things—Christmas, waiting for bread to rise, long car trips to somewhere special. But it wasn't nice for others. Waiting for certain female guests to leave, for example.

Every morning, just before dawn, Tyler would meet Claire in the garden. They would touch and kiss and he would say such things to her, things that made her blush in the middle of the day when she thought of them again. But then, just before the horizon turned pink, he would leave and promise, "Just three more days." "Just two more days." "One."

Claire had Rachel and Tyler over for lunch the day before Rachel was to leave, under the guise of good manners— because it was a Southern tradition to do all sorts of things under the guise of good manners—but really because she wanted more time with Tyler and the only way to get it was with Rachel.

She set up a table on the front porch and served turkey salad in zucchini blossoms. She knew Tyler was immune to her dishes, but Rachel wouldn't be, and zucchini blossoms aided in understanding. Rachel needed to understand that Tyler was hers. It was as simple as that.

Bay had taken her seat at the table and Claire had just set out the bread when Tyler and Rachel walked up the steps.

"This looks lovely," Rachel said. As she sat, she gave Claire a once-over. She was probably a perfectly nice person. Tyler liked her, and that said something. But it was clear that she wasn't entirely over Tyler, and her sudden presence in his life was curious. There was a long story to her.

One Claire had absolutely no desire to learn.

"I'm glad the two of you get to spend some time together before you leave tomorrow," Tyler said to Rachel.

"You know, my schedule is flexible," Rachel said, and Claire nearly dropped the water pitcher she was holding.

"Try the zucchini," she said.

It turned out to be a disastrous meal, passion and impatience and resentment clashing like three winds coming from different directions and meeting in the middle of the table. The butter melted. The bread toasted itself. Water glasses overturned.

"It's strange out here," Bay said from her seat, where she was trying to eat. She picked up a handful of sweet-potato chips and left for the garden, where she didn't think anything was strange at all about the tree. Strange, after all, depended on your personal definition.

"I guess we should go," Tyler finally said, and Rachel stood immediately.

"Thank you for lunch," Rachel said. What she didn't say was, **He's leaving with me and not staying with you.** But Claire heard it anyway.

When Sydney came home from work

that evening, Claire was in the shower, the water on her hot skin causing such steam that the entire neighborhood was enveloped in the moist fog. Claire heard the bathroom door open and jumped when Sydney's hand appeared and shut off the water.

Claire poked her head around the curtain. "Why did you do that?"

"Because you can't see your hand in front of your face for an entire block. I walked into Harriet Jackson's house, thinking it was ours."

"That's not true."

"It could be true."

Claire blinked through the water dripping into her eyes. "I had Rachel and Tyler over for lunch," she admitted.

"Are you crazy?" Sydney said. "Do you want her to leave, ever?"

"Of course I do."

"Then stop reminding her that Tyler wants you, not her."

"She's leaving in the morning."

"You hope." Sydney walked out of the

bathroom, her hands out in front of her like she couldn't see. "Don't take another shower. She won't be able to see to leave."

Claire couldn't sleep that night. In the early-morning hours she crept to Sydney's room and knelt at the window that over-looked Tyler's house. She stayed there until daybreak, when she saw Tyler walk with Rachel out to her car, carrying her luggage. He kissed her cheek, and Rachel drove away.

Tyler stood there on the sidewalk, look-ing at the Waverley house. He'd been doing that all summer, watching the house, want-ing in to her life. It was time to let him in. She was going to live or she was going to die. Tyler was going to stay or he was going to go. She had lived thirty-four years keep-ing everything inside, and now she was let-ting everything go, like butterflies released from a box. They didn't burst forth, glad to be free, they simply flew away, softly, grad-ually, so she could watch them go. Good memories of her mother and grandmother were still there, butterflies that stayed, a little too old to go anywhere. That was okay. She would keep those.

She stood and started to walk out of Sydney's room, but she gave a start when Sydney said, "Has she finally left?"

"I thought you were asleep," Claire said. "Has who left?"

"Rachel, you goof."

"Yes, she's gone."

"Are you going over there now?"

"Yes."

"Thank God. You kept me awake all night."

Claire smiled. "I'm sorry."

"No, you're not," Sydney said as she covered her head with a pillow. "Go be happy and let me sleep."

"Thank you, Sydney," Claire whispered, sure Sydney didn't hear her.

What she didn't see was Sydney peek out from under the pillow with a smile.

Still in her nightgown, Claire went downstairs and out the door. Tyler's eyes followed her across the yard. He met her halfway and twined his fingers with hers.

They stared at each other, their conversation silent.

Are you sure?
Yes. Do you want this?
More than anything.

Together they walked to his house and made new memories; one in particular would be named Mariah Waverley Hughes and would be born nine months later.

Sydney and Henry walked around the green downtown one afternoon a few days later. Henry had met her after work for what was becoming an almost daily coffee date. Their walks lasted only about twenty minutes, because she had to get home to Bay and he to his grandfather, but every day around five o'clock she would start looking forward to seeing him, unconsciously watching the clock and looking toward the reception area for him to appear. As soon as he did, carrying two iced coffees from the Coffee House, she would call out to him, "Henry, you're a lifesaver!"

It was common knowledge that single

men in beauty shops were descended upon like carrion, and all the girls she worked with liked Henry and flirted and teased him while he waited for her. But when Sydney told her coworkers that she and Henry were just friends, they all looked disappointed in her, like they knew something she didn't.

"So, can you and your grandfather come to Claire's dinner party?" Sydney asked as they walked. Inviting people over was something Claire had never done before. Like their grandmother in her later years, she never liked having guests. But Claire had Tyler now, and love made her different, less like their grandmother and more like herself.

"I put it in my calendar. We'll be there," Henry said. "I think it's nice how you and Claire have been getting along. You both have changed a lot. Do you remember the Halloween dance our junior year of high school?"

She thought a moment. "Oh, my God," she groaned, sitting on the rock bench around the fountain. "I'd forgotten about that."

That was the year Sydney dressed up as Claire for Halloween. She thought it was hilarious at the time. She'd bought a cheap black wig and pulled it back with combs and she wore jeans covered in dirt and Claire's old gardening clogs. Claire had become famous for unknowingly going out with flour on her face, and sometimes girls at the grocery store would make fun of her, so Sydney put streaks of flour on her face. The pièce de résistance was the **Kiss the Cook** apron she wore to the dance, which everyone had a good laugh over, because the whole town knew that no one would kiss oddball Claire, who was only in her early twenties at the time but already ridiculously set in her ways.

"I think you did it back then to make fun of her," Henry said, sitting beside her. "These days I see you dressing like her, but I think you're trying to be like her in earnest this time."

Sydney looked down at Claire's sleeveless shirt she was wearing. "True. And it helped that I didn't bring a lot of clothes with me when I moved back."

"You left in a hurry?"

"Yes," she said, not explaining any further. She liked the way things were, the relationship they had, like when they were kids. David was nowhere in that picture. David didn't even exist when they were together. And there was no pressure for anything beyond their friendship, which was a huge relief. "So you were at that dance?"

He nodded and had some of his drink. "I went with Sheila Baumgarten. She was a year ahead of us in school."

"Did you date a lot? I don't remember seeing you at any of the date spots."

He shrugged. "Sometimes. My senior year and a year after that, I dated a girl from Western Carolina University."

"A coed, hmm?" She nudged him with her elbow playfully. "You like older women, I take it."

"My grandfather is a huge believer in the fact that Hopkins men always marry older women. I do it to make him happy, but there's probably some truth to it too."

Sydney laughed. "So **that's** why your grandfather asked me how old I was when we went to your place for ice cream."

"That was why," Henry said. "He's always trying to set me up. But he insists they have to be older."

Sydney had been putting this off because she was so fond of her time with Henry, but she honestly thought she was doing him a favor by finally saying, "You know Amber, our receptionist, is almost forty. She likes you. Let me set you up with her."

Henry looked down at the drink in his hands but didn't respond. She hoped she didn't embarrass him. She'd never thought of him as shy.

With his head tilted down and the sun shining on him, Sydney could see his scalp through his closely cut hair. His skin was getting pink from the sun. She reached up and rubbed his head affectionately, like he was a little boy. That's how she saw him, that friendly, dignified little boy she once knew. Her first friend ever. "You should wear a ball cap. Your head is going to burn."

He turned his head and gave her the strangest look, almost sad. "Do you remember your first love?"

"Oh, yes. Hunter John Matteson. He was the first boy to ever ask me out," Sydney said ruefully. "Who was yours?"

"You."

Sydney laughed, thinking he was joking. "Me?"

"The first day of sixth grade, it hit me like a rock. I couldn't talk to you after that. I'll always regret it. When I saw you on the Fourth of July and it happened again, I was determined that this time it wouldn't stop us from being friends."

Sydney couldn't quite get her mind around it. "What are you saying, Henry?"

"I'm saying I don't want to be set up with your friend Amber."

The dynamic changed in a flash. She was no longer sitting beside young Henry.

She was sitting beside the man in love with her.

Emma walked into the living room that afternoon after unsuccessfully trying to make herself feel better by shopping. She had bumped into Evanelle Franklin downtown, and Evanelle said she'd been looking for Emma all day because she needed to give her two quarters.

And, as proof of how bad her day was, taking money from a crazy old woman had actually been the bright spot.

Her big mistake had been in meeting her mother for lunch to show her what she'd bought. Her mother scolded Emma for not buying enough lingerie and immediately sent her off to get something sexy for Hunter John. Not that it would work. She and Hunter John hadn't had sex in more than a week.

She dropped the bags suddenly when she saw Hunter John sitting on the couch, flipping through a large book on the coffee table. He'd taken off the jacket and tie he'd worn to work that morning, and his shirt-sleeves were rolled up.

"Why, Hunter John!" she said, smiling brightly, but at the same time an uneasiness settled in the pit of her stomach. "What are you doing here at this time of day?"

"I took the afternoon off. I was waiting for you."

"Where are the boys?" she asked, hoping to take this to the bedroom. She glanced down, ready to grab the pink bag, the one that contained the sheer black bra and the thong with the tiny red bows.

"The nanny took them to the movies, then out to eat. I thought we needed to talk."

"Oh," she said, fisting her hands at her sides anxiously. Talk. Discuss. Dissolve. No. She pointed at the book in front of him to distract him. "What are you looking at?"

"Our senior-high yearbook," he said, and her heart sank. **What could have been.** She had his office at home decorated with his old football photos and trophies. She even had his old jersey framed. It was a time he could be proud of, when anything was possible.

A time she took away from him.

The bags and packages left on the floor, she walked to the couch and sat beside him, gently, cautiously, afraid that if she moved too fast he would bolt. The yearbook was turned to a two-page layout of candid photos. Sydney and Emma and Hunter John were in nearly all of them. There they were in the Dome, the covered picnic area outside the cafeteria where they would sometimes sneak puffs of cigarettes. There they were on the senior bench in the rotunda, an exclusive seating area claimed by the most popular in school. Hamming it up in front of the camera at their lockers. Celebrating at the homecoming game that year when Hunter John threw the winning pass.

"I was in love with Sydney," Hunter John said, and Emma felt strangely satisfied. Or maybe justified. He was admitting it. He was admitting that she was the problem. But then he continued, "As much as a teenager can feel love. It felt real to me at the time. I look at these photos, and in every single one of them, I'm staring at her. But then I see you, and in every single one, you're staring at her too. I forgot about her a long time ago, Emma. But you didn't forget, did you? Has Sydney been in this marriage for ten years without my knowing it?"

Emma stared at the images, trying not to cry. She was ugly when she cried. Her nose swelled and her mascara ran like river water. "I don't know. I just know that I've always wondered, if you had to do it all over again, would you still do it? Would you still choose me?"

"Is that what this is all about? You've been trying so hard, the sex, the perfect house, because you thought I didn't want to be here?"

"I've tried so hard because I love you!" she said desperately. "But I took away your choices! I made you stay home instead of

going off to college. You had children instead of spending a year in Europe. There's
always been a part of me that thought I ruined everything for you because I hated
Sydney so much, because I hated that you
loved her and not me. I hated it so much I
had to go and seduce you. And I ruined all
your plans. I've been trying to make it up
to you every day since."

"My God, Emma. You didn't take away
my choices. I chose you."

"When you saw Sydney again, didn't
you think about what could have been?
Didn't you compare her to me? Didn't you
think for just a moment what your life
would have been like without me?"

"No, I didn't," he said, sounding honestly confused. "I haven't spared her more
than a moment's thought in ten years. And
barely that since she's been back. But **you**
keep bringing her up. **You** think that her
being back has changed things. But it
hasn't changed anything for me."

"Oh," she said, turning her face away to

wipe under her eyes, where tears were pooling, threatening to fall.

He hooked a finger under her chin and made her look at him. "I wouldn't change a thing, Emma. I have a great life with you. You are a joy and a wonder to me, every single day. You make me laugh, you make me think, you make me hot. There are times when you confuse the hell out of me, but it's a pleasure to wake up to you in the mornings, to come home to you and the boys in the evening. I am the luckiest man in the world. I love you so much, more than I thought it was possible to love another human being."

"Sydney—"

"No!" he said harshly, dropping his hand. "No. Don't start that again. What have I ever done to make you think I regretted my choice? I've spent days trying to figure out how I could have prevented this from happening, but you know what I realized? This isn't between me and you. This is between you and Sydney. I also suspect this might be between you and your mother. I love you. I don't love Sydney. I want a life with you. I don't want a life with Sydney. We're not those people anymore." He closed the yearbook in front of him, closing the book on childhood dreams of football stardom and backpacking through France. "At least I'm not that person anymore."

She put her hands on his leg, high on his leg because that was who she was and she couldn't help herself. "I don't want to be that person, Hunter John. I really don't."

His eyes searched her face. "I think she's here to stay, Emma."

"I think so too."

"I mean in town," he said. "Not in our lives."

"Oh."

He shook his head. "Try, Emma. That's all I'm asking."

CHAPTER
13

Fred sat at his desk in his office, staring at the mango splitter in front of him.

What did it mean?

James liked mangoes. This could mean that Fred was supposed to call him and . . . invite him to eat fruit?

Why couldn't this have been

clearer? Why couldn't it have come earlier?

What in the hell was he going to do with a mango splitter? How was it supposed to help him get James back? He'd been agonizing over this for days now, waiting for some sort of sign, some sort of instruction.

There was a knock at the door and Shelly, his assistant manager, poked her head in. "Fred, there's someone out here who wants to speak to you."

"I'll be right out." Fred grabbed his jacket from the back of his chair and put it on.

When he went out, he saw Shelly talking to a man standing by the wine racks. She pointed to Fred, then walked away. The man was Steve Marcus, a culinary instructor from Orion College. They'd had some good talks over the years about food and recipes. It took a moment for Fred to make himself walk. The last thing James had said to him was that he should go out with Steve. This had nothing to do with that, he told himself, but he still found himself hating every step he took. He didn't want to date Steve.

Steve extended his hand. "Fred, good to see you."

Fred shook his hand. "What can I do for you?" **That doesn't involve marriage.**

"I wanted to invite you to join a free community class I'm teaching, sponsored by the university," Steve said affably. He was a stout, good-natured man. He wore his chunky college ring on his right hand, and Fred had always liked that his nails were neat and shiny. "It's going to be a fun course on making cooking easy with gadgets and shortcuts. You'd be a real asset to the class, with your knowledge of food and what's available locally."

This was all too much. It was too soon. Fred felt like someone was trying to wake him up too early in the morning. "I don't know . . . my schedule . . ."

"It's tomorrow night. Are you busy?"

"Tomorrow? Well . . ."

"I'm asking everyone to bring any tricks

they've learned and gadgets they use that most people wouldn't know about. No pressure, okay? Tomorrow night at six if you can come." He reached into his back pocket and brought out his wallet. "Here's my card with my number if you have any questions."

Fred took it. It was warm from his body. "I'll think about it."

"Great. See you later."

Fred walked back to his office and sat down hard in his chair. **Bring any tricks and gadgets most people wouldn't know about.**

Like a mango splitter.

He'd waited so long for Evanelle to give him something. This was supposed to make everything right. Fred picked up the phone stubbornly. He would call James. He would **make** this the thing that brought them back together, no matter what.

He dialed James's cell phone number. He began to worry after the tenth ring. Then he started saying to himself, after the twentieth ring I'll know this wasn't meant for him.

Then the thirtieth.

The fortieth.

The fiftieth.

Bay watched the party preparations from under the tree. Everything seemed fine, so she couldn't figure out why she felt so anxious. Maybe because there were tiny vines of thorns starting to sprout along the edge of the garden, so small and so well hidden that even Claire, who knew everything that happened in the garden, couldn't see them yet. Or maybe she had seen and had decided to ignore them. Claire was happy, after all, and being happy made you forget that there were bad things in the world. Bay wasn't quite happy enough to forget. Nothing was perfect yet. Still, Tyler had stopped roaming his yard at midnight and giving off those purple snaps that looked like Pop Rocks. And it had been more than a week since Bay or her mother had smelled Bay's father's cologne, and Sydney smiled more because of it. Sydney had even started to talk more about Henry, bringing him up in nearly every conversation they had. Bay should be pleased about all this. She was even registered for school now, and in two weeks she would start kindergarten. Maybe that's what was bothering her. She knew her mother had lied about Bay's name at registration. It was a bad start.

Or maybe it was just the fact that Bay still couldn't figure out how to make the dream she'd had of this place real. Nothing worked. She couldn't find anything that made sparkles on her face, and her mom wouldn't let her take any more crystal from the house outside to experiment. There was no way to replicate the sound of paper flapping in the wind either. There hadn't even been any wind for days, not until that afternoon when, as soon as Sydney and Claire tried to spread the ivory tablecloth over the table in the garden, out of nowhere the wind suddenly kicked up. The tablecloth snapped out of the sisters' hands and floated across the garden like a child had draped it over his head and was running away with it. They laughed and chased it.

Sydney and Claire were happy. They stirred rose petals into their oatmeal in the mornings, and they stood side by side at the sink as they did the dishes in the evenings, giggling and whispering. Maybe that was all that mattered. Bay shouldn't worry so much.

Big clouds, white and gray like circus elephants, began to lumber across the sky with the wind. Bay, on her back by the tree, watched them pass.

"Hey, tree," she whispered. "What's going to happen?"

Its leaves shook and an apple fell to the ground beside her. She ignored it.

She guessed she would just have to wait and see.

"Excuse me," a man said from the other side of the gas pumps.

He appeared in front of Emma suddenly, the elephant thunderheads in the sky haloing him as she looked up into his dark eyes.

Emma was standing beside her mother's convertible, pumping gas for her while Ariel sat in the driver's seat and checked her makeup in the rearview mirror. At the sound of his voice, Ariel turned. She smiled immediately and got out of the car.

"Hello there," Ariel said, coming to stand beside Emma. They'd been out shopping again that day. Emma and Hunter John were going to Hilton Head for the weekend, just the two of them, then they were taking the boys to Disney World before school started. Ariel had insisted on buying Emma a new bikini, something Hunter John would like, and Emma went along because it was easier. But no matter what Ariel said now, Emma felt good about where she was with her husband. She didn't blame her mother for her bad advice. Seduction always worked for Ariel, after all. But Ariel thought Clark women constantly needed to prove their abilities, even to strangers. Case in point: She saw a man talking to her daughter and had to get out of the car and lean forward so that her cleavage peeked out from her halter top, to prove she still had the touch.

The man was handsome and a little heavy. His smile was megawatt. He was good at whatever he did, that much was clear. He had that confidence. "Hello, ladies. I hope I'm not bothering you. I'm looking for someone. Maybe you can help me?"

"We can certainly try," Ariel said.

"Does the name Cindy Watkins sound familiar?"

"Watkins," Ariel repeated, then shook her head. "No, I'm afraid not."

"This is Bascom, North Carolina, isn't it?"

"You've got your toe just over the town limit, but yes. Down the highway. That way."

He reached into the pocket of his very nice tailored jacket and brought out a small stack of photos. He handed Ariel the one on top. "Does this woman look familiar to you?"

Emma flipped the tab on the handle of the nozzle to keep it pumping, then leaned over to look at the photo with her mother. It was a black and white of a woman standing outside what looked like the Alamo. She was holding a sign that said, very clearly, she didn't care at all for North Carolina. Judging by the style of her clothes, it was taken more than thirty years ago.

"No, sorry," Ariel said, and started to hand it back to him before suddenly looking at it again. "Wait. You know, this might be Lorelei Waverley."

Emma looked more closely at the photo. Yes, it did look like her.

"But this was taken a long time ago," Ariel said. "She's dead now."

"Do you have any idea why this woman," he handed her another photo, a more recent photo, "would have photographs of this Lorelei Waverley?"

Emma could hardly believe what she

was looking at. It was a photograph of Sydney standing next to the man. She was wearing a very tight and tiny evening dress, and his arm was looped around her possessively. This was a photo from her time away. She didn't look happy. She didn't look like she was doing wild and adventurous things. She looked for all the world like she didn't want to be where she was.

Ariel frowned. "That's Sydney Waverley," she said flatly, then handed the photos back to him, as if they weren't fit to touch now.

"Sydney?" the man repeated.

"Lorelei was her mother. Lorelei was a ne'er-do-well. Between you and me and the fence post, Sydney's just like her."

Sydney," he said, as if trying out the name. "She's from here, then?"

"She grew up here and surprised us all by coming back. She tried to take my daughter's husband."

Emma looked at her mother. "Mama, she did not."

"**This** person is Sydney Waverley?" He held up the photo of her. "Are you sure? Does she have a child, a little girl?"

"Yes. Bay," Ariel said.

"**Mama,**" Emma said with warning. That was something you simply didn't tell strangers.

The man immediately backed off, sensing that Emma was growing uncomfortable. Oh, he was good. "Thank you for your help. Have a wonderful day, ladies." He walked to an expensive SUV and got in. The sky grew darker as he drove away, like he was somehow causing it.

Emma frowned, feeling funny. She took the nozzle from the car and put it back on the pump. There was no love lost between Emma and Sydney, that was for sure. But something was wrong.

"I'll pay for the gas, Mama," Emma said, hoping to get to her purse in the car, where her cell phone was.

But Ariel had her credit card already out. "Don't be silly. I'm paying."

"No, really. I'll get it."

"Here," Ariel said, putting the card in Emma's hand and getting back in the convertible. "Stop arguing and go pay the clerk."

Emma walked into the convenience store and handed the clerk the card. She couldn't stop thinking about that man. While waiting for the approval on the card, she put her hands in the pockets of her windbreaker and felt something. She brought out two quarters. She'd been wearing this jacket when Evanelle came up to her that day and gave her the money.

"Excuse me," she said to the clerk. "Do you have a pay phone?"

The wind kept up all afternoon. Sydney and Claire had to tie the ends of the tablecloth to the legs of the table, and they couldn't use candles because the wind blew out the flames. In lieu of candles, Claire brought out sheer bags in amber and raspberry and pale green, and she put the battery-powered lanterns from the storeroom in them, which made them look like gifts of light set around the table and tree. The tree didn't like them and kept knocking over the ones nearest it when no one was looking, so Bay was in charge of keeping the tree in line.

Birds and flying bugs were never a problem in the garden—the honeysuckle swallowed them—so a garden dinner was a fine idea, really. Sydney wondered why no one in their family had ever done it before, then thought of the tree and realized why. It tried so hard to be a part of the family when no one wanted it to be.

She thought back to the night before, when she couldn't sleep and went to check on Bay. Claire was over at Tyler's, and it was quite possibly the first time Sydney had ever spent a night alone in the house, responsible for everything.

She found Bay sleeping peacefully. Sydney bent to kiss her, and when she straightened, she noticed two small pink apples resting in the folds of the quilt Bay had pushed to the bottom of her bed in her sleep. Sydney picked them up and went to the open window. There was a trail of three apples on the floor leading to it. She picked those up as well.

She looked out the window and saw some movement down in the garden. The apple tree was stretching its branches as far as they would extend toward the table Tyler had helped them move into the garden that day. The tree had actually gotten a branch wrapped around one of the table legs and was trying to pull it nearer.

"Psst," she whispered into the night. "Stop that!"

The table stopped moving and the tree's branches bounced back into place. It stilled immediately, as if to say, **I wasn't doing anything.**

Evanelle was the first to arrive that evening at what Sydney was affectionately calling Claire's Celebration of Her Deflowering.

Claire made her promise not to call it that in front of other people.

"Hi, Evanelle. Where is Fred?" Sydney

asked when Evanelle walked into the kitchen.

"He couldn't come. He has a date." Evanelle set her tote bag on the table. "Mad as a fire ant about it too."

Claire looked up from checking the tenderness of the corn on the cob boiling on the stove. "Fred's dating someone?"

"Sort of. A culinary instructor at Orion asked Fred to join a class he was teaching. Fred thinks the class tonight is a date."

"Why is he mad about it?"

"Because I gave him something that led him to the instructor instead of back to James, like he hoped. So naturally Fred thinks he has to spend the rest of his life with that teacher. He cracks me up sometimes. He's soon going to realize that he makes his own decisions. All I do is give people things. What they do with them is out of my hands. You know, he even asked if I would sneak him an apple from your tree tonight, as if that would tell him what to do."

Claire shivered slightly, even though she

was encompassed by the steam from the boiling pot in front of her. "You can never know what that tree will tell you."

"That's true enough. We didn't know what it showed your mother until she died."

The kitchen went still. The water stopped boiling. The clock stopped ticking. Sydney and Claire instinctively moved closer to each other. "What do you mean?" Claire asked.

"Oh, Lord." Evanelle put her hands to her cheeks. "Oh, Lord, I promised your grandmother I would never tell you."

"Our mother ate an apple?" Sydney asked incredulously. "One of **our** apples?"

Evanelle looked up at the ceiling. "I'm sorry, Mary. But how can it hurt now? Look at them. They're doing all right," she said, like she was used to speaking to ghosts who didn't talk back. She pulled out a chair at the kitchen table and sat with a sigh. "After your grandmother got the call about Lorelei dying in that huge car pileup, she figured it out. She told me after she had taken to her bed, about two months before she passed away. As close as we can figure, Lorelei ate an apple when she was about ten. The day she ate that apple she probably saw the way she was going to die, and every wild thing she did afterward was to try to make it not come true, to make something happen that was even bigger than that. We figured that you two brought her back here, that for a while she accepted her fate because you needed taking care of. Mary said that the night Lorelei disappeared again she found her in the garden, for the first time since she was a child. She might have eaten another apple that night. Things seemed to be going well here; maybe Lorelei thought that her fate had changed. But it hadn't. She left you girls here to be safe. She was supposed to die alone in that huge wreck. The tree always liked your mother. I think it knew its apples would show her something bad. It never tossed apples at her like it does the rest of the family. It's always trying to get us to know something. But Lorelei had to drag a ladder into the garden to pick one. Mary remembered finding the ladder outside the garage after Lorelei left. Are you girls all right?"

"We're fine," Claire said, but Sydney was still a little stunned. Her mother didn't pick her fate. She didn't pick the way she lived. But Sydney, in imitating her, had **chosen** to do those things.

"I'll just head outside, then," Evanelle said.

"Watch out. The tree is cranky today. It keeps trying to move the table. Even Bay can't reason with it," Claire said. "We're hoping it doesn't freak Tyler and Henry out."

"If those boys are going to be in your lives, you better tell them everything. The first thing I said to my husband when I was six years old was, 'I have to give people things. It's who I am.' Intrigued him so much he came to my window that night." Evanelle took her tote bag and walked outside.

"Do you think she's right?" Sydney said. "About Mom, I mean."

"It makes sense. Remember, after we

got the phone call that Mom had died, Grandma trying to set fire to the tree?"

Sydney nodded. "I can't believe I left, wanting to be like her, when she left because she saw how she was going to die. How could I have gotten it so wrong?"

"You're a Waverley. We either know too little or we know too much. There's never an in-between."

Claire seemed to have let the hurt go, but Sydney shook her head sharply. "I **hate** that tree."

"There's nothing we can do about it. We're stuck with it."

Sydney looked at her, exasperated. Claire obviously didn't want to share in the drama. "Your deflowering has made you stoic."

"Will you stop saying that? You make me sound like a dead plant." Claire took a platter over to the stove and started taking the corn on the cob out of the pot. "And Evanelle is right. We should probably tell Tyler and Henry."

"Henry already knows. That's one of the

good things about someone who has known you, accepted you, your whole life. He already knows how strange we are."

"We're not strange."

"Henry told me something the other day," Sydney said, stepping over to Claire. She rubbed at an invisible spot on the countertop by the stove. "Something I didn't know. I've been thinking about it a lot."

"He told you that he loved you?" Claire said, cutting her eyes at Sydney.

"How did you know that?"

Claire just smiled.

"I like having him around," Sydney said, thinking out loud. "I should kiss him. See what happens."

"And Pandora said, **I wonder what's in this box?**" Tyler said as he entered the kitchen. He walked up behind Claire and kissed her neck. Sydney turned her head away, smiling.

Henry had called earlier and said he was running late, so Tyler and Evanelle and Bay were already seated and Sydney and

Claire were bringing the last of the dishes out to them when Henry finally knocked at the front door.

Sydney set down the sliced tomatoes and mozzarella and went to the door as Claire went ahead to the garden with the blackberry corn bread.

"You're just in time," Sydney said as she opened the screen door for Henry. He was acting as he always did. She was acting as she always did. So what had changed? Maybe nothing. Maybe this had been here the whole time, and she just didn't see it because Henry was a good man and she didn't think she was that lucky.

"Sorry I couldn't get here sooner," he said as he entered.

"It's too bad that your grandfather couldn't come."

"It was the strangest thing," Henry said as he followed her to the kitchen. "Just before we were going to leave, Fred drove Evanelle out to the house. She said she needed to give Pap something. It was a book he's been dying to read. He wanted to stay home with it. His leg's been acting up, and I think it was a good excuse not to come. I had to wait for Yvonne to come out to sit with him."

"Evanelle didn't tell us she went out there."

"She was in a hurry. She said Fred wanted to get some class he was going to over with. So," he said, rubbing his hands together, "I finally get to see the famous Waverley apple tree."

"Two things you need to know. One, don't eat the apples. And, two, duck."

"Duck?"

"You'll see." She smiled at him. "You look nice tonight."

"And you look beautiful." Sydney had bought a new skirt for the dinner, a pink one with sparkling silver embroidery, and she preened a little. "Did you know I used to sit behind you in North Carolina History class in eighth grade? I used to touch your hair without you knowing."

Sydney felt a curious sensation in her chest. Without another thought, she took two steps over to him and kissed him. The force of her body sent him falling back against the refrigerator. She went with him, not losing contact, and colorful paper napkins Claire had stored on the top of the refrigerator fell over the edge and fluttered down around them like confetti, as if the house was saying, **Hooray!**

When she pulled back, Henry looked shell-shocked. He slowly, softly brought his hands up to touch her arms, and she felt goose bumps.

Was that . . . did she really feel . . .

She kissed him again to make sure.

She felt it again, more this time, and her heart beat faster and faster. Henry's hands went to her hair. She'd kissed many men who wanted her, but it had been a long time since she'd kissed one who loved her. She'd forgotten. She'd forgotten that love made anything possible.

When she pulled back again, Henry asked breathlessly, "What was that for?"

"I just wanted to make sure."

"Make sure of what?"

She smiled. "I'll tell you later."

"You know, this means that there's no way I'm going out with Amber from the salon now."

Sydney laughed and lifted the plate with the tomatoes and mozzarella with one hand and led Henry out the back door with the other.

The phone rang as they stepped outside. She didn't hear it or the answering machine as it picked up the call.

"Sydney? This is Emma. I . . . I wanted to call to tell you that there's someone looking for you and your daughter. He doesn't look . . . I mean, there's something about him that . . ." There was a pause on the line. **"I just wanted to tell you to be careful."**

They ate and laughed well into the evening. Sydney and Henry's legs touched under the table and she didn't want to move, even to get up for a bottle of beer or cherry ginger ale from the aluminum tub full of ice by the table. As long as she touched him, she wasn't going to change her mind, she wasn't going to say he deserved better or that she didn't deserve something so good.

Claire lifted her glass after everyone had eaten. "Everyone make a toast. To food and flowers," she said.

"To love and laughter," Tyler said.

"To old and new," Henry said.

"To what's next," Evanelle said.

"To the apple tree," Bay said.

"To—" Sydney stopped when she smelled it.

No, no, no. Not here. Not now. Why would thoughts of David come to her now?

The tree shivered, and something only Tyler and Henry thought was a bird zoomed over their heads.

There was a thud as the apple made contact with someone at the front of the garden, near the gate. "Fuck!" a male voice said, and everyone but Sydney turned.

She felt her bones break. Bruises

popped out on her skin like a rash. The hollow space between two of her back teeth began to ache.

"Hello?" Claire called brightly, because this was her home. She didn't think anything this bad could happen here.

"Shh!" Sydney said curtly. "Bay, go behind the tree. Run. Now!"

Bay, who was very aware of who it was, shot up and ran.

"Sydney, what's wrong?" Claire asked as Sydney stood and slowly turned around.

"It's David."

Claire immediately got to her feet. Tyler and Henry looked at each other, feeling the fear radiating off Sydney and Claire now. They stood simultaneously.

"Who is David?" Henry asked.

"Bay's father," Claire answered, and Sydney could have cried in relief that she didn't have to say it herself.

From the shadows of the honeysuckle by the gate, David finally materialized.

"Can you see him?" Sydney asked desperately. "Is he really here?"

"He's here," Claire said.

"You threw a party and I wasn't invited?" David asked, and his shoes made loud exploding sounds on the gravel walkway as he approached, not a crunch like with normal footsteps, but angry, heavy bangs like stomping on paper caps. He was a large, confident man. His anger had never been to make up for any physical inadequacy or insecurity. His anger didn't need a reason so profound. He would get angry if Sydney didn't wear what he wanted her to, without first telling her what he wanted. That was why she didn't bring many clothes with her. She had so few pieces that she had actually picked out herself.

She tried to tell herself that maybe this wasn't so bad, maybe he was worried or wanted to see his daughter. But she couldn't fool herself. She wasn't going back to him. And he wasn't there to take her back. That left only one thing.

She had to protect Bay and Claire and everyone else there. The simple act of her coming back had placed them in a danger she never thought would follow her here. Or maybe the day she left ten years ago had caused this to happen, a series of events that led up to this one. Either way, this was all her fault.

"It's all right, everyone. David and I will leave and talk," she said. Then she whispered to Claire, **"Take care of Bay."**

"No, no," David said. As he got closer, Sydney felt her body jerk, like an electrical shock. Tears came to her eyes. Oh, God. He had a gun. Where did he get a gun? "Please don't let me interrupt."

"David, this doesn't have anything to do with them. I'll go with you. You know I will."

"What in the hell is going on?" Tyler said when he noticed the gun. He gave an incredulous laugh. "Put that thing down, man."

David steadied the gun on Tyler. "Is he the one you're fucking, Cindy?"

She knew what Henry was going to do mere seconds before he did it. These people were so innocent. They had no idea what they were up against.

"Henry, don't!" Sydney screamed as he lunged for David. A shot burst into the silence like thunder. Henry was suddenly very still. A stain of bright red started to grow over his shirt at his right shoulder.

Henry sank to his knees. After a few moments, he fell onto his back and stared up at the sky, blinking rapidly as if trying to wake up from a dream. Evanelle, as light and small as a leaf, floated over to him, unseen by David.

"All right," David said. "I guess we know now which one you're fucking. Everything here looks just **fabulous.**" He lifted a foot, and with one push the table went over, plates breaking, ice skittering into the chicory. Tyler had to jerk Claire back to keep her from getting hit by the falling debris.

"How did you find me?" Sydney asked, to get him to look at her, not Claire. If he kept that up, Tyler was going to do something about it and get shot too. She glanced at Henry. Evanelle had taken a blue crocheted scarf out of her tote bag and was pressing it to his shoulder. There was blood everywhere.

"I found you with these, you stupid bitch." He held up a stack of photos. One mistake. One of many mistakes. She'd done everything to deserve this, but Henry hadn't. Claire hadn't. Maybe she should try to run, give the others time to call for help. Or grab an icicle-size piece of glass from the broken dishes on the ground and try to stab him. She thought she was getting stronger here, but he could still terrify her into submission. She didn't have the courage to stand up to him then, and she didn't know how to now.

David was carelessly leafing through the photos. "This one in particular was of great help. **No More Bascom! North Carolina Stinks!**" He held up the photograph of her mother at the Alamo. The tree shrugged, as if recognizing Lorelei. He tossed the photos at Sydney as she backed away from him, away from the table and everyone she loved there.

"Do you realize how you made me look? I brought Tom home from L.A. Imagine my surprise when you and Bay weren't there." Her fingertips had gone numb with that news. Tom was his college buddy and business partner in L.A. Looking foolish in front of him had driven David to find her with a gun. He hated to look foolish. She knew that. She knew that over every inch of her body. "Stop backing away, Cindy. I know what you're doing. You don't want me," he turned and faced Claire, "to notice her. And who might you be?"

"I'm Claire," she said fiercely. "Sydney's **sister.**"

"**Sydney,**" he laughed, shaking his head. "I still can't get over that. Sister, hmm? You're taller, more sturdy. You don't look like you'd break as easily. You're not quite as pretty, I think, but you have bigger tits. But you're probably just as stupid or you would have **known** not to take in what was mine."

Tyler stepped in front of Claire, and David never turned down a fight. He took a step toward Tyler, but Sydney said, "Don't!"

David rounded on her. "What are **you** going to do about it? You'll let me do anything. And you know why." He smiled evilly. "Where is Bay? I saw her here. Come out, kitten. Daddy's here. Come give Daddy a hug."

"Stay where you are, Bay!" Sydney yelled.

"Don't you ever undermine my authority in front of our daughter!" David advanced on her, but then an apple rolled to a stop at his feet. He looked over to the apple tree bathed in shadows. "Is my little Bay behind the apple tree? Does she want Daddy to eat an apple?"

Sydney, Claire, and Evanelle all watched, afraid to move, as David picked up the apple.

Tyler started to move, to take advantage

of David being distracted, but Claire caught his arm and whispered, "No, wait."

David brought the perfectly round pink apple to his lips. The juicy crack of him biting into it echoed throughout the garden, and the flowers twitched and shrank as if in fright.

He chewed for a moment, then he went unnaturally still.

His eyes darted back and forth, like he was watching something only he could see, a movie projected only for him. He dropped the apple and the gun at the same time.

He blinked a few times and looked at Sydney. He then turned and met the eye of everyone in the garden. "What was that?" he said, his voice trembling. When no one answered, he yelled, "What in the hell was that?"

Sydney looked down at the photographs of her mother, scattered around the grass at her feet. She felt a strange sense of calm come over her. She could remember clearly when David found her in Boise, when he beat her with such force in the back of his car. At one point, she knew she was going to die. As his fists came down, she was positive she was watching him kill her. It had been such a surprise to wake up, to find him on top of her. It might have been a surprise to him too. The death of someone else meant nothing to him, after all. But what he just saw meant something. It meant a lot to him.

"You just saw your death, didn't you?" she said. "Was it your biggest fear coming true, David? Was someone actually hurting you this time?"

David went white.

"Years and years of doing it to other people, and finally someone is going to do it to you." She walked up to him, close, not intimidated now, not scared anymore. Somewhere in her she had believed he would always be around to scare her at night, to torment her thoughts. But David was going to die one day. And now they both knew it. "Go as far away as you can, David," she whispered. "Maybe you can outrun it. As long as you're here, it will come true. I'll make damn sure it will come true."

He turned and stumbled a few steps before he ran out of the garden.

As soon as he disappeared, Sydney called out, "Bay! Bay, where are you?"

Bay came running from the side of the garden, nowhere near the tree. She ran into her mother's arms. Sydney held her tight before they both went to Henry. Sydney went to her knees beside him.

"He's going to be okay," Evanelle said.

"You've got to stop being a lifesaver," Sydney said tearily.

Henry smiled slightly. "You really think I'm going anywhere before you tell me what you were trying to make sure of in the kitchen?"

She couldn't help but laugh. How could he love someone so bad for him? How could she love someone so good?

"I'll go call the ambulance," Evanelle said.

"Get the police out here too! Give them

a description of him," Tyler yelled after Evanelle, going for the gun and picking it up. "They might be able to catch that lunatic. What kind of car does he drive, Sydney?"

"He's gone for good," Sydney said. "Don't worry."

"Don't worry? What is the matter with you people?" Tyler was looking at them, suddenly realizing they all, even Henry, knew something he didn't. "Why did he go crazy like that? And how in the hell did an apple roll to a stop at his feet if Bay was all the way over there?"

"It's the tree," Claire said.

"What about the tree? Why am I the only one wigged out about this? Did you see what just happened here? Someone needs to get his license-plate number." Tyler started to run out, but Claire grabbed his arm.

"Tyler, listen to me," she said. "If you eat an apple from this tree you'll see the biggest event in your life. I know it sounds impossible, but David probably did see how he was going to die. It chased him away. It chased our mother away. To some people, the worst thing to ever happen to them is the biggest thing to ever happen to them. He's not coming back."

"Oh, come on," Tyler said. "I ate one of those apples and I didn't go off screaming into the night."

"You ate an apple?" Claire asked, aghast.

"The night we met. When I found all those apples on my side of the fence."

"What did you see?" she demanded.

"All I saw was you," he said, which made Claire's features go soft as she looked up at him. "What—" He didn't get to say anything else, because Claire had decided to kiss him.

"Hey," Bay said. "Where did all the photographs go?"

PART THREE

Foresight

CHAPTER
14

I can't reach them," Sydney said. Bay was lying on her side on the grass, her head resting on her arm. She'd been dozing that Sunday afternoon in the garden, but the sound of her mother's voice caused her to open her eyes. Claire and Sydney had propped an old wooden ladder against the trunk of the apple tree. Sydney was at the top, reaching toward the branches. Claire was holding the bottom of the ladder steady.

"I might be able to reach that one," Sydney said, pointing to a lower branch on the other side, "if we move the ladder."

Claire shook her head. "It will move it before we get there."

Sydney made an exasperated sound, hissing through her teeth. "Stupid tree."

"Hey, I thought I'd find you out here," someone called. The sisters looked over their shoulders. Evanelle was walking down the path.

"Hi, Evanelle," Sydney said as she backed down the ladder. She stopped at the fourth rung from the ground and jumped the rest of the way, her skirt billowing in the air like a parasol. That made Bay smile.

"What are you girls doing?" Evanelle asked as she got closer.

"Trying to get the photographs of Mom away from the tree," Claire said, even though she was only doing it because

Sydney wanted to. Bay noticed that Claire had been distracted lately. Today she was wearing two different earrings, one blue and one pink. "It's been six weeks. I don't understand why it won't let us have them."

Evanelle looked up at the black-and-white squares sticking out among the leaves and apples on its highest branches. "Let it have the pictures. That tree always loved Lorelei. Leave it be."

Sydney put her hands on her hips. "I'm going to cut off its branches."

"The branches won't break," Claire reminded her.

"It'll make me feel good to try."

"It will conk you with apples." Claire sighed. "Maybe we can get Bay to talk to it again."

"The only time we've even been close to getting to the photos was when Bay said she wanted to see what her grandmother looked like," Sydney explained to Evanelle. "It lowered a branch to show her but snapped it back when we tried to grab it." Sydney turned to Bay, who closed her eyes quickly. Ever since that night, the only time she got to hear the good stuff was when no one thought she was listening. "Let's not wake her."

"I see she's still wearing that pin," Evanelle said affectionately.

"She never takes it off."

Bay wanted to touch the pin, like she did when she got worried. But they were all watching.

"What brings you by, Evanelle?" Claire asked. Bay cracked an eye open. They had their backs to her now. "I thought you and Fred were having lunch with Steve today."

"We are. I can't wait. Steve is going to make something fancy again. I told Fred he was lucky he had a culinary instructor in love with him. He looked at me like I'd told him he had bees in his hair."

"He still thinks he has to date Steve because of the mango splitter?"

"Oh, it gets better. I might as well be dating Steve these days. Just about everywhere they go now, Fred wants me to come along. He's having a good time. He's happy. He just doesn't want to admit it yet. He's going to figure it out sooner or later. I'm not going to tell him what to do. And Steve is letting Fred call the shots, which is what he needs to do. In the meantime, I get to eat fancy cookin'. I ate snails for the first time last week! How about that." Evanelle gave a little cackle. "I like gay men. They're a real hoot."

"I'm glad you're having fun, Evanelle," Claire said.

"Fred's waiting in the car, but I had to stop by to give you this."

Bay couldn't see what it was, just a flash of white paper as Evanelle took something out of her tote bag.

"Baby's breath seeds?" Sydney said. "For which one of us?"

"Both of you. I had to give it to both of you. Fred took me to the garden shop by the farmers' market to get it. Oh, and I saw Henry at the market. He was buying apples. He looks real good. He said his shoulder was coming along nicely, that he'll be as good as new soon."

"Yes, and he thinks it's because of the apples." Sydney smiled and shook her head. "Ever since that night, he can't eat enough apples."

"I wish Tyler felt that way," Claire said. "He won't go anywhere near the tree now. He still can't get over it. He says it's probably the only official police report in history that claims an apple tree ran the suspect off and no one found that unusual."

They all tried to keep the details of what happened to David after he ran out of the garden that night from Bay, but she would hide behind doors or put her ear to the furnace grates to secretly listen when they talked about it. Her father had been arrested just outside Lexington, Kentucky. He wrecked his SUV during a police chase. When they hauled him out of the wreckage unhurt, he begged them not to take him in. He couldn't go to prison. He **couldn't.** He begged them to kill him first. That night he tried to hang himself in the county jail. Something bad was going to happen to him in prison, and he knew it.

That had to be what he saw when he ate the apple, the reason he ran, the reason he didn't want to get caught.

When Bay thought about him, she felt sad. Her father had never belonged anywhere. It was hard not to feel sorry for a life that had no purpose of its own. He was the son of faceless parents who died many years ago. He was the friend of many who were too scared not to be. His only purpose, it seemed, was to come into her mother's life in order to send her home.

For that, Bay decided, she would be grateful.

For the rest, though, she wondered if she would ever be able to forgive him. She hoped she wouldn't remember him long enough to find out.

It had been so scary, seeing her father here. She'd almost forgotten him, what he looked like, how angry he could get. She'd been lulled into happiness before he showed up, and she wanted to be lulled again. It was already starting; just lying in the garden made things better. It was going to take her mother a little longer, but Sydney was being lulled again too. Sometimes Bay would sit at the bottom of the staircase inside the house while Henry and her mother were on the porch, and she would hear Henry sing to her mother, not in song, but in promises. Bay wanted Henry in their lives in a way she couldn't fully explain. It was like the way you wanted sunshine on Saturdays, or pancakes for breakfast. They just made you feel good. Her father never did that. Even when her father would laugh, it made everyone around him cringe with the anticipation of that good humor ending. And it always ended.

But she wasn't going to think of that.

"These must be for you," Sydney said, handing the seed packet to Claire. "Baby's breath is for a bride, right? You and Tyler have a wedding date."

"No, they're for you," Claire said, trying to hand them back. "You and Henry are going to elope if he has anything to say about it."

Bay hoped that was true. Some nights Sydney would sit on the edge of the bed before Bay drifted off to sleep, and she would talk about Henry. She spoke in broad and tentative terms, obviously not wanting to overwhelm Bay with the thought of a new man in their lives. But Bay wasn't overwhelmed. She was **impatient.** With her dream not exactly replicated yet, Bay was anxious about the way things were going to turn out. What if her father had ruined everything? What if his coming here had thrown everything off?

"Maybe the seeds don't mean marriage, maybe they mean a baby," Evanelle said.

Sydney laughed. "Well, that rules me out for now."

Claire looked thoughtfully at the packet in her hand.

"Claire?" Sydney said.

Claire looked up with a small knowing smile, one that Bay had never seen before, but one that Sydney seemed to immediately recognize.

"Really?" Sydney exclaimed, taking her

sister's face in her hands. Bay thought she'd seen her mother growing happier lately, but she'd never seen her like this. Yellow joy was radiating from her. When you're happy for yourself, it fills you. When you're happy for someone else, it pours over. It was almost too bright to watch. "Oh, my God. **Really?**"

Claire nodded.

Bay watched the three of them hug, then they walked out of the garden in a Waverley cluster, talking with their hands, touching, laughing.

The tree was shaking with excitement, like it was laughing along with them.

It threw an apple after them.

Bay rolled onto her back after they'd left the garden. She stretched in the grass under the tree. As the tree shivered, there was the sound of paper flapping above her. She looked up at the photographs the tree had picked up that night six weeks ago. They were fluttering slightly. The sun was now beginning to fade the images, and Lorelei was slowly disappearing.

The longer Bay stayed out here, the more her father faded too.

She loved this place so much.

Things were only halfway perfect, because there still weren't any sparkles and rainbows on her face, but wasn't this good enough? Everyone was happy. It was as close to her dream of this place as she was probably going to get. And it was close. So close. She really shouldn't worry.

She put her hand to the brooch automatically, for comfort.

Her fingers suddenly clutched the pin.

Wait a minute.

Was that it? Was it really so easy?

She pinched her lips together as she unhooked the brooch from her shirt. She was so excited that her fingers were clumsy and it took several tries.

The grass was soft like in her dream. And the scent of herbs and flowers was exactly like in the dream. There was the sound of paper flapping all around her as the tree continued to shake. She lifted the starburst rhinestone pin above her head breathlessly. Her hand was trembling now, not wanting to be disappointed. She moved the pin back and forth until suddenly, like a Christmas cracker, the light broke through and multicolored sparkles rained down on her face. She could actually feel them, the colors so cool they were warm, like flakes of snow.

Her entire body relaxed and she laughed. She laughed like she hadn't laughed in a long time.

She needed this. She needed this proof.

Yes, everything was going to be okay now.

Perfect, in fact.

From the Waverley Kitchen Journal

Angelica - Will shape its meaning to your need, but it is particularly good for calming hyper children at your table.

Anise Hyssop - Eases frustration and confusion.

Bachelor's Button - Aids in finding things that were previously hidden. A clarifying flower.

Chicory - Conceals bitterness. Gives the eater a sense that all is well. A cloaking flower.

Chive Blossom - Ensures you will win an argument. Conveniently, also an antidote for hurt feelings.

Dandelion - A stimulant encouraging faithfulness. Frequent side effects are blindness to flaws and spontaneous apologies.

Honeysuckle - For seeing in the dark, but only if you use honeysuckle from a brush of vines at least two feet thick. A clarifying flower.

Hyacinth Bulb - Causes melancholy and thoughts of past regrets. Use only dried bulbs. A time-travel flower.

Lavender - Raises spirits. Prevents bad decisions resulting from fatigue or depression.

Lemon Balm - Upon consumption, for a brief period of time the eater will think and feel as he did in his youth. Please note if you have any former hellions at your table before serving. A time-travel flower.

Lemon Verbena - Produces a lull in conversation with a mysterious lack of awkwardness. Helpful when you have nervous, overly talkative guests.

Lilac - When a certain amount of humility is in order. Gives confidence that humbling yourself to another will not be used against you.

Marigold - Causes affection, but sometimes accompanied by jealousy.

Nasturtium - Promotes appetite in men. Makes women secretive. Secret sexual liaisons sometimes occur in mixed company. Do not let your guests out of your sight.

Pansy - Encourages the eater to give compliments and surprise gifts.

Peppermint - A clever method of concealment. When used with other edible flowers, it confuses the eater, thus concealing the true nature of what you are doing. A cloaking flower.

Rose Geranium - Produces memories of past good times. Opposite of Hyacinth Bulb. A time-travel flower.

Rose Petal - Encourages love.

Snapdragon - Wards off the undue influences of others, particularly those with magical sensibilities.

Squash and Zucchini Blossoms - Serve when you need to be understood. Clarifying flowers.

Tulip - Gives the eater a sense of sexual perfection. A possible side effect is being susceptible to the opinions of others.

Violet - A wonderful finish to a meal. Induces calm, brings on happiness, and always assures a good night's sleep.

ABOUT THE AUTHOR

SARAH ADDISON ALLEN was born and raised in Asheville, North Carolina, where she is currently at work on her next novel, which Bantam will publish in 2008.